For Kevin
Hope you enjoy
Joe
LWC

Night of the Raven

Joseph Coughlin

Order this book online at www.trafford.com
or email orders@trafford.com

Most Trafford titles are also available at major online book retailers.

© Copyright 2013 Joseph Coughlin.

All rights reserved. No part of this publication may be reproduced, stored in a retrieval system, or transmitted, in any form or by any means, electronic, mechanical, photocopying, recording, or otherwise, without the written prior permission of the author.

Printed in the United States of America.

ISBN: 978-1-4669-7487-6 (sc)
ISBN: 978-1-4669-7489-0 (hc)
ISBN: 978-1-4669-7488-3 (e)

Library of Congress Control Number: 2012924330

Trafford rev. 12/28/2012

 www.trafford.com

North America & international
toll-free: 1 888 232 4444 (USA & Canada)
phone: 250 383 6864 ♦ fax: 812 355 4082

Contents

Prologue	vii
One	1
Two	13
Three	30
Four	41
Five	65
Six	81
Seven	103
Eight	114
Nine	126
Ten	138
Eleven	158
Twelve	173
Thirteen	186
Fourteen	204
Epilogue	229

Prologue

THE SNOW HAMMERED UNMERCIFULLY DOWN from the darkened sky. The wind roared in from the east, sending the slashing snowflakes that battered the paralyzed city unmercifully down on the helpless streets below. Cars were already buried under the massive veil of white that had started the day before. Forecasters were predicting up to four feet before the storm receded. New York was a sheet of white hiding the dirt and filth that was so prevalent on a daily basis. Traffic had come to a standstill, and the lights that shone around the clock covered the streets below in an eerie sheen.

The roads were deserted as the battered station wagon slowly made its way toward the tavern where the lights glimmered, their sparkle dancing magically across the eerie sky. As the car turned into the parking lot, sounds from the jukebox emanated from the bar. The shrill laughter from the crowd that had decided to stay in the city to ride out the storm could be heard above the raging blizzard that had turned New York from a vibrant, pulsating mecca into an almost hushed silence.

The man in the car sat quietly. His eyes flickered as he looked around slowly in all directions, his head barely moving. As he stepped silently from the car, he glanced around once more at the deserted parking lot. There was no movement, a sure sign that everyone was settled in for the night. He silently walked across the lot, his footsteps hushed by the wind and snow.

He was in no hurry. Pulling the collar of his overcoat up around his face, he made his way down the darkened street. There were a few snowplows out, barely making a dent as they began to pile the snow into the many hills that only the kids loved. Keeping his head burrowed into his overcoat, he had to glance up several times as his depth perception was hindered by the elements. Three blocks later, he was standing across from the luxury apartment building that was his destination. He looked both ways. Seeing that all was quiet, he hurried across the street, stepping into the parking garage that sloped into the building. He made his way in until he was standing under the overhead.

Unhurriedly, the man shook the snow from his coat as he silently moved across the garage. The booth that held the security guard was empty. He was gambling that the storm had kept him home or he had bolted when it hit. The garage was deserted. It looked to the man that all the cars were parked in their designated spots. No one was going out tonight.

He moved quickly around the garage until he spotted the Lincoln Continental. Next he gauged the distance from the car to the elevator that exited in the garage. Since he had scoped the parking garage out the week before, he knew where the car and elevator were. He was confident that nothing had changed. Slipping out of his overcoat, he stepped in behind the pillar he had picked and began his wait.

For the man, this was always the hardest part. It was at this point that he felt the muscles tighten in his neck; the trickle of sweat that slid down his back was just a part of it. As cold as it was outside, the man felt warm and flush. This did not bother him. It went with the territory. The waiting, always the waiting.

He tensed as he heard the noise from the elevator as it made its descent. Glancing once to be sure the arrow was pointing down, his hand moved inside his jacket. The iron fit his hand like a glove. With his other hand, he screwed on the silencer, his hands quick and sure. The parking garage was as silent as a tomb. His steel gray eyes were glued to the bank of elevators. The door to the elevator opened with a whoosh. The man's eyes were piercing as he watched one of the three men who occupied the elevator step out.

The man who had stepped out of the elevator was a big man, his face scarred from too many bouts in the ring. Stepping silently across the floor, he stopped. Looking in all directions, making sure no one was around, he turned back to the elevator. Without a sound, he beckoned with his head to the other two men. They cautiously stepped out of the elevator.

The sound of silence was deafening as the three men moved swiftly to the Lincoln Continental that was parked two spaces from the elevator.

The man took a deep breath moving easily out of the shadows, his every move silent as death. Taking his time, he waited until one of the men glanced again around the silent garage. His hand inside his jacket, he motioned to the other. Opening the back door, the nervous man, his frightened eyes darting in all directions, climbed quickly into the back seat. The first man climbed in beside him. When the other man opened the door to the driver's side and got in, the man made his move.

Like a cat, he moved quietly across the wet floor of the garage. Opening the back door with one hand, he raised the gun, pumping two slugs into the back of the man in the driver's seat, his head slamming against the steering wheel, the blood splattering the window. Swinging the piece around, the other man was groping inside his coat for his gun. He never made it as two more slugs tore the back of his head off.

He looked at the frightened man cowering in the corner, fear gripping him like a vise, unable to scream as the words formed on his lips. The man hesitated briefly then emptied the weapon of death into the terrified man, watching as he slumped forward, his head dangling obscenely against the window. Dropping the gun in the car, the man shut the door and turned slowly, moving back to the pillar.

Shrugging into his coat, he walked silently to the entrance of the garage. Stepping out into the blizzard that had paralyzed the city, he pulled the collar of his coat up and headed back in the same direction he had come from. As he ascended the deserted garage the man glanced around quickly, his eyes darting cautiously through the blinding snowstorm, looking warily to see if anyone was in sight. Satisfied, he walked silently back in the direction he had come from.

The lights of the gin mill could be seen eerily glowing through the white flakes that descended from the blackened sky. As he disappeared into the night, the music and laughter could barely be heard above the deafening wind that accompanied the storm. The battered car he had arrived in was already covered with snow. The man glanced quickly at the bar. Then his steps silently drifting across the snow, he disappeared into the night.

Silence followed.

ONE

THE AER LINGUS FLIGHT LEFT John F. Kennedy at 8:00 p.m. The passengers were made up of vacationers who were visiting Ireland, many of them to see family that had stayed behind when others had migrated to New York. Then there were the natives returning from their stay in New York after visiting with relatives and the few businessmen who had already dozed off as the plane left the ground.

At 6:00 a.m. the following morning, the plane touched down at Shannon Airport. The passengers that hadn't had too much to drink and were fighting morning hangovers, their tongues like cotton, were beginning to stir anxiously, some not even sure where they were. Some would be shocked into sobriety when they arrived at the terminal. They would have no idea that they had booked a flight to Ireland while they were drunk. Others were excited they had arrived and were already out of their seats chattering to each other. Harried-looking flight attendants were patiently working to bring them into some sort of order as the passengers bunched up at the exit.

The people began disembarking excitedly from the plane. The attendants were standing at the door, weary smiles on their faces greeting everyone as they arrived at the door exiting the plane.

As the passengers moved quickly toward the baggage claim, one man unhurriedly moved through the throng of people. His carry-on bag was the only luggage he had. The man moved slowly, his eyes missing nothing as he sized up the exiting passengers. He stopped at one of the pubs in the airport, ordered a coffee, and waited for the crowd to thin out. This was not his first trip to Ireland, and he was thoroughly familiar with Shannon's layout.

Seeing that most of the passengers had gone, the man followed the signs leading to customs. No one paid any attention to him as his bag was checked and he was waved through by the customs agent who welcomed him cheerfully to Ireland.

As he moved toward the exit, he contemplated stopping at one of the pubs again for a second cup of coffee, giving the last of the crowd time to thin out. He decided against it. He watched as some passengers were being picked up by family members. Others were lined up at the car rental desks. Still others were moving in groups, herded together for a week of organized sightseeing. He decided that everything was kosher and moved through the exit doors. Standing on the curb, he spotted some of the group being ushered onto the waiting buses. His first impulse was to step onto one of the buses and then changed his mind.

Seeing an empty taxi, the man waved him over. Taking one last glance around the airport, he climbed into the car. The taxi pulled away from the terminal, leaving the organized chaos of Shannon Airport behind.

The traffic was horrific following the storm that had paralyzed New York. Cars were left abandoned wherever the driver happened to hit the wall when the storm hit. Snowplows were already beginning to build the never-ending mounds of snow that would freeze and mesh with the winter, waiting for the spring thaw before it began to melt. Trucks spraying salt would add to the slush-covered streets. The dirt that had been hidden beneath the sheet of white that accompanied the first falling of snow would rise to the surface, giving New York a dank and forlorn look that would linger for months.

Streets were already beginning to develop the silvery ice that followed the storm as temperatures dropped. The office buildings, most of them empty, many of the employees not even making an attempt at getting in to work, added to the eerie solitude that had gripped the city and was holding it hostage like some alien life-form that showed no mercy. The clouds that drifted across the darkened sky covered the sun, adding to the hopelessness that hovered below. They moved slowly, bringing with it the promise of another snowfall that would only fracture an already broken city.

The sidewalks were impassable. The few diehard shopkeepers that had ventured out were fighting a losing battle as they halfheartedly shoveled the drifts in front of their stores. The other people who had tried getting out were stumbling and sliding, some falling into the mounds of snow that was piled against the sidewalks. The sky overhead was dark as night, the sun having acquiesced to the raging storm that had paralyzed New York. There was more snow to come.

The skyscrapers, the bastions of business that dominated the city, were eerily silent. Where ordinarily the city teemed with the ebb and flow of the hustling people, it had now come to a screeching halt. The only sign that New York was still functioning was the never-ending stream of taxi drivers that drifted slowly up Broadway looking for that lone fare that would justify their being out in this weather.

One of the cabs pulled up in front of one of the office buildings on Fiftieth Street and Broadway. Coming to a stop as close to the curb as he could get, the cabdriver waited as two men climbed out, making their way over the mound of snow that had formed in front of the building. The cab pulled away, its tires spinning as it continued its search for more passengers. The two men moved hurriedly into the building, heading directly to the elevators.

The building they entered was deserted, save for two maintenance men who were moving at a snail's pace, not encumbered by a supervisor who would tell them to stop fucking off. The two men ignored them and headed directly to the elevators. They waited anxiously as the elevators made their slow descent to the first floor. Stopping, the door to the elevator slowly opened.

Stepping into the vacant elevator, one of the men hit one of the buttons and they both stepped to the back. The two men were staring straight ahead, each caught up in his own thoughts. They didn't speak. The tall man stood about six feet one with a rugged face that could be called handsome. He was lean with the build of an athlete. He had dark hair that was combed straight back, a small scar on his left cheek that highlighted the piercing blue eyes that looked as though they could bore through steel. The other man was short and compact, the muscles rippling in a rock-hard frame straining through the overcoat. His blond hair was cut military-style and sat atop a hard face that once you saw it you knew this was a man of violence. His hands clenched and unclenched inside his overcoat.

The elevator stopped at the twentieth floor. The two men step out into the deserted hallway. They moved quickly toward the end of the hall, stopping in front of one of the offices. Looking both ways, making sure they were not observed, the tall man nodded to the other. The name on the door of the office they entered said World Wide Shipping. Without knocking, they entered the sparsely furnished office. Sitting at the desk facing the door was an attractive woman who barely glanced up as they entered. Her desk was almost completely bare, save for a phone and a computer. The woman reached for the intercom. Speaking softly into the mouthpiece, her lips barely moving, she nodded to no one in particular.

"He's waiting for you," the woman said, hitting one of the buttons.

Without answering, the tall man nodded, and they opened the door marked Private, stepping quietly inside. The man standing behind the desk was speaking into the phone.

"Thank you, Carol. Hold all my calls please," the man said in a deep voice that reeked of authority.

This office was in direct contrast to the outer office in the plush lavishness that surrounded the man. The wall-to-wall carpeting was soft and deep, giving one the feeling that they were walking in quicksand. The walls were darkly paneled and stretched around the length of the office. They were adorned with pictures and heads of animals that were meant to be intimidating. The large oak desk that the man stood behind was remarkably uncluttered. This was a man of perfection. Gesturing without speaking, the two men sat in the two chairs in front of the elevated desk. As they silently waited, the man glared at them.

The tall gray-haired man walked over to the window, looking out over the city below. He was about sixty years old with a granite jaw that jutted out from a lean, hard face. He was tall, a spare tire beginning to show the softness around his middle that did not belie the fact this was not a man to take lightly. The two men waited as he continued to look out at the street below. He did not turn around when he spoke.

"I love this city," he said in a deep baritone with a hint of hardness. "There is something magical about New York that gives it a life of its own. I can't envision living anywhere else. Even looking out at the disaster created by the snowstorm, New York still holds a magical beauty about it. By tomorrow, New York will be bustling as though nothing happened, thanks to the peasants working to get it back into shape."

The two men waited, knowing they were not required to answer. The man would get around to them in his own time. They had learned this in the years working for him. They didn't like it, but said nothing.

Turning back from the window, the man's hands folded behind his back, John Childers faced two of his best operatives, their eyes showing the hardness of their chosen profession, hardness and experience that only people who killed for a living could have. They were two men who had done very dangerous and selective work for Childers. He addressed the two men without moving.

"Well, gentlemen, is there anything you have to tell me?" Childers asked quietly. "And please don't refer to the weather," Childers continues in an attempt at levity. From Childers, this didn't fly.

The taller of the two men, Al Reynolds, turned in his chair, facing Childers. "The contract on Deacons has been fulfilled, sir. Deacons is dead."

Walking over to his desk, Childers sat down ramrod straight. The ex-military man smiled at the two men. "Congratulations, Mr. Reynolds. I would like to commend you and your team for doing such an excellent job. Deacons was a thorn in our side, particularly when he had an attack of conscience. Announcing he was sick of what he was doing and then telling us that he intended to bare his soul was not in our best interest."

"No, sir, it wasn't."

"Is there anything else you have to tell me?" Childers asked, a knowing smirk on his face.

"Yes, sir," Reynolds answered. "We do have a problem."

The smile slowly left Childers's face as he leaned forward in his chair. Hands folded on the desk, his voice was barely audible as he spoke.

"What kind of problem, Mr. Reynolds?" Childers asked.

"Raven has disappeared. After Deacons was terminated, Raven vanished. We have a procedure that everyone is expected to follow. He didn't follow that procedure, and for all intents and purposes, Raven has vanished," Reynolds answered, trepidation in his voice as he glanced over at Jack Harris.

"That is an unacceptable response, Mr. Reynolds," Childers answered coldly, his eyes boring into the two men. "No one can just disappear, gentlemen, and you know that. We are the eyes and ears of a very big country and just about every other country on the planet. *Disappear* means many things, but one thing it doesn't mean is 'can't be found.' What are you doing about this situation?"

The office was deathly silent as the three men stared at each other in awkward silence. The sun fighting its way through the clouds sent a sliver of light through the room. The paneled walls adorned with artifacts felt as though it was closing in on them. Finally, Jack Harris nervously broke the silence.

He leaned forward, speaking hurriedly. "We have bottled up all the exits in and out of the city. It would be virtually impossible for him to slip through our fingers."

Turning to look at Harris, Childers, a disgusted look on his face, shook his head sadly. He turned back to Reynolds. "Mr. Reynolds, did you hear what Mr. Harris said?"

"Yes, sir."

"Then I strongly suggest you get together with Mr. Harris after our meeting and acclimate him as to our friend Raven. If Mr. Harris wishes to live long enough to draw his retirement, it would be beneficial for him to be aware of the caliber of man he is dealing with." Leaning back in his chair, Childers directed his attention to Reynolds, subtly dismissing Harris as though he wasn't in the room. "What precautions have you taken so far?"

"We have alerted only the necessary people, keeping this on a need-to-know basis," Reynolds answered, shifting uncomfortably in his chair. "Before meeting with you, I made my own inquiries regarding Raven. At first I thought he might have just decided to take some time off. He has been talking about it for some time now. When I found he had not gone through the proper channels, I suspected something was wrong."

Childers, his voice as cold as ice, addressed Reynolds. "If you will recall, Mr. Reynolds, we have had this conversation before. I have never liked the fact that Raven has virtually operated on his own. He has always been given the freedom to fulfill his contracts as a freelance operative, always outside the guidelines of this organization. Too much freedom.

He is supposed to be one of ours, and yet no one, Mr. Reynolds, and that includes you, have been capable of reining him in."

Childers got up angrily and walked over to the window. Staring down at the street below, John Childers face was set in stone. Al Reynolds and Jack Harris waited in silence, knowing Childers would get to it in his own time. The ticking emanating from the grandfather clock that sat in the corner of the office could be heard. The silence was deafening.

John Childers had been a career military man. He had moved up through the ranks garnering favors with his superiors, always with his eye on his own career. He felt he had found his niche when assigned to counterintelligence and he began to make a name for himself. Retiring abruptly after twenty years under a cloud of suspicion over a botched operation in which three operatives had been killed, John Childers moved into the shadow world where deceit and cleverness and a world where scruples and rules had no place for the faint of heart. It was in this environment where men like Childers plotted and planned the assassinations of people without feeling compassion and coldly calculating their every move.

Operating in a department unknown to the United States intelligence agency, Childers bided his time knowing that given the opportunity he could again move into the world he craved and envied. But for now he had to deal with inferiors such as Harris and Reynolds. He cursed the day Raven became part of his organization. He turned back to the two men. Before he could speak, Jack Harris's raspy voice broke the silence.

"Excuse me, sir. But just who is this Raven?"

Childers, still staring out the window, the unlit pipe that has become his trademark still in his mouth turned and looked at Jack Harris, the annoyed look on his face not betraying his dislike for Harris. He turned to Al Reynolds.

"Mr. Reynolds," Childers gestured to Al Reynolds, "please fill our young friend in on Raven and just what his capabilities are." Childers dismissed them with a wave of the hand, turning his attention back to looking out at the street below.

"Jack," Reynolds began, "officially, Raven doesn't exist."

"I don't follow," Harris answered, looking confused. "What do you mean he doesn't exist?"

Reynolds looked over to Childers. Childers took his pipe from his mouth, shrugging his shoulders. "You might as well tell him since Mr. Harris will be working with you on this problem."

Reynolds turned to face Jack Harris. "Raven basically works in the shadows. When we recruited him years ago, he was freelancing as a mercenary. Since coming to the agency, Raven has worked alone. Other than myself, Mr. Childers and one or two others alone know of his existence."

"Why the big secret?" Harris asked.

"Because we wanted it that way," Childers answered agitatedly. Walking over to the window again, Childers gestured to Reynolds. "Continue, Mr. Reynolds."

"Jack, you have been with the agency long enough now too know we have several high-profile clients we deal with. Raven is able to operate quietly and anonymously without fear of recognition. For all intents and purposes, Raven is unknown to anyone. You couldn't find three people that even know what he looks like."

Childers impatiently turned from the window and returned to his desk. "Let's cut to the chase, gentlemen. Raven is loose cannon. He has to be neutralized as quickly and quietly as possible. What he knows about our organization makes me shudder to think of the consequences should that information end up in the wrong hands."

A soft sprinkling of snow started to fall as Al Reynolds looked out the window. As bad a shape as New York was in right now, another snowfall would devastate the city. Childers looked suspiciously at Al Reynolds.

"Is there something on your mind, Mr. Reynolds?" Childers asked. "It's easy to see that something is bothering you. Out with it."

"Sir," Reynolds began tentatively. "I have known Raven since he came to the agency."

"If I remember correctly, Mr. Reynolds," Childers interrupted, a sarcastic tone to his voice, "you were the one who recruited him. If my memory serves me right, you knew Raven from Vietnam. Is that right?"

"Yes, sir, it is," Reynolds continued. "I would be willing to stake my career on it that Raven has no intention of divulging anything about our organization."

Childers leaned back, a troubled look on his face as he contemplated what Reynolds had said. Leaning back across the desk, directing his remarks to Reynolds, he was curt and blunt. "We can't take any chances, Mr. Reynolds. I want him found and terminated. Do you have a problem with that?"

"No, sir," Reynolds answered.

At this point, Jack Harris, who has been sitting quietly by during the exchange between Reynolds and Childers, chimed in. "You have nothing to worry about, Mr. Childers. If Raven is just a gun, we'll find him and take him out."

Looking disgustedly at Jack Harris, Childers turned to Reynolds and shook his head. Turning his attention back to Harris, Childers asked, "How long have you been with us, Mr. Harris?"

"Two years, sir."

"If you want to last another two years, Mr. Harris, I suggest very strongly that you have a talk with Mr. Reynolds," Childers answered. "It may save your life. That will be all, gentlemen. The next time I hear from you, I will expect this problem to be resolved."

Childers swung his chair around, turning his back on them, and resumed staring out the window. It was a signal that they had been dismissed. Getting up, Reynolds and Harris headed for the door, shutting it silently behind them. After they had gone, Childers watched the falling snow as it began to cover an already paralyzed city, a frown creasing his brow as he chewed on the empty pipe that dangled from his mouth.

After leaving Childers's office, Jack Harris and Al Reynolds sat in Reynolds's office. Unlike Childers's office, Al Reynolds's office was sparse with very little furniture. There was an ominous silence hanging between them. Both men looked thoughtful and unhappy. Reynolds got up and began pacing the floor, a bottle of water clutched in his hand. Harris was sitting back in the standard government-issue uncomfortable chair, his eyes following Reynolds as he moved around the room.

"Al, give it a break, will you?" Harris asked. "You're making me nervous with all your pacing."

Ignoring Harris, Reynolds continued moving. Stopping, he looked across the room at Harris. "Officially, Raven is a phantom," Reynolds began. "Since coming to the organization, he has worked anonymously and for the last several years has reported directly to me. Even you, Jack, didn't know of his existence." Holding his hand up to cut Harris off from responding, Reynolds continued. "It's no reflection on you, Jack. It's just the way it has been set up. I see no risk in his disappearance, and unlike Childers, I am certain Raven will not divulge anything that could affect us. I know Raven as well as anybody, and my guess is all he wants is out." Reynolds paused to look at Jack Harris to see what his reaction would be.

"Would this Raven talk, Al?" Harris asked. "Do you wonder whether he is damaged or dangerous?"

"It doesn't matter what I think, Jack. Childers wants him neutralized, and on Childers's behalf, this agency cannot afford a single leak. Ever." Reynolds had an ominous look. "If this ever reached anyone in the seat of power, you and I would be the next ones eliminated. Let's not forget that, Jack."

Harris shrugged. "No matter what you and Childers think of this guy Raven, to me he's just a pistol. We find him and take him out just like any other gun."

"Let's hope you're right, Jack. But for your own sake, don't underestimate Raven. That would be a big mistake."

A smile crossed Harris's face. "I'm looking forward to meeting him."

The small farmhouse sitting on a lush piece of green land was surrounded by rolling hills with a brook whose water gently flowed under a scarlet sky, gently sitting in a valley nestled among the trees calmly and peacefully. In the distance, the roar of the ocean could be heard. Overhead, the ominous dark clouds bringing the threat of rain danced across the sky.

A man was bicycling along the dirt road that led up to the door of the farmhouse. The cattle and sheep were grazing lazily in the meadow. Parking his bike, the man walked up the path and knocked on the door. The door was opened by a smiling woman who greeted the man warmly.

"Good morning, Matthew," she said softly, her voice barely above a whisper. The woman was Catherine Fallon, a stunningly beautiful woman with soft brown hair and blue eyes that radiate when she smiles. Catherine Fallon was a tall, slim woman with the graceful movements of a dancer. "Would you like to come in for a cup of tea, Matthew?"

"Thank you," Matthew answered as he moved back to retrieve his bike. "I have several more stops to make. I'll take a rain check if you don't mind."

"Of course not. You're always welcome. Have a good day now."

"That I will," Matthew answered, waving as he pedaled down the path and headed down the unpaved road, dust swirling up behind him. Catherine Fallon watched and waved back. Turning, she went back in the house. Dropping the mail on the dining room table, Catherine Fallon walked into the kitchen where a tall, wiry man was looking out the kitchen window, a cup of coffee in his hand. She noticed his eyes as they followed Matthew down the road.

"That's only my neighbor, John," Catherine replied.

The man turned to face Catherine Fallon. The resemblance was remarkable. John Fallon, a ruggedly handsome man with a shock of blond hair, was easy to see as the twin brother of Catherine Fallon. He stood about six foot two, a small scar two inches long running across the left side of his chin. He has the build of an athlete, slim and wiry. But it was the dark eyes that magnetize. He moved to the kitchen table and sat down.

"Old habits die hard, Kit," he said in a deceptively soft voice as he nursed his coffee.

Smiling, Catherine Fallon sat down across from her brother. "Sure it's been a long time since someone has called me Kit."

"I had forgotten how peaceful it was here," Fallon said, continuing to look out the window until Matthew was out of sight. "There were times in my life when I was sure I would never see Ireland again."

"You're home now, John," Kit answered, reaching across the table to take his hand. "You can begin to put the past behind you. You are staying this time, John, aren't you? It would break my heart if you left again."

"No, Kit, I'm home for good. There is nothing left for me back in America," Fallon answered, a distant look in his eyes.

Catherine Fallon couldn't help but notice the sad and faraway look on her brother's face. The look saddened her heart as she reached across the table, taking his hand in hers.

"Give it time, John," she said gently. "The bad times are over now. Sure in no time at all you'll be your old self."

Smiling, John Fallon patted his sister's hand. "I hope you're right, Kit, I truly hope you're right. It's been a long time since I've known peace."

"You don't have to say anything, John. You're here now and that's all that matters. Put the black days behind you. It's time to put the past to rest."

"It's a long story, Kit, and maybe someday I'll be able to talk about it," Fallon said. "Not yet though. Coming home to Ireland is my last chance at finding serenity in my life. I hope you understand, Kit."

"John, you're my brother, of course, I understand. I love you and there's no explanation necessary." A flicker of sadness crossed her face. "There hasn't been much peace in Ireland for a long time though. To see the young men and women dying in the streets would break your heart. Our only wish now is for the peace talks to continue and maybe we'll see an end to the violence."

"It's big news back in the States too, Kit, and the newspapers are giving it a big play. They say the talks are going well."

"These are troubled times, John. It breaks my heart to see Irishmen killing Irishmen." Catherine Fallon paused and looked out the window at the rolling green hills. She turned back to her brother. "Sometimes I wonder if the killing will ever stop. I feel this is our last chance at gaining any kind of stability in our country."

There was an edge to Fallon's voice when he answered. "I wouldn't worry too much, Kit, it can't last forever. Someday someone will look around and realize there is never a winner in war. When that happens, the killing will stop."

They sat quietly. Fallon stared out the window at the lush green land, his thoughts a million miles away. Catherine Fallon watched her brother, a worried look on her face.

Two

John and Catherine Fallon had been born to Patrick and Bridget Fallon in the town of Belmont, Offaly. The father, a hardworking man, was a seaman in the Merchant Marine. The Fallon family had always been farmers, and the family farm had been handed down to Patrick Fallon. Patrick Fallon, from the time he was a small child, always had that feeling of wanderlust, his inquisitive mind always wondering what was on the other side of the hill. Farming was never to his liking, and at an early age, Patrick Fallon was drawn to the sea.

The adjoining farm was owned by the Devery family. Patrick Fallon and Bridget Kenney were childhood sweethearts, and it came as no surprise when they announced they were going to marry. Both families had trepidations about Patrick's being gone for weeks, sometimes months at a time. Being a seaman, Patrick knew it left him at the mercy of the steamship companies and it was not something he had any control over. When he was assigned a ship, it was either take it or run the risk of developing a reputation as someone who was not reliable.

Patrick and Bridget discussed this before getting married, but they had loved each other all their lives and felt that they could handle Patrick being away at sea. It was almost two years before John and Catherine Fallon were born. Patrick and Bridget were ecstatic. Patrick made a promise that as soon as they had saved enough money he would get off the ships and settle down with his family. Seven years later, Patrick Fallon was lost at sea after a collision with another merchant ship.

The happy, carefree life of the Fallons had come to a shattering and devastating end. For Catherine and John Fallon, only seven years old at the time of their father's death, it was a confusing and tragic loss of a man who loved and worshipped them. They drifted through the days leading up to the funeral not fully comprehending what had happened. Family and friends came in and out of the house helping to console their mother who had been swallowed up in grief and was barely able to function. Catherine and John were left to pretty much fend for themselves, at this time unaware that their lives were about to take a drastic turn.

After Patrick Fallon was buried in the family cemetery, the townspeople of Belmont returned to their lives, still giving as much emotional support to Bridget Devery as they could. The Fallons remained on the farm, but Bridget Fallon never fully recovered from the loss of her husband. The extended family was the first to notice, mainly Patrick's sister Ann.

Ann Fallon, the sister of Patrick, was a nun who taught in the local grammar school. Patrick and Ann Fallon were the only children, and with her duties at school and church, it was extremely difficult for her to maintain the raising of her niece and nephew.

It wasn't long after the funeral that Bridget Fallon began drifting in and out of a melancholy state, several times being hospitalized because of her severe bouts of depression. It was after the second attempt at suicide that Ann Fallon realized that something had to be done.

Several years prior to Patrick Fallon's death, two of Bridget Fallon's brothers had immigrated to the United States. They were both married, but one of them, Michael Devery and his wife Helen, were childless. Contacting them, Ann Fallon found that they would be overjoyed to take one of the Fallon children and raise them as their own. After much soul-searching, it was decided that John Fallon would be sent to the States to live with Michael and Helen Devery. It would be the first time in their lives that Catherine and John Fallon would be separated.

When the time arrived for John Fallon's departure, it not only turned out to be a traumatic change in their lives, but for John Fallon it was also the beginning of a change in his life that would alter his life forever. Even before he left, everyone noticed the change in him.

Ann Fallon knew she was breaking a bond between the two children but had little knowledge of the effect it would have on John. Even as he boarded the plane that would take him to America, John Fallon had all but isolated himself from everyone. There was a cold iciness about him that had seeped into his personality, and as the plane lifted off, Catherine Fallon cried tears of sadness, seemingly knowing that her beloved brother had changed forever.

One year after arriving in the States, Michael Devery contacted Ann Fallon requesting permission to adopt John Fallon. Knowing the Deverys were good people and would raise John Fallon in a loving and caring home, Ann Fallon granted permission. It was at this point in time when John Fallon became John Devery, another drastic change in his life that would further alienate him from society. Feeling betrayed by his family and feeling that they had stolen his name and identity, John Fallon drifted further into the world of isolation he had created for himself.

John Devery was a brilliant student, athletically gifted and had an uncanny ability to read and assess anyone he came in contact with. Growing up, John Devery never caused the Deverys any problems though they lived in a tough hard-nosed neighborhood in Harlem. John Devery held himself apart from any gangs, made few friends, and pretty much stayed to himself. What he was to become became very evident early on in his life.

John Devery never gave his aunt or uncle an ounce of trouble. He was polite, well mannered, and excellent in school; and though he was a talented and gifted athlete, he never participated in any organized sports much to the chagrin of his coaches at Bishop Dubois High School. In the neighborhood, he shied away from gangs and never bought into the temptations, even threats, from some of the gang members to join.

John Devery, because of his status as a loner, was depicted as arrogant, aloof, and by his peers as seeing himself better than they were. He was sixteen years old when it came to a head.

The toughest gangs in John Devery's neighborhood were the Riffs. The leader was a tough hard-nosed piece of work named Benny Macklin. Macklin had established his reputation by taking on all comers locally and even branching out his gang fights in other neighborhoods by taking on and whipping the best they had. Benny Macklin was feared by all, and as big and tough as he was, no one wanted a piece of him.

John Devery stuck in his craw. Several times Macklin had goaded him, mainly by trying to embarrass him in front of others but was unable to get a rise out of him. Until one day he cursed out his Aunt Helen who was on the way home from the store.

Benny Macklin and several of his crew were hanging out in the park that evening drinking. Benny Macklin was older than most of the gang at eighteen, and most of them were awed by him. When John Devery walked into the park that night, he headed straight for where Benny Macklin was standing. Moving toward Macklin without any warning or hesitation, John Devery clocked Macklin, sending him sprawling across the bench, blood spurting from his mouth.

The rest of Macklin's gang stood in shocked silence, not knowing what to do. Macklin, sprawled obscenely on the ground, looked up in astonishment at John Devery standing calmly above him. Wiping the blood from his mouth, Macklin started to get up.

"You son of a bitch," Macklin rasped. "Devery, I'm going to take you apart."

"Not with your mouth," Devery said softly, stepping in and burying his fist in Macklin's stomach, causing him to double over with a grunt. Devery stepped in, dipping a little and bringing a shot up from the deck, breaking Macklin's nose and sending him crashing back to the ground. One of Macklin's cronies moved toward Devery.

"You bastard," he started, and before another word came out, he threw a looping right that Devery sidestepped. Devery drilled two shots to the head, causing him to crumple next to Macklin.

Devery turned to the others, standing poised with his hands at his side he waited. No one moved. Turning back to Macklin who was on all fours with blood streaming from his nose and mouth, Devery crouched down, bringing his mouth up to Macklin's ear.

"Now listen up, Macklin, I'm only going to say this once," Devery said, his voice barely above a whisper. "If I ever hear of you saying anything to my aunt again, if I even hear you went near her, I'm going to kill you. Do you understand?"

Barely able to move, Macklin nodded his head. As he started to get up, Devery came up with another haymaker, sending Macklin off to never-never land. Standing over the unconscious Macklin and the other flunky who had not moved, Devery scanned the group once, turned, and walked slowly out of the park. Later on when they talked about it, the gang spoke not only of the meticulous way Devery took Macklin apart, but also of the ice-cold eyes that sent shudders through the group.

The Deverys were caring and loving parents to John, and even though he had never given them any problems, the Deverys always felt that there was a void between them. Maybe it was the way John Devery came off as not needing anyone, being able to care for himself, and never asking for anything. Nonetheless, the Deverys were happy to have John as their son and in time were able to come to grips with this fact and showed him the love and understanding as if he were their own.

John Devery graduated from Bishop Dubois High School with honors. His aunt and uncle were extremely proud of him, particularly since he had offers from several prestigious colleges based on his academic achievements. John though had other plans. The Vietnam War was raging, and it came as a shock and surprise when John Devery informed them that he had joined the army. His aunt and uncle were devastated.

Two months after graduation, John Devery left for boot camp. He never saw his aunt or uncle again.

"What are your plans now, John?" Kit asked while clearing the table.

Before Fallon could answer, there was a knock on the door. Fallon stiffened as Kit moved quickly to the door. Fallon moved his chair against the kitchen wall that faced the door.

Instinctively, he reached behind his back for the gun that wasn't there.

From the living room, Fallon could hear the muffled voices of his sister and a man and a woman. He couldn't hear what they were saying as he sat quietly, the tenseness leaving his body. Recognizing Kit's laughter, he assumed they were neighbors. Fallon waited as Kit entered the kitchen followed by the man and woman.

The man who came in behind Kit was hard and wiry, with quick, dark eyes. He stood about six foot two and moved with an easiness that proved deceptive. He had dark hair and appeared to be in his late thirties. The haunted look in his eyes held the same look Fallon had seen in many other men. It was the look of a radical, angry and distrustful, and Fallon knew this was someone that bordered on dangerous.

It was the woman that captured Fallon's eye. She was stunningly beautiful with clear blue eyes and long brown hair that flowed across her shoulders. She was in her early thirties, and her slender, athletic body moved gracefully into the room. Her smile was infectious, but there was an anxious look about her that told Fallon that this woman had been touched by or was involved in the struggle in Ireland.

"John," Kit said, gesturing to them both. "This is Megan Clark and Sean McGuire. Megan and Sean, this is my brother John."

The man McGuire took Fallon's hand in a forceful grip, a grip that was a shade too forceful. His dark eyes were piercing, and the sly smile at the corner of his mouth took the measure of John Fallon. It was easy to see that Sean McGuire didn't like what he saw.

"You're the one from America," McGuire said none too kindly. "We've heard a lot about you here in Offaly."

"It's nice meeting you, Sean," Fallon answered, watching McGuire closely. Something about him didn't ring true with Fallon. Turning away from McGuire, Fallon's eyes came to rest on Megan Clark.

The woman was beautiful. Taking her hand gently, Megan met his gaze then looked away with a flush crawling up her cheeks. Sean McGuire followed this exchange with wary eyes and was not unaware of the significance, and it was plain to see that he did not like what he was witnessing. At that moment, he took an immediate dislike to Fallon.

"Your sister Kit has spoken often about you, John," Megan responded in a soft, gentle voice. "I'm glad we're finally getting a chance to meet you."

Fallon, letting his hand slip from hers, smiled. Megan found herself smiling back, the flush returning to her cheeks. Fallon's smile, against his better judgment, went deeper, penetrating his heart.

McGuire, who had positioned himself now by the fireplace, was taking in the exchange between Megan and Fallon. He began to scowl, not liking what he saw. Pulling out a pack of cigarettes, he fired one up, letting the smoke drift slowly toward the ceiling.

Kit Fallon, completely unaware of the play that was unfolding in front of her, put an arm around Megan. "Megan has been like a younger sister to me." Kit smiled, looking at Megan. "I don't know what I would do without her."

Megan's face was glowing as she hugged Kit. "After my parents died, it was Kit who took me in. She is the only family I have."

Before Megan could elaborate, McGuire, who had stepped away from the fireplace and was sitting in one of the chairs by the couch, spoke. "Will you be staying long?" McGuire asked, looking directly at Fallon.

Fallon, turning to look at McGuire, did not answer. Instead he moved across the room, standing by Megan and Kit, his back to McGuire. For the first time, Kit sensed the uncomfortable tenseness in the room. "Would anyone like a cup of tea?" Kit asked. "I know I could use some."

"I would love a cup of tea," McGuire answered gregariously, sitting back and making himself comfortable, his eyes never leaving Fallon. "Are you sure it won't be too much trouble now, Kit?"

It was a finger in the eye, and Fallon knew the battle lines had been drawn between him and McGuire.

"Of course not." Looking at Megan and John, Kit asked, "Would the two of you like some tea?"

Shaking his head no, Fallon, who has not taken his eyes off Megan Clark, said no.

Getting up from where she was sitting, Megan, sensing Fallon's gaze, took Kit's arm. "Kit, let me help you with the tea."

Megan and Kit left the room, making their way to the kitchen. Megan turned once to look back, her gaze shifting from Fallon to McGuire. Nervously, she followed Kit Fallon into the kitchen.

Fallon waited until they had left room then turned to look at McGuire, who has settled comfortably in his chair. "Sit down, Yank, and make yourself at home," McGuire stated, gesturing to the chair Megan had vacated. Fallon sat down and waited. Experience had taught him patience and, if nothing else, how to read people.

Fallon knew Sean McGuire. He has dealt with them all his life, and the arrogant, condescending front he was putting on was all show. McGuire, for all his bluster, did not know how to figure Fallon. On the one hand he was curious, wanting to find Fallon's weaknesses and shortcomings, knowing that if he can tap into them, he could manipulate and eventually bring Fallon to his knees, another notch in McGuire's arsenal.

On the other hand, he was afraid of Fallon. McGuire too was a master at reading people, and there was something about John Fallon that disturbed him. It was that part of him that was insecure and not sure of himself, something he had been able to keep from other people. With Fallon, McGuire had not been able to peg him, and deep down, he sensed that this was a man that he knew he needed to be wary of. Shrugging these thoughts to the back of his mind, McGuire leaned forward, a forced smile on his lips.

"With the ladies gone, John," McGuire began, "maybe now would be a good time to get to know something about each other."

"What do you want to know?" Fallon asked softly.

Fallon's directness unnerved McGuire. For a moment, he lost his train of thought. McGuire quickly recouped. "For starters, how long will you be staying? You didn't mention whether this was a vacation trip, business trip, or if you were just visiting your sister."

"No, I didn't," Fallon answered casually, his gaze never leaving McGuire's face. He was making him uncomfortable and enjoying it. Whatever it was about McGuire that rubbed him the wrong way, John Fallon did not trust him or particularly like him. Fallon could see that McGuire was not used to being put on the defensive. "As to how long I will be staying, I am not sure. In fact, I'm probably going to be putting down roots here."

"Stay in Ireland?" a surprised McGuire asked.

"That's right."

"But why?" McGuire asked. "Sure I would think with all the troubles that have shaken our country, the last place anyone would want to settle would be Ireland."

"This is my home, I was born here," Fallon said casually, watching the shocked look on McGuire's face.

Sitting straight up in his chair, McGuire looked, puzzled, at Fallon. "I thought you and your sister Kit were born in America and Kit came back to Ireland while you stayed in the States?" Seeing Fallon was not about to elaborate, McGuire continued. "A Yank from Ireland, huh? Well, isn't that something."

At that moment, Kit and Megan returned from the kitchen. Megan was carrying a tray with a pot of tea on it and four cups. Putting the tray on the coffee table, Megan stood and addressed the two men. "And sure what have you two been talking about?"

"Fallon here was telling me he was born right here in Ireland and is coming back to live. Now isn't that something," McGuire said. "Sure I would welcome that if our grand country wasn't overrun with the bloody British bastards that make our life a holy hell. They want our land, our money, even our guns. And they won't be satisfied until they have it all."

Both women were looking at McGuire now. His anger was clearly evident, and he was talking excitedly; both of them knew McGuire was ready to begin one of his tirades about the injustices that plagued Ireland. Fallon looked on, an amused smile on his face.

Before he could get started, Kit intervened. "Please, let's have no more talk of fighting. It appears to be a topic that never ends. Every day, I pray for peace to come to our country."

McGuire was not about to let it go. "But what I have said is true, Kit. The British have taken our land over. What I would like to hear is how someone from another country, someone like your brother John, feels about that. Especially since he was born here."

Letting his glance take in everyone in the room, seeing that no one was going to respond, McGuire gestured toward Fallon. His face was hard, eyes flashing as he continued. "It's something that will never end and for a good reason," McGuire continued harshly. "Maybe Fallon can enlighten us on what the feeling is in America. I would also be interested in what he thinks of our plight here in Ireland."

Kit and Megan turned to look at Fallon. There was an amused look on his face as though he was the participant in some comedy. When he spoke, his voice was soft and sadness could be felt emanating from it. "I can't speak for the rest of the country as I am not involved in the politics and how others feel."

"What about yourself?" McGuire pushed Fallon now as though he had to take him down a peg.

Megan and Kit, sitting quietly now, feeling the tension that has descended upon the room, knew there was no disputing the fact that no love was lost between John Fallon and Sean McGuire. They sat and waited.

"Since the beginning of time men have killed other men," Fallon continued, his voice never rising. He was focused on McGuire now, and the weariness in his tone was hard to dispel. "They kill using noble words like *patriotism*, *causes*, and *beliefs*. They are not above waving flags and spouting sanctimonious babble like so much garbage."

Fallon had everyone's attention now. Megan looked on with a shocked look on her face. Kit sadly lowered her head, knowing deep down that her brother John still carried the wreckage of the past inside him. Fallon continued.

"To me it, all just goes to prove what I have believed all along. At the end of the day, it's just the number of dead bodies and, whether they believe in what they are fighting for or not, they are just as dead."

McGuire's scowl deepened as he looked from Megan and back to Kit. When he turned back to Fallon, there was viciousness in his voice. "No reasonable person would object to our cause based on political beliefs. We can't be denied rights of citizenship, one of the reasons being we are Catholic and the Anglo-Irish Council is powerless to help."

"Reasonableness is irrelevant in politics," Fallon said to McGuire, leaning easily back in his seat. "If someone can use a gun to get what they want, they will. That's the way it has been the world over, and that's the story in Ireland today."

Stunned, not receiving any input from Megan or Kit, McGuire found himself groping for words, trying to penetrate Fallon's shield. He himself did not totally disagree with Fallon, but what started out as a game to goad Fallon into losing his temper has backfired. McGuire now found himself on the defensive. "Ireland is just a tragedy of people who are trying to simply live their lives every day without bloodshed," McGuire stated weakly.

"That's true of all tragedies," Fallon smilingly said. "The fact is everybody dies. How we choose to do it is simply a matter of choice."

"Armed struggle isn't a matter of choice," McGuire answered angrily. "It's the only way we can end this conflict and get our land back. Being a pacifist, Fallon, or turning to look the other way is taking the easy way out. It takes a strong stomach to last in a war and strong men to wage that war."

"What you say, McGuire, has a nice ring to it," Fallon said, his disinterest evident in his voice. McGuire knew he had lost this round. "Direct talks and a government that represents everyone equally is the only solution to the problem that continues to plague men. The simple fact is governments don't get along, and as hard it is to kill and keep killing, it takes more work to get them to the bargaining table."

Megan, who had been sitting quietly, looked toward the bedroom door where Kit had excused herself earlier to leave and get ready for work, looking uncomfortable and confused. Watching McGuire and Fallon, Megan was not sure what to make of it. She looked pleadingly over to where Fallon was seated.

Fallon recognized the look on her face and smiled. It was a small smile, but it caught her eye and lessened her discomfort. McGuire, already frustrated at what has transpired, abruptly stood up.

"We had better be leaving, Megan," McGuire said, draining the last of his tea. "I still have to meet Cassidy."

Megan slowly got to her feet, as did Fallon. "What about Kit?" Megan asked McGuire who was already moving to the door. Megan Fallon had excused herself earlier to leave and get ready for work. McGuire stopped at the front door.

"John," Megan asked, "will you tell Kit we had to leave and I will stop by to see her this weekend?"

"Yes, I will," Fallon responded. "I'm sure Kit will be sorry she missed getting the chance to say goodbye."

"It has been a pleasure meeting you, John," Megan said, extending her hand. Fallon took her hand, lingering a little too long to suit McGuire who has shown his distaste for Fallon's obvious attraction to Megan Clark. He said nothing.

"I've enjoyed meeting you, Megan, and I hope we get to see each other soon." Turning to McGuire, a smile on his face, Fallon addressed him. "It's nice to have met you, McGuire. Maybe we can get together soon."

"You can count on it, Fallon," McGuire said harshly, the threat in his voice hard to disguise. Megan was outwardly uncomfortable with the situation. Megan and McGuire started out the door. Megan turned back to Fallon.

"You really didn't mean what you said, did you, John?" Megan asked.

"I'm afraid I did."

"It sounds so cold," Megan said, a flash of anger for the first time showing in her eyes. "You make it all sound so matter-of-fact. These are people's lives we are talking about. Don't you have any feelings about what is happening in Ireland today?"

Shrugging, Fallon answered softly, "Not particularly. Quite frankly since I know so little about what is going on, I'm not for anybody right now."

"It sounds a little like you're a British lover," McGuire shot back viciously.

Fallon didn't rise to the bait. Sensing that he was not going to say anything else, McGuire stormed out the door. Megan reluctantly hesitated, looked back at Fallon sadly, and followed McGuire out the door. Fallon watched through the window as they headed down the path leading away from the house. Fallon couldn't take his eyes off Megan Clark as she descended down the path and onto the road leading to the village. He turned at the sound of his sister's voice.

"Have they left, John?" Kit asked.

Fallon turned to see his sister Kit standing at the entrance to the living room. He smiled warmly. "Kit, I don't think I will ever get used to seeing you in that outfit."

Kit Fallon was standing regally dressed in her nun's habit. Kit smiled back. "You better, John. In Ireland, we are not as liberal as the order in America where they can dress in formal wear. We still hold on to the old ways."

It was about five years after John Fallon migrated to America when he received word that Catherine Fallon had entered the convent. Growing up, she had always been a gentle and kind person, so it came as no surprise to the family when she informed them that she wanted to become a nun. Only John Fallon had trouble with it when they contacted him.

Kit Fallon taught at Saint Mary's Catholic School in Belmont. She was a brilliant teacher and was loved by all the students. It came as no surprise when she was elevated to principal of the school when the opening presented itself. Kit Fallon loved teaching though and still kept her hand in by carrying a couple of classes. Until she had gotten the word that John Fallon was returning to Ireland, Kit had lived in the nuns' residence in town. She had an overseer taking care of the land during this period.

Stepping into the living room, she stood by her brother who had resumed looking at Megan and McGuire. Kit looked at John and knew it was not McGuire he was interested in. Deep down, this pleased her. She took his hand.

Sergeant Charles Wilson of the British Forces strode quickly into the building that housed the British Battalion stationed in Ireland. It was a large dank structure that sat in the middle of an antiseptic-looking compound. Wilson was a short dark man built ruggedly compact in a deceivingly hard frame with a mouth screwed into a sneer that passed for a smile. It was his eyes though that showed the sadistic, hateful glimmer that let you this was a man capable of being genuinely joyous when inflicting pain.

As Wilson crossed the marble floor, his boots resounded sharply throughout the structure, and he moved nimbly up the set of stairs the led to the offices of his superior. Reaching the top, Wilson turned sharply left until he was standing in front of the office of Major James Wilson. Wilson knocked on the door and waited. From the other side, a voice rang out. "Come in."

Wilson opened the door and entered the sparsely furnished office where a man was standing behind a deserted secretary's desk. Standing at attention, Wilson waited, irritated as Major Neville, apparently oblivious to his presence, continued fingering the papers on the desk.

"Damn incompetents," Neville grumbled. "I told her before she left for lunch I needed that report. Now I can't find it in this clutter she calls a desk."

Wilson looked on as Neville, stroking his mustache, continued his search and finally threw his hands up in desperation. "I give up. I'll have to wait until she gets back. All right, Wilson, let's go into my office."

Wilson followed Major Neville into his office. Unlike the secretary's office that had the sparest of essentials, Neville's office was plush and intimidating. The walls were adorned with several deer, moose, and boar heads. The pictures, spread along the dark paneled walls, were those of Churchill, Napoleon, Hannibal, and several other warriors who have left their mark in history.

The furniture was plush and expensive, and Neville's massive oak desk offset the power that was meant to be reflected in the room. Wilson could feel his feet sinking into the carpeting. Two chairs were directly in front of

Neville's desk. Gesturing, Wilson dropped into one of the chairs that were just a fraction of enough lower and he will be looking up at Neville.

Major Neville was a tall, slim man, fit in a ruggedly handsome way. His hair was short-cropped military-style, and his dark eyes nestled under bushy eyebrows. One look could tell that this was a man to be reckoned with. When he addressed Wilson, it was in a curt, almost threatening, manner.

"Well, Sergeant, what have you found out about the American?"

"His name is John Fallon," Wilson began. "He is the brother of Catherine Fallon. He was born here but raised in America by an aunt and uncle."

Major Neville spread his hands out in a questioning manner. "Who is Catherine Fallon, Sergeant?"

"She is the nun, sir," Wilson answered. When he noticed the still puzzled look on Major Neville's face, he hurriedly explained who Catherine Fallon was. "She is the one who is the principal at the Catholic school, sir. The Fallon farm is located just outside of Belmont."

Neville nodded his head in an understanding way. "Yes, now I know who you are talking about. It's a waste to see a beauty like that as a nun. They're brother and sister, you say?"

"Actually they are twins, sir," Wilson continued. "After their father died, it appears the mother couldn't handle it and went bonkers. They sent the son off to America to live with relatives. Evidence leads us to believe he was raised in New York, but to be honest, sir, my sources find very little information available at this point. Apparently he is just another Yank who has come home to what the Irish lovingly refer to as 'the old country.'" Wilson closed the book he had been reading from. Neville looked at him coolly.

"What we don't want, Sergeant," Neville said evenly, "is some bleeding-heart American, sympathetic to the IRA cause, coming here and making a name for himself by bemoaning the way the bloody Irish bastards are being treated. We don't want any cowboys running around yapping to the newspapers if you know what I mean."

Wilson sat quietly, listening to his superior rant on about the American. Having served with Major Neville for over ten years, Sergeant Wilson was more than attuned to his wild mood swings and vivid imagination—that and the fact that Neville was paranoid about anyone and anything that doesn't fit into his carefully crafted niche.

Neville continued, unable to keep the disdain out of his voice. "We have enough on our plate now what with being surrounded by them as it is. Beyond that, the man's politics is the question that I want answered."

"From what my informer tells me, we don't have to worry about his leanings," Wilson told Neville as he watched Neville continually fiddling with his mustache. Wilson, hoping that one day he will have the opportunity to burn the infernal thing off his face, continued smiling with cruel satisfaction. "McGuire and his girl had a session with the American, and it appears he doesn't have the stomach for fighting. The word going around is that McGuire thinks he's a coward and has had no qualms about saying as much."

Major Neville was staring out the window, the bleak sky overhead making the surroundings of the compound more depressing than usual. There was a noise in the courtyard as the changing of the guards was taking place. Footsteps could be heard in the hallways, their sound like echoes in a graveyard. Neville was lost in thought. Each sound a reminder of where he was and what he was doing there, he was jolted out of his reverie when Sergeant Wilson cleared his throat. He turned back to where Wilson was sitting.

"This is a godforsaken country, Sergeant," Neville stated coldly. "If I had my way, I would give it back to the bloody rebels and let them wallow in it for all eternity. It has caused us nothing but problems for too long and for what? To protect another segment of Irish filth located in the north of this country."

Sergeant Wilson has learned over the years to keep still, knowing that when Neville goes into one of his tantrums, the prudent path was to let it run its course. It was not something Wilson was unfamiliar with. Wilson knew how deeply Neville's hatred of the Irish, all Irish, ran. Neville rambled on as though Wilson was not in the room. Abruptly, Neville swung back to the topic at hand, bringing his fist down hard on the desk.

"The thing about the Americans, Sergeant," Neville pushed on, "especially those that are born here, was that you never know what side they are going to fall on. They have no problem playing both sides of the fence."

"I wouldn't worry too much bout what this American, sir," Wilson said softly, hoping to keep Neville on track.

"Okay, but keep tabs on him anyway. At least until we can uncover some background information on him," Neville said curtly. "The fact that he seems to have materialized from nowhere disturbs. Now what have you got on the latest rumor?"

"Nothing beyond the fact that the rebels will likely make a move in the next couple of weeks. My guess is they are going to make a move on trying to free the prisoners," Wilson added with a shrug.

"You don't have to be a genius to figure that one out, old man," Neville responded angrily. "The question is whether they try to make their move while the bastards are in jail or when we move them. One thing we have going for us is they have no idea where they are headed."

The prisoners Neville and Wilson were talking about were locked in the cells located in the basement of the building that the British used as their headquarters. It had been one month since the five had been arrested and jailed after a failed bombing attempt on a British outpost at the border leading to Belfast; two of their comrades had been killed. The five were waiting to be transferred to a maximum security facility at an undisclosed destination.

Major Neville, understandably obvious to Sergeant Wilson, had been on edge ever since. Wilson, for his part, had no trepidations whatsoever. Looking across the desk at the worried Neville, Wilson had to stifle a smile. In all the years he had been with Neville, Wilson had found him to be a pompous, arrogant ass. He came across as a tough, hard-nosed leader, but Wilson knew better. Deep down he was a coward.

Wilson stayed with Neville for the simple reason that he was a sadist. Prior to being assigned to Major Neville's staff, he had almost been drummed out of the army for the cruel and inhuman treatment of his own men. Neville had been a godsend. Sergeant Wilson, who had found it ridiculously easy, had managed to endear himself to Neville, mainly by taking on all the jobs and responsibility Neville sent his way. It was to the point now that Sergeant Wilson all but ran the operation in Ireland. This left Neville free to pursue his true calling, and that was to try to get every woman in Belmont and the surrounding areas to sleep with him.

"We could bring that McGuire in and squeeze him a little bit," Wilson suggested with some pleasure of hope. "We know he's the rebels' contact in the area."

"No, not yet," Neville decided after mulling it over. "The last thing we want to do is give these lunatic bastards another hero to hang their hat on. The Irish seem to have this propensity for raising upward the least likely candidates at their disposal." Stroking his mustache, Neville pointed out. "Besides, Sergeant, if we want McGuire, we can pull him in whenever we need to. As far as I'm concerned, he's nothing, really."

"Yes, sir," Wilson said. "I always know where I can put my hands on McGuire."

"By the way, Sergeant, your informer? Put some pressure on. Let him feel our weight. He's in too deep to back out now."

"Yes, sir."

Neville nodded his head in satisfaction. "I want to stop whatever it is they think they are going to pull." Leaning across the desk, eyes flashing, his voice hard and cold, Neville looked directly at Wilson. "I want to break them, Sergeant. I want to break them once and for all. I want them, Sergeant, I want them all."

"Yes, sir," Wilson answered as Neville got up from his desk and walked over to the window, looking blankly at the courtyard below. Wilson waited momentarily, then stood and headed for the door. Dismissed, Wilson let himself out of the office.

Three

At the same time that Major Neville and Sergeant Wilson were holding their meeting, McGuire, along with several of his companions, were sitting in the Three Oaks Pub in Belmont. Occupying a table in the far corner of the almost deserted bar, they were far away from any conversations or loud distractions.

The pub sitting in the middle of the town square was an old oak-paneled dwelling, with the distinctive circular bar with about seven stools and the proper number of small tables and chairs that are dotted throughout. At the far end of the pub was an elevated stage that offered music every night and enough of a dance floor that the locals who frequent the Three Oaks were able to congregate and socialize. At this time of the morning, it was comparatively quiet with about four patrons sitting at the bar.

Sitting with McGuire were Mike Cassidy, Dermot Collins, and Patrick Casey, all good men with a gun and loyal to the cause. They all had pints and cigarettes going and were speaking in low tones out of taut, hard faces. Collins and Casey could have been cut from the same cloth. Both were in their late twenties, fresh faced and fair skinned. Both could be deemed handsome in a rugged way with no distinguishing marks other than the scar that ran down the side of Collins's left cheek. It was the compliments of one of the girls at a dance who reminded Collins that the next time he wouldn't get off so lucky.

Mike Cassidy was another matter. Like Wilson, Cassidy was without conscience, enjoyed inflicting pain, and bordered on the psychotic. He was a huge man standing six feet three with shoulders hard as an axe handle. His thinning hair only highlighted the brutal face with craggy lines and a meanness that seemed frozen there. The only drawback to this hardened outlaw was the stomach that dropped over the beltline from drinking too much beer. He was McGuire's closest confidant, and like an obedient puppy, he worshipped McGuire and was at his beck and call to handle any dirty work that came their way.

"It's less than two weeks away," McGuire said. "I want to go over the plan again to be sure everyone here knows what they are supposed to be doing. Our brothers are coming up from the South, and I don't want them to think we are not prepared for what we have to do. We can't afford any mistakes now," he reminded them, looking both glum and annoyed. "As far as I am concerned, we are Ireland's last hope."

"Let's run the British bastards out," Collins said with some irony that no one questioned. "This is our country and time we showed them that."

"For Christ sakes, Sean, how many times are we going to go over the same old territory before we finally get it done?" Cassidy wanted to know, his voice tempered by the drinking. "We've been talking about it for so long, sure I think I could pull this one off alone in my sleep. I've been ready, so let's do it."

Dermot Collins started laughing and quickly stopped when McGuire shot him a baleful look and a sneer.

"We'll go over it until I say we don't have to go over it anymore, and if you have a problem with that, Cassidy, I can take care of that too," McGuire said, his steely eyes glaring at Cassidy. Though he was a much bigger man than McGuire, and from the looks of the old scars that dotted his face and hands, Cassidy looked away nervously.

"Take it easy, Sean. Take it easy. Sure I was just having myself a bit of fun," Cassidy said, moving his glass of beer around the table in nervous circles. Collins and Casey were outwardly uncomfortable, not saying anything. McGuire, not taking his eyes off Cassidy, continued addressing them.

"Is there anyone else sitting here that thinks what we are talking about is anything to joke about?" McGuire asked bitterly. "Because if they do, now is the time for him to speak up about it and answer to me."

The only sound in the pub was the low murmur of voices from the few drinkers at the bar. The sound of the fans overhead and the bartender cleaning glasses seemed overly loud. McGuire let his glance slide around each of their faces, but each of them avoided his look, occupying themselves with their beer and making a project out of lighting their cigarettes. Not satisfied, McGuire continued to stare them down, saying, "Come on now, let's hear what you have to say.

Any one of you."

McGuire, slowly letting his gaze drift from one man to the other, watched smugly as they averted their eyes when braced. Their nervousness was evident, and McGuire's silence wasn't making any of them feel all that comfortable. Continuing to stare at each of them, McGuire kept pushing. "Come on now, let me hear that man speak up."

It was Collins who finally broke the silence. "Sean, sure everything is going just the way you said. We all know how serious this is."

"I meant nothing by it, Sean," Cassidy apologized. "You know I'm all in, and whatever you call, I'm with you."

"You're the boss," Casey chimed in, "and whatever you tell us you want to do is fine with me." Casey raised his glass in a toast and downed the rest of his lager, patting McGuire on the shoulder. "You're my man, Sean," Casey said, finishing off his drink, giving McGuire a crooked smile.

McGuire liked Casey. The lad was crazy as a loon but could be depended on when the chips were down. Giving him a nod and a smile, McGuire looked over at the bar.

The barman, Pete Donohue, was working the sticks like the old pro that he was. Donohue was a good Catholic in the predominantly Catholic province of Offaly. Though Donohue was married to a Protestant woman from the north of Offaly, he was well liked and ran a good establishment. The people of Belmont forgave him for his wife.

Donohue, not one to talking too much which was unusual for a bartender, was as round as he was tall. Bald, with a bright red face that carried the lines of broken blood vessels that were beginning to take a toll on his drinking, moved as nimbly as a dancer behind the bar. McGuire caught his eye, gesturing for another round of drinks; and Donohue, nodding, began pouring pints into frosted glasses he kept under the bar for special customers.

"All right, gentlemen," McGuire began. "Let's get down to business. There's much to do, above all, timing is of the utmost importance. We know that for sure. I also want to make sure that when our comrades from the north show up, we're ready. This is a big step for us getting our foot in the door, and I am personally going to make sure we don't bungle it."

"How many men will they be sending this time, Sean?" Cassidy asked, a look of suspicion crossing his face.

"They have informed me they will be sending at least five men, Cassidy. Why do you ask?" McGuire inquired suspiciously.

"I remember that the last time we needed help, the bloody bastards never showed up," Cassidy answered, unable to keep the venom out of his voice.

"That was a different situation," McGuire said testily. "It was simply a matter of getting our dates mixed up. Listen. They have a lot invested in the success of this operation, and I can assure you, they'll show."

"Do you think five men will be enough?" Collins asked, a worried look on his face. "The bloody Brits will have an army guarding our lads, don't you think?"

McGuire pondered what Collins had asked. McGuire knew that the British were hell-bent on making an example of the prisoners and would surely have made provisions to bring more men in to help in transporting them. He also knew that their small company of men was not regarded in high esteem by the commander of the IRA. With this operation, McGuire was looking to see that the situation was changed.

"It will have to do," McGuire answered, "because that's all we are going to get. Besides, we have our contingent of men, at least six more we can rely on. We will just have to strike the bastards fast and hard." McGuire uttered these last words with a great deal of relish, envisioning how it would go down in his head.

Donohue arrived at their table with a round of drinks. "Here we go, lads," Donohue said, smiling as he put the lager down in front of each of them. "Enjoy your drink, and if you need anything else, just let me know."

"Thanks, Donohue," Casey said as Donohue prepared to leave.

It was then that a strange thing happened. McGuire leaned back in his chair, the back of it resting against the wall, and a small chuckle escaped through his lips. The others all turned to look at him.

"What is it, Sean?" Casey asked.

McGuire pointed in the direction of the bar. The others turned to John Fallon standing at the railing waiting to be served. "Well, well," McGuire said after a moment of watching Fallon standing at the bar, seemingly oblivious to McGuire and his companions.

They all looked at Fallon and then back to McGuire to see what was about to transpire. Being a small town, everyone in Belmont was aware of the confrontation between McGuire and Fallon at Catherine Fallon's home.

Donohue looked nervously over at the bar, wondering what McGuire had in mind. Being aware of his violent nature, Donohue knew McGuire had the sound of trouble in his voice. Donohue, being a coward by nature, dreaded what would come next.

"Donohue," McGuire said, not taking his eyes off Fallon, but directing himself to Donohue, pushed himself away from the wall. When he spoke, it was in a low sinister tone. "It appears you are not too particular about who drinks in your establishment." He looked at Donohue with cruel amusement.

Donohue frowned uneasily at McGuire. He was keenly aware of the cruelty that ran through McGuire's veins, having witnessed it many times over the years. Not wanting to alienate McGuire, Donohue tried nervously to diffuse the situation. "Easy now, lads, let's not be having any trouble here today. Sure it's just another Yank stopping in for a drink. We get them all the time."

"Save it for another day, Donohue," McGuire shot back even more bitterly. The thought of Fallon standing casually at the bar after McGuire's encounter with him at the Fallon home was more galling than even he imagined. Deep down, he knew he had already judged Fallon, and in the same feeling he held for the Brits and their loyalists, he felt the same about Fallon.

"What's the problem?" Collins asked, unaware that the man standing at the bar was the same one McGuire had told them about.

Cassidy, knowing McGuire better than the others, knew who he was though he had never met him and turned to Collins. "The bloody Yank waiting at the bar for a drink is the cowardly bastard Sean met at the Fallon farm. He's the one that told Sean he isn't interested in what we are doing to take our country back." Cassidy spit the last of the words out. "If Sean thinks he's a coward, then so do I."

""So that's the one, Sean," Casey said, letting his eyes drift to John Fallon, who was still calmly waiting at the bar, a look of unconcern on his face. "Maybe we should join him and have a little chat with him. Give him a good Irish welcome."

"This would be a bad time for having a brawl," Donohue warned, sensing that no matter what he said it was inevitable that there would be a confrontation. "The bastard Brits have been snooping around too much lately."

"You're worse than an old woman, Donohue," Cassidy said acidly, looking disgustedly at Donohue. Everyone knew there was no love lost between him and Donohue. "The Brits are always checking up on us, so get your arse behind the bar and see what our friend wants to drink. And don't be worrying, Donohue, anything we break we'll pay for."

"As usual," Collins replied, laughing. "Now do what Cassidy said and get the hell away from us or we just might include you in the fun."

With that, Donohue, tray in hand, hurried away from where they were sitting and resumed his position behind the bar. Donohue' eyes were anxiously darting from Fallon and over to the table where McGuire and the others were seated, knowing that trouble was coming.

McGuire, never taking his eyes off Fallon, nodded to the others at the table. "Maybe you boys should visit our American friend. Keep him company at the bar."

McGuire was not forgetting how John Fallon and Megan Clark exchanged looks at the Fallon farm. What was especially sticking in McGuire's craw was the fact that Megan Clark responded. That was even worse. It was true that of late, he and Megan were having their problems and she had suggested they stop seeing each other for a while. But as far as McGuire was concerned, Megan was still his girl and some peace-loving American just over from the States was going to move in on him.

Cassidy was the first to get up from the table, which was not surprising. He usually was the one who smelled trouble. One thing the big ox was good for was getting into it as long as he had the chance to hurt someone. "Well, I for one wouldn't mind welcoming him to Ireland now," Cassidy said in a booming voice that resounded off the walls of the pub.

"You're no Department of Irish Tourism," Casey said to Cassidy, amused as he got to his feet. "Maybe you'll be needing some help."

Collins was already up as they all stood, their chairs making loud scrapes across the barroom floor. The other people in the bar were alert now to the trouble that was brewing and were looking over to where McGuire and the others were sitting. The tension in the air could cut like a knife. McGuire continued staring at Fallon, his small cruel smile obvious to all. Fallon continued standing where he was, patiently waiting, seemingly oblivious to what was transpiring around him.

Cassidy, Collins, and Casey made their way across the room, the eyes of the other bar patrons watching nervously as they approached the bar. Taking a place at the end of the brass railing, Donohue, outwardly nervous now, made his way to their end of the bar.

"Please, lads." Donohue leaned toward them, his whiny voice pleading. "Let's be having no trouble now. Sure this round is on the house."

"Shut up, Donohue," Cassidy snarled, staring at Fallon. Turning to the other two, he continued. "Well, I see we have a stranger in our midst, boys. Let's go over and welcome him to Belmont. What do you say?"

"Good idea, Cassidy," Casey chimed in.

The three men moved over to where Fallon was standing. McGuire was following everything with satisfied eyes. Fallon did not seem to hear them approach. He slowly sipped the beer that Donohue had placed in front of him.

They came up on both sides of him and flanked him at the bar. Collins and Casey watched as Cassidy took his spot right next to Fallon who continued to drink his beer with a deep and quiet satisfaction.

When the three men had positioned themselves, satisfied with the way they had boxed Fallon in, Cassidy looked over to where McGuire was seated. McGuire nodded and Cassidy leaned in on Fallon.

Fallon's drink spilled onto the bar. The three men tensed as Fallon signaled to Donohue. Donohue hurried over to Fallon.

"I'm sorry, but I seem to have spilled my drink," Fallon said without looking at anyone. "May I have another one please?"

Cassidy, puzzled and unsure of what to do next, looked again at McGuire. McGuire, who was losing his patience, nodded forcefully.

"I'm sorry, Yank," Cassidy said without sincerity. Collins and Casey, alert now knowing something was bound to happen, waited.

Fallon turned to Cassidy and smiled. His voice was gentle when he spoke. "That's no problem. It happens all the time."

"I'll bet it does," Cassidy said, frustrated he hasn't gotten a rise out of Fallon. Cassidy, his violent nature legendary in Offaly, was at a loss with how to proceed with Fallon. The bar patrons were looking on with interest, noting Cassidy's discomfort.

Casey and Collins had shouldered their way into Fallon and were pressing him from both sides, unsure what to do next. They looked at Cassidy to give them the word. When none came, they began to feel uncomfortable.

Fallon felt the pressure, judging it physically and knowing what it might mean. The three of them had been drinking, and that made for a dangerous mix. Pushing himself away from the bar, Fallon, casually turning, took in the full scope of the patrons who were by now curious to see what was about to happen.

Fallon took stock of the situation and knew without a doubt what could transpire depending on his actions. His shoulders slumped slightly from the weariness that accompanied situations like this and how in the past he had reacted to them. A feeling of sadness rushed through him as he wondered if it would ever be over.

He had three men on him waiting for some sort of reaction. Given how close they stood to him, he knew he could take them out in less than ten seconds, and that was without the use of a gun. "Old habits die hard," Fallon thought to himself. Since he didn't know the cause of the confrontation, but guessing what it was, he just stood and waited. He knew the reason would present itself; it always did.

It came loudly in the form of McGuire's voice that bellowed from where he was sitting. "Was it true what you said, Yank?" McGuire called over. "You are not sympathetic to our cause? Even though you are supposed to be one of us, you can just turn your back on what we are fighting for?'

Fallon, turning away from the others, gave his full attention to McGuire. "I don't believe that is what I said."

"You're not about to be calling me a liar now, are you?" McGuire asked sarcastically.

"No, I'm not."

The whirring of the fan, the soft wind that whistled through the doorway, Donohue, nervously working behind the stick, became even more pronounced over the deathly silence that had settled over the bar. The drinkers were alert now to the play that was unfolding around them. Cassidy and the others, like Fallon, had let their gaze come to rest on McGuire, waiting to see what his next move would be.

"Well, Fallon, that's what it sounded like to me the other day," McGuire answered loudly in response to Fallon.

Fallon turned from McGuire, giving his attention to the three men surrounding him. He knew they were of no threat right now. He turned back to McGuire. "I didn't come in here looking for trouble, McGuire, just a drink."

"Well, you came to the wrong place then," McGuire told him. "This establishment only serves Irishmen."

"Sure his sister is Irish, Sean," Donohue said amiably, hoping there was a chance he could still diffuse the situation. "And the man himself was born here. Just a stone's throw from here. Isn't that so?"

"Shut up, Donohue," Cassidy hissed.

Something shifted in the perception of the small crowd gathered in the pub. It was a level of sympathy if not understanding. Fallon could sense it even if no one else could. But he knew it didn't matter. McGuire had made their play, and there would be no backing off.

He could make his presence felt here and have advocates right here in the pub, but he did not want to bring his violence home. Fallon wanted to leave it where he had left it, two thousand miles from here.

"That doesn't make him Irish by any stretch of the imagination, and you know it," McGuire said to Donohue and also to the other silent patrons of the pub. "There are plenty of people in Ireland I wouldn't call Irish either, and they have been here for centuries. It takes more to being an Irishman than being born here."

Fallon, sensing what was coming and wanting to pass it by, reached into his pocket, pulled out his wallet, and left money on the bar. All the while he was doing this his body was tense as he watched them all from the corner of his eye.

"I'll be taking off now," Fallon said agreeably to Donohue. Turning, he came face-to-face with Cassidy. Looking him directly in the eye, he moved toward the door. "Excuse me please," he said.

Cassidy, seeing something in Fallon's eye that unnerved him and made him hesitate, moved, giving Fallon enough room to step away. Unsure of just what to do, Cassidy glanced over at McGuire, hoping for some signal from his boss what to do next. Fallon smiled to himself. A situation like this was easily ignited. Fallon was intimately familiar with the ramifications. But it was also easy to defuse.

Cassidy, as big as he was, probably had the size and strength to intimidate people. And maybe a history with a gun or a bomb, Fallon judged. He could probably be judged as a hard man. But Fallon knew from experience that most hard men are usually only hard on the surface. It takes many years of training to be hard all the way through.

As for the other two who stood like puppets beside Cassidy, though he did not yet know their names, they were weak; and the only thing you had to worry about a weak man was he sometimes pulled the trigger at the wrong time. But even that could be judged. Fallon had already pegged the one closest to Cassidy on the left to be the craziest. That was evident by his hyper demeanor.

"That's right, Fallon," McGuire said from his table as he watched Fallon head for the door. "Keep moving, the door is on your left."

Fallon looked over at McGuire on the way out, hesitating briefly. McGuire still had that small smirk on his face and the hard eyes that never left Fallon. But Fallon also noted something else.

Fallon pegged McGuire to be the head of the local cell in Offaly. ASUs they were called if Fallon remembered correctly. Active service units. It was the IRA's latest attempt at restructuring their organization. He remembered it from some directive back in the States. Fallon had not been directly involved in any operations with the Irish. As a freelance operative, he managed to stay away from the Irish problem. Though he did remember what had been noted on the directive.

There were two to four people per cell, with only one man having all the information of any given operation, given out to the others only on a need-to-know basis. It was almost impossible for the British to infiltrate without having an informer. It was the reason the IRA structured it this way.

McGuire was undoubtedly part of the revolutionary movement in Ireland. He had to have been a man who had killed and a man who left some grisly scenes behind for the British and even the Irish people to sort out.

As Fallon stepped outside, he looked back once more at McGuire before he left. If one did not know better, you would swear he did not want to forget his face.

McGuire had seen something in Fallon's eyes. His smirk faltered, and he wondered what it was he had seen.

Then Fallon was gone into the gray Irish day. Cassidy and the others wandered back to where McGuire was seated, silently taking their seats. A low murmur could be heard throughout the pub.

Just another Yank, they thought. Not too worry.

FOUR

THE SNOW THAT HAD COVERED the streets had been pushed up against the sidewalks after the snowplows had gone through. Huge mounds of snow were dotted throughout the community, and the children who had been given the day off from school were romping and playing, their voices echoing throughout the neighborhood.

It was a quite neighborhood, made up mostly of hardworking middle-class families. Many in the development were policemen, firemen, accountants, post office employees, and a smattering of retirees. The homes were mostly ranch-style with well-kept lawns that would not be visible until the spring. It was a neighborhood that during the summer, the smell of barbecue filtered through the air and laughter came from homes where people gathered to enjoy the warm summer days and nights.

It was a modest home nestled in a cul-de-sac at the end of the street. It had a winding driveway with a lattice-framed door sitting in the center of the house. There was a two-car garage, but like most of the neighbors when snow or ice was in the forecast, a car was parked at one end of the driveway in case residents had to make a run to one of the stores and weren't snowed in.

Sitting in the comfortable living room in front of a fireplace that gave a golden glow to the room, Dan Morehead was sitting in his favorite chair reading. He was a sixty-eight-year-old and looked fifty. He was ruggedly handsome, with silvery gray hair. His hazel eyes were gentle, with a perpetual twinkle as though he knew something funny was happening and he was keeping it secret. Standing at six feet, he was rock hard and someone would be hard-pressed to find a soft spot on his frame.

Alice Morehead, Dan's wife of thirty-five years, stepped into the room. She was small, petite, and an extremely beautiful woman of sixty-five. She moved with all the grace of a dancer. Heading over to where Dan sat, she put her hand on his shoulder.

"Dan," Alice said softly.

"Yes, Alice," Dan said, looking over his shoulder.

"It's for you."

Dan Morehead had heard the phone when it rang. He had made it a policy since retiring to avoid answering it whenever possible. If Alice was out, he made a point of letting the answering machine take a message.

"Take a message please, Alice," Dan said, sounding annoyed.

"It's John Childers," Alice answered, not sounding all that happy.

Dan Morehead, putting the book down on the coffee table in front of him, looked out the bay window into the distance. Something inside him tilted a few degrees. It couldn't be anything he wanted to hear if it was John Childers.

Pushing himself up from his chair, nodding his head in annoyance at Alice, he made his way into the foyer and picked up the phone.

"Hello," he said. Then he listened.

Reynolds had found something interesting in Sudan. Reynolds got up, poured himself another cup of coffee, just to be doing something, and returned to sit down in front of the terminal he was working with. Harris, noting Reynolds's actions, raised an inquisitive eye at him, shrugged, and returned to his terminal that was zeroing in on South America.

Darfur, Reynolds knew, was a hot spot right now. They were in the middle of a civil war or ethnic cleansing or radical uprising or whatever the hell else they wanted to call it. For Reynolds, for all the political and media crap that was being spun out of Washington, he saw it as the usual land/money/ power grab that is the constant movement of countries around the world.

The vice president had been in Darfur on a fact-finding trip when three car bombs were detonated as his caravan passed. Three of his aides in one of the cars were killed, though they missed the vice president's car and he was quickly shuttled out of the area and back to Washington.

Whatever label they wanted to pin on it, depending on which way the political wind blew, to a hardened field operative like Reynolds, it was a perfect destination for the many mercenaries who killed for money. Places like Darfur never failed to attract these ex-soldiers, killers, or any of the other cretins who made their living selling their guns to the highest bidder. But to Reynolds, that wasn't the interesting part.

What Reynolds found interesting was that not a day later (in fact, as far as anyone could determine, only hours after sundown of the same day as the incident with the car bombs) six men were executed in their homes. What witnesses there were, mostly with conflicting stories, the killings were done by one man who could not be identified.

Presumably, a lone gunman had moved swiftly and silently, entering the homes and killing the men without question or verbal contact. The men, looking up the barrel of a gun, had yelled or screamed out in protest, but the silent stranger came and went in less than an hour, leaving six dead bodies behind.

That was swift retaliation, and it made Reynolds's skin go cold with excitement. As usual, the relatives of the victims swore that the men were innocent of any crimes, and the inevitable finger-pointing began in earnest. Reynolds, hardened to this scenario, understood as the cries of corruption, intimidation, injustice, and all the usual catchphrases were being bandied about and he ignored them. That was not what Reynolds was focused on. Reynolds saw it in a different way.

Naturally the newspapers from around the world had picked up the story. They reported the confusion, the carnage; and in their best blood-and-guts way, reported on the killings in Darfur in whatever way suited their countries' needs. The rebels, the janjaweed, the Sudan People's Liberation Movement, UN officials, the victim's families, anybody and everybody involved all blamed whoever it was in their best interest to blame.

Reynolds, reading the report carefully for the second time, saw it in another way. While everyone was focused in on who was to blame, Reynolds coolly and methodically deciphered it in such a way that he was able to derive from it what he was looking for. For Reynolds, it had nothing to do with politics.

Reynolds was able to zone in on what he was looking for. The killings were carried out by a well-trained assassin, dispatched by an organization he was more than familiar with. They were guns for hire, letting the government know that would-be car bombers or anyone looking to take someone out could be gotten to no matter where they lived whenever the government wanted without consequence or problem. The vice president, in his familiar arrogant manner, was saying "go to hell."

To Reynolds, the body count, method, and success of the assignations by a well-trained operative was possibly American, possibly World Wide, possibly Raven. Stroking his chin thoughtfully, Reynolds leaned over and tapped Harris on the shoulder.

"Look at this," he said.

Harris, leaning toward Reynolds's terminal frowning, leaned closer. "What?" Harris asked, puzzled.

"Read this and tell me what you think."

Harris moved closer and started reading.

Three hours later, a World Wide operative that lived a nondescript but deeply complex and even harrowing life just outside of Darfur was contacted through a UN agent in place.

Two hours after, he was working his way through the levels of local government via the usual gifts of cash—pounds to be exact.

The rolling green hills lushly hovered in the background, the clouds danced across the ominous skyline like quicksilver. The winding road bordered on both sides by the man-made barriers that the rocks, which were plentiful in Ireland, protected the dusty paths that led into town. Several men on bicycles were making their way into Belmont now. These were hardy men who looked upon cars, trucks, anything that took gasoline as intruders to the beauty and the air of their beloved Ireland.

Fallon was contemplating his options as he slowly walked beside Kit's slow-moving sheep. Kit didn't have that many, but she had enough that required constant care. The sheepdog was endlessly running throughout the herd, nipping at their heels, keeping them moving. He was fascinating to watch and brought memories of long ago when his mother was alive.

The farm was comparatively small and just on the edge of sustaining itself. Fallon imagined that was how it had always been.

Fallon knew he could stay here, but it would be impossible because he could not hide forever. Ambling silently down the hill, the sheep picking up their pace as the sheepdog stayed on their heels, Fallon knew World Wide would locate him soon enough. He was well aware of their methods.

They would be searching world databases for hot spots throughout the world, looking for any extraordinary actions taking place. One of the first things that World Wide had to figure was that Fallon had sold his gun to a higher bidder. Once that trail petered out, they would relentlessly dig into his mercenary past.

The first order of business would be to make direct contact with his previous employers; those that were still alive, which probably weren't all that many. Fallon was well aware of World Wide's reach, and he knew there was no one they couldn't get to. Eventually they would wind up in Ireland.

In the World Wide database, Fallon would show up as John Devery. His aunt and uncle's name were on the birth certificate they attained after adopting him. Though he never spoke of it and seemed to have no connection to it, the original birth certificate said Ireland. For World Wide, that would be worth checking. How long would it take them to search all of Ireland, the North and the South? In a country the size of Ireland, not that long.

His first thinking was that maybe he could cut a deal. Let World Wide know that he just wanted out, he had his fill of killing and was just looking to end his days in peace. Knowing Childers, that one wouldn't even fly.

Maybe he could go further under, but Fallon knew that would be tiring and more to the core and he did not want to. Fallon was determined to live the remainder of his life, whatever time he had left, on his own terms. He knew that was not an option with World Wide. Reluctantly giving them their due, he had to look at it from their point of view. Fallon, with what he knew about World Wide, would be a loose cannon they could not afford the luxury of having running around free. He scratched that opening quickly.

Then there was Dan Morehead. Fallon stopped and looked off the soft blue horizon. When he thought about Dan Morehead, it was with fond memories. It was Dan Morehead who trained him, mentored him, and guided him through those first few years with World Wide. But even Dan Morehead was not that far away.

They could and would reel him back in whenever they wanted. It was the one constant with World Wide—no one ever really got out. Knowing Childers, he had no qualms about altering the course of anyone's life. Childers, though he never worked in the field and would be a liability if he ever had to take on a contract, was a company man through and through. If Fallon had Childers figured right, Dan Morehead had already been brought back in.

Dan Morehead was as close to a friend that was possible at a place and time, in a life that afforded no friends. At World Wide, they found it more feasible if friendships were discouraged. At World Wide, you have no friends and they thrived on everyone distrusting everyone else. To someone like Childers and his cronies, it was another way of keeping people on a string. Having friends was a joke. For Fallon at least, when he first started with World Wide, that type of game of cat and mouse was exhilarating. It got old in a hurry.

But a man can't live or function in a life without friendship. So at World Wide, you developed them slowly, surreptitiously, with one eye over your shoulder, each man taking stock of the other, smelling the others like animals. Over the years, Dan Morehead had proved to be reliable and a constant. In the end, Fallon and Morehead knew they could trust each other. That was friendship at World Wide. That was enough.

As he rounded the bend at the bottom of the hill, Fallon knew the question was not if World Wide would find him, but when. And when everything factored in, Fallon always came back to that conclusion. Obviously it was something to think about.

The burning question now was, who would they send? That would determine the outcome to some extent. Fallon was fairly sure who it would be, but knowing Childers and the way he thought, there was always the chance he could be wrong. "Maybe I'm becoming paranoiac," Fallon thought. Given that, it was what had kept him alive all these years.

And as Fallon walked his family's land, sheep in tow, heading toward the sea, he now had to factor in World Wide's options. He could not deceive himself into believing they would leave him alone. Mulling it over, he came back to the same conclusion. They were closely aligned with his own. Again. Still.

"It's over, Kit." The sun sent slivers of light through the open windows. A soft breeze had settled across the sky, gently guiding the clouds as they made their way across the endless sky. Megan Clark and Kit Fallon were sitting at the kitchen table in the small neat Fallon cottage drinking tea. Megan, looking drawn and distressed, continued. "I have told Sean that I don't want to see him anymore."

Kit Fallon had changed from her nun's outfit, her stunning face masking the sadness she felt for Megan. In all the time she had known Megan, this was the first time she had spoken so openly about her relationship with Sean McGuire. Though Kit had suspected for some time now that all was not right between them, she had never spoken with Megan about it.

"What was his reaction when you told him, Megan?"

"He got very angry," Megan responded nervously. "I have seen Sean angry before, but this time he scared me. He started ranting that there was no way I could just call it off. Kit, Sean and I have known each other all our lives. For the first time, I saw the true side of him. It frightened me."

Kit watched Megan's eyes. She was looking at genuine fear. "I suppose everyone has assumed that you and Sean would marry someday. For myself, Megan, I have to say I am not totally surprised this happened. I have known you both all my life and have never felt you and Sean were made for each other."

"You are smarter than me then, Kit," Megan answered, smiling. "What's funny is that I have known it was coming for a long time now. God knows we have been arguing over everything. Mainly though it has always come back to the same thing."

"What was that?" Kit asked.

"The fighting and killing that has gripped our country, Kit." Hesitating, looking out the window at some far-off place, Megan turned back to face Kit. "You know at the beginning, Kit, I was all for Sean and the others, believing in what they were fighting for. God knows if anyone was brainwashed, it was me. But now that I have seen what they stand for, I truly feel they do not want peace."

"Have you discussed this with Sean? Does he know how you feel about what is happening in Ireland?" Kit asked.

"Yes, I have. Kit, he just doesn't want to listen." Leaning across the table, her eyes flashing, Megan continued. "What Sean and the others don't understand is I would like nothing better than to have the Brits and the Prots leave us to ourselves. But when I see our own people being killed, it makes me sick."

Kit got up and went to the kitchen, bringing back two fresh cups of tea. Sitting back down, Kit said to Megan, "I couldn't agree with you more, Megan. God knows I have prayed the killings would stop. I've known so many that are not among us anymore."

"How many more bullets, how many more bombs are going to take before everyone wakes up and realizes all we are doing is killing our own people?" Megan said, a distressed sound to her voice. "It's becoming a war of attrition. That's all I would ever hear from Sean, how it was the Brits' fault as though we had nothing to do with it."

"I know, Megan dear, I know," Kit answered, taking Megan's hand. "I'm sorry for the sadness you feel. Is there anything I can do for you?"

"Even breaking up with a man you don't love anymore, or even respect, can still hurt, blast it," Megan said. Then Megan and Kit both burst out laughing. "It's Sean that's having the problem, really. I tried being reasonable, but Sean is angry, too angry to listen to reason, and that makes it more difficult."

"I can see how that could be a problem for you, and it should be. He's losing you, Megan, and you're the best thing that ever happened to Sean McGuire," Kit told Megan. Kit smiled as she watched Megan's eyes light up a bit.

"Excuse my language, Kit, but Sean's a stubborn bastard," Megan said. "He is also a hard man too."

Kit just nodded her head.

"Enough about me and my woes, Kit. Even I am getting tired of listening to myself," Megan said, smiling. "Tell me about your brother John. Is he getting along all right?"

"John has taken to the farm well enough," Kit replied. "Like a fish to water, really. It's good to have him back. Sometimes I feel he has never been away."

Kit noticed that there was a plaintive look on Megan's face. "What manner of man is he?" Megan asked. "It was hard to read him the first time I met him."

"You couldn't tell what exactly?" Kit asked.

"When the discussion turned to talk of the ongoing battle between Britain and the Irish," Megan continued, "it was hard to tell whether John was for us or against us. Is he a pacifist? Or is he just afraid, Kit?"

Kit looked at Megan for a moment before answering. "You know, Megan, John is my brother and I love him. It has been many years, and I am just now beginning to get to know him again."

"Please, Kit," Megan said anxiously. "Please don't think I am criticizing John or saying he is a coward. I should just keep quiet, it's really none of my business."

"I know, Megan, but I can assure John is no coward," Kit replied. "As far as for what he stands for or what he believes in, I really don't know, and to be honest, I don't ask. Half the time I don't know what I stand for. Megan, I have my work, but for all the years we have been apart, I have missed my brother terribly. Just having him back home to me is a blessing. I do know Ireland is a strange country and can do strange things to you."

"The only reason I bring it up, Kit, is there has been talk in town," Megan told Kit. "There was an incident in one of the pubs."

"Talk and an incident?" Kit said narrowly. "What happened?" Kit wanted to know.

Knowing this is a sensitive issue for Kit having seen how she felt about her brother, Megan was having second thoughts about how much she should divulge. Megan remembered that she and Kit had never had any secrets between them.

"Well," Megan began, looking uncomfortably at Kit, "our darling Sean tried to instigate a fight with John at the Three Oaks Pub. Of course, he had his three cronies with him."

Kit looked surprised. "I haven't heard. John hasn't said a word."

"It appears that Sean, Cassidy, and some of the others started pushing John trying to find out if he was with them or a British sympathizer, and he didn't feel it necessary to respond to them," Megan replied. "Then Sean, in his vicious manner, turned the men loose on John, treating him like scum and running him out of the pub."

"What did John do?" Kit asked.

"It appears John did nothing," Megan said. "Word around town is he never spoke to them, just turned and left the pub."

"That was a smart move on John's part," Kit said. "Knowing Sean and the way he operates, it would have been John against the bunch of them."

"Sean and Cassidy are spreading the word that John is a coward," Megan said solemnly. "That's not true, is it, Kit?"

"John a coward?" Kit looked at Megan in true surprise. "Not hardly. There hasn't been a Fallon born yet that has been a coward," Kit added, incensed. "I can assure you, Megan, John is no coward."

"Well, he backed down from them, Kit, and left the pub," Megan continued, a puzzled look on her face.

"What else was he supposed to do, Megan? Fight Sean?" Kit wanted to know. "From what I know of your Sean McGuire, to fight him means you are going to fight all of his men," Kit said with disgust. "Sean is the type of man who gets others to do his fighting because that's the type of man he is. If there is a coward, it's Sean McGuire."

Megan thought about that and then nodded her head in agreement. "That is true, Kit. When I look back now through all the years I have known Sean, he has always had somebody else do his dirty work and his fighting. He comes across with a lot of bravado, but deep down, Sean is a bully and a bad man. I'm embarrassed to have known him as I have."

"Oh, you were just young and didn't know any better," Kit told her. "What could you have learned growing up here on the farm? Megan, it's my fault. I should have spent more time with you, taught you better. Or at least have told you more. Alas, when it comes to men, I don't know all that much myself."

They both shared another laugh. Even as a nun, Kit had always looked upon Megan as a daughter or younger sister. After the loss of her parents, Kit had taken it upon herself to watch over Megan. Sadly, Kit's work at school and in the community had left her little free time. Kit could not help but feel some form of guilt when it came to Megan.

"From what I gather, Megan, men are hard to read," Kit said. "That's about the extent of what I know about them, especially Irish men in particular. They are the worst." Kit continued and they both smiled with wry understanding.

"How about your brother?" Megan asked.

"What about him?"

"I don't want to pry," Megan began nervously. "But is he okay? His lack of concern about what is happening in Ireland that we were discussing the other day seemed rather strange to me. He seems kind of dark."

"John may be a loner," Kit began, "and for all intents and purposes, he may have his reasons like we all do about certain things. But the one thing I am certain of John is he is a good man and is surely no coward. I don't know what he would do in a situation that entailed violence, but then most men don't either. I would venture to guess that once the violence starts, they would hope for the best and let their guns do the work."

"I suppose you're right on that last part," Megan said to Kit.

"You can't go by me, darling. My life has been somewhat sheltered living in the convent for so many years."

"Well, in any case, Kit," Megan said, blushing, "your brother is a handsome man. I'll give him that, even though he seems a little dark."

"He's got the Fallon looks, that's for sure," Kit said mischievously, smiling. "And that includes the dark side." Megan smiled back. They both knew what Megan was thinking.

They both knew Kit was pleased.

Fallon was thinking about Sean McGuire and his revolutionaries as he walked along the coast of the Irish Sea. The waves were crashing in across the rocks that jutted out from the shore, the water slapping in across the shore and twisting and turning back to sea. The sky was dark and ominous; the promise of rain was on the horizon.

As Fallon stared off in the distance, he could not shake that old feeling that began in the pit of his stomach, the feeling that he was being drawn into something he wanted no part of. You could not help but think about the troubles here in Ireland. Their situation was your situation, and everyone was included in it whether they wanted to be or not. Fallon, so happy to be home at last, was now having second thoughts that maybe it would be better to cut and run.

Ireland was a small country, and tragedy spreads fast. A bomb that kills three touches twenty. Three men break into a house in one of the counties and slaughter an entire family. The British, their hatred obvious, kill innocent civilians. The fight for independence, even if fought by the few, included them all.

World Wide did some work here, but very little. Little was needed. It was a small fire, barely a blip on their radar screen and easily watched. The purpose of the war in Ireland was brutally simple, yet it had a great arc of tragedy to it, so fitting to the Irish. Fallon, smiling to himself, thought that the Irish loved romanticizing everything.

The purpose of the IRA was to keep Ireland ungovernable so the British would get sick of supporting it financially and sick of watching their men dying here for a patch of land that didn't amount to a hill of beans. That was the purpose of all the killing and instability.

The problem the British faced was they that were so firmly entrenched in Ireland; it looked as though there was no possibility of getting out. That was where their frustration took over.

The methods they used were the same as when they started—violence by gun and bomb and physical harm, always with the threat of intimidation behind it. The only problem being as the years went on was that the weapons became more sophisticated and the threats more dangerous. But that was true for all wars in all countries. The Irish couldn't be blamed for that, though they learned very quickly how to utilize it. You use what you have. Only you have more and more because man keeps striving for better ways to kill man. Better ways to go to war.

Despite the long-incoming, long-to-wait peace process, the war was still on. ASUs operated throughout North and South Ireland. The Catholics in the North needed the Catholics in the South to back their operations, and though the majority in the South appeared not to want the bloodshed it cost, a strong minority let the North know the cause was worth fighting for. Ireland was a small country. Ballots and bullets was a phrase known to all.

As Fallon looked across the raging ocean, whitecaps dotting the tops of the waves as they roared in across the beach, his thoughts were elsewhere. Even knowing there is no chance for peace, the British and Ulster Protestants have other notions. While some called it just a war, some called it genocide.

Fallon was well aware of the workings of the different sides, the different armies and cells and organizations. And in Ireland, there were many to be made aware of. He had known men doing work on all sides and known many who had died fighting for their respective causes. That did not discount the fact that most of these men joined these causes with high ideals, dreams of making their land a better place to live. Most of them were good men who believed in what they were fighting for.

Then there were the fanatics, the ones whose vision was warped by the sense of power they could attain, not really caring who was killed in the process. Most of them bordered on the insane belief that it was their duty to keep the battle raging, peace not being an option. They killed senselessly and viciously, terror and intimidation being their calling card. Fallon had known men like this.

Then there were the ones who played both sides of the fence. These were the most dangerous. These men were mercenaries who fought for the highest bidder. They came from all over the world, and peace was never something they worried about. To them, as long as their gun was needed, they could care less about peace or the people who were fighting for it. At one time after the war, Fallon had been one of them.

Fallon also knew he didn't want any part of this any longer. He continued walking slowly down the beach, weighing his options. It would break Kit's heart, but if he had to leave Ireland, Fallon was prepared to do so.

Fallon even knew that had he not spent his life growing up in America and naively defending American interest, he still did not want a part of this war they were raging in Ireland. He had been used too many times to believe in who was right and who was wrong. He knew a loss when he saw one coming, and Ireland without peace was a loss. Pausing in his tracks, Fallon's thoughts drifted to Sean McGuire.

Fallon sensed it from their first meeting. McGuire had the look of someone that had plans, an agenda that could only spell trouble. Fallon was certain that McGuire was planning something, and his cockiness told Fallon he was fairly sure he could pull it off. For that one reason alone, he had walked out of the Three Oaks Pub the day McGuire had his men brace him.

Fallon had had his share of trouble, and the last thing he was about to do was let some local drunks with grandiose ideas draw him into a confrontation. He knew McGuire was disappointed that he had backed off. But if Fallon had learned anything in his days as an assassin, anything that went down would be on his terms. For now, just to be away from the trouble that was on the way was all that counted. Being looked on as coward was something that Fallon found to be amusing.

He saw that look on McGuire's face, and he saw it on the faces of the other three men. Someone else's opinion of him had never mattered to Fallon, and he wasn't about to let this episode change that.

Fallon stopped walking, and the sea came in strong at his feet. The smell of the salt air and the wet sand made him feel some sort of contentment he hadn't felt in years. Though he had faint recollections of his father, his uncle had told Fallon that his fascination for the sea came from him. Whatever the reason, Fallon had always gravitated to the water, and it was at this time he found serenity.

Fallon had been walking and standing at the water's edge and taking in the coast for hours, and now stopping to rest again, he looked off in the distance and spotted a figure on top of one of the hills behind him. He watched as the figure he couldn't make out headed in his direction. Fallon, ever alert, felt his body tense up.

As the figure became clear, Fallon was already assessing the distance and, if they had found him, what were his options. He didn't have a weapon, which put him in a precarious position. He had a fleeting thought of having bought the farm on a beach in Ireland.

Fallon, his breathing returning to normal, felt his body relax when he saw that approaching him now across the sand was the woman Megan Clark. A beautiful Irish woman if ever there was one, Fallon thought. Watching the graceful way she walked, her hair billowing in the wind that coursed across the sea, Fallon gasped at her beauty.

He stood and watched her walk through the coarse sand toward him. When she was close enough to hear him, he said smilingly, "Good morning, Ms. Clark." Fallon wondered if Megan Clark could hear the relief in his voice.

As she moved closer, Fallon waited. When she spoke, Fallon noted that her voice was soft, with the gentle Irish lilt of a songbird. "Good morning," Megan said. "I do wish you would call me Megan. Ms. Clark does sound rather formal, doesn't it?" She had a teasing smile that made Fallon laugh.

"I would find it very easy to call you Megan," Fallon answered, noticing the deep blue eyes that a man could get lost in. "Megan is such a beautiful name. It's not one you hear too much of in America."

"Thank you," Megan said and blushed a little like he had seen her do the first time he had met her. "And I'll call you John if you don't mind."

"I don't mind at all," Fallon said.

"You mentioned America," Megan asked hesitatingly, unsure whether she should go on. She plunged ahead. "Do you miss it?"

Fallon hesitated for a moment, looking out to sea again before answering. "No, Megan, I don't miss it. Don't get me wrong, I just about lived my whole life there and will always love it. But being back in Ireland, I realize how much I have missed it. To be honest with you, I think of this as home."

A look of pleasure crossed Megan's face. She followed his gaze as they both looked out at the sea. Megan noticed there was a comfortable silence that passed between them. She didn't know why, but she was at ease with him. Megan found this disconcerting. John Fallon was a comparative stranger, yet she felt as though she had known him all her life. Megan broke the silence.

"I love the sea," Megan said. "It makes me feel lucky to be living in Ireland sometimes. Just to have that." Megan pointed to the rows of incoming waves as they made their way toward the shore to drift in across the sandy beach. "It takes hold of you and doesn't' let you go. I suppose that sounds rather foolish to you."

"Not at all. I think it's a beautiful thought," Fallon said, turning to look at her. There was a serene and peaceful look on her face.

"Just a thought," Megan asked him somewhat playfully, somewhat honestly.

"You can love something, and it doesn't have to love you back," Fallon said plaintively. Megan noticed him looking off across the horizon, lost in his own thoughts. "We can love anything we put our minds to, whether it deserves to be loved or not." Fallon continued. "That said, Megan, I feel the same way myself."

Fallon turned back to Megan and smiled gently at her. Megan turned to look at him, and a feeling that she could not explain rushed through her. After a moment, Megan spoke. "Kit said the Fallons were dark and strange people. I think she may be right."

Fallon started laughing as they began walking along the shore. They were comfortable with each other, and it showed in the way they enjoyed being together.

"When I was a child, I would come down to the water and dream about living in some far-off place beyond the sea, you know," Megan said wistfully. "My mind conjures up those faraway places that exist only in the mind of a child. But the years have come and gone and I still haven't left Ireland," she said and laughed. It was a small laugh with not much happiness in it. "Do you know I have never been beyond these shores?"

"It's never too late, Megan," Fallon said. "Planes fly out of here every day." Speaking gently, Fallon continued. "Megan, if you really want to travel, see other places, experience new adventures, you are still young. These things can happen to you."

"Sadly, I don't believe that anymore," Megan said sadly. "With all that has happened in my country, all the things I dreamed of as a child doesn't exist in any of the countries out there. That much I know."

"That sounds terribly jaded, Megan."

"I suppose it does. But unfortunately it's the way I feel." Megan, pausing to gaze at the horizon, turned to look at Fallon. "Dreams are dead to me now."

"Dreams don't die, Megan," Fallon answered softly. "People kill them."

Megan, a frown creasing her forehead, looked strangely at Fallon. For the first time, she began to see John Fallon in a different light. "That's an odd thing to say, John. It sounds as though you have been hurt in the past." Megan watched as the wall that she felt Fallon had let down was suddenly back up. Looking closely at him, Megan sensed that Fallon was a million miles away from Ireland.

"We should be getting back," Fallon said, a smile on his face. "Kit has me working so hard on the farm I think she is determined to make a farmer out of me yet."

Megan laughed as they turned and headed back along the shore. Megan was still not ready to let it go. "I hear what you are saying, John, about dreams and aspirations, but I am not sure you fully understand what it is like living in this country. You have been away for a long time and things have changed."

Megan waited for a response from Fallon. When none came, she continued speaking as they slowly made their way back toward the Fallons.

"John, when you live in a country like this . . ." The frustration evident in her voice, Megan stopped and faced Fallon. "You might not understand, but living in a country that is set on killing itself makes you think you know what reality is. And that reality is the dream of peace. No offense, John, but you come from America. You don't have violence and the threat of violence as an everyday occurrence. You fought your civil war over two hundred years ago."

Fallon did not bite at the sarcastic tone that emanated from Megan. Experience had taught him that people looking for a reaction sometimes tried to draw you into a verbal battle. He spoke very gently when he did respond. "There's plenty of violence to go around, Megan. Not everyone has it as easy in America as you think. People are dying every day."

"I'm not talking about random shooting or drunks hitting people with their cars. I'm talking about when every day someone is planting a bomb or arbitrarily bursting into someone's home and killing an entire family. There is a difference, John."

Fallon was silent as he looked at the anguish on Megan's face. Sorrowfully, he knew there was no reaching her or trying to explain how it was in the States "You're right, Megan, we in America don't have to contend with the violence and unrest that pervades throughout Ireland. But in America, all is not hail fellow well met. We have our share of killings, muggings, burglaries, and the rate of gangs that inhabit the city cannot be kept under control by the police."

Looking at Megan, Fallon knew she did not grasp what he was talking about. "Megan, most people in America are free to work, raise families, and have social lives all in comparative safety. But even there we have our problems. For one thing—"

Before he could continue, Fallon heard the sound of Megan's name being carried on the wind. Megan turned at the same time as Fallon at the sound of her voice. Fallon knew immediately who it was. He could see Sean McGuire off in the distance, about ten men with him as they came over one of the sand dunes, heading in their direction.

Fallon knew from the raucous laughter, the loud voices, and the barroom banter they had brought with them where they were coming from. At the head of the crew that was headed their way was Sean McGuire. Fallon and Megan, having stopped, waiting to see what was about to transpire, looked at each other. Fallon noticed the worry on Megan's face.

When they were close enough, Fallon made a mental note of just how many men there were. He counted twelve. Having encountered situations like this in the past, Fallon knew most of them were there out of curiosity and posed no threat. Fallon had already designated the ones he would have trouble with, and trouble was coming.

After observing very quickly who the men were, the look of trouble on their faces and their swaggering frames, Fallon figured he would have at least five to contend with. He knew they had all been drinking, some to excess, as they had trouble even keeping their balance. That wasn't what concerned him. It was Sean McGuire.

Fallon knew any trouble that came, the lead would come from McGuire. Positioning himself just in front of Megan, making sure he could make eye contact with McGuire, Fallon waited. Fallon found it interesting that McGuire, flanked by Cassidy and the other two who had braced him in the Three Oaks, was not as drunk as the others.

The weak one, Casey, though Fallon did not know his name yet, was the drunkest. He had the wildest eyes and the craziest smile on his alcohol-heated face. Fallon knew he would prove to be more reckless than the others. He would also be the easiest to take out. It now became a waiting game to see when they would make their move.

Standing next to Megan, Fallon could feel the concern course through Megan's body. McGuire and his men were coming on strong, and he forced his body to relax and locked onto McGuire's eyes. Watching McGuire, Fallon could see that he was unnerving him. The sardonic smile he was showing was a façade, and Fallon was sure he caught a glimpse of uncertainty cross McGuire's face. McGuire broke first.

"Will you look at this now," McGuire said sarcastically. "It's my lovely Megan and what should she be doing but strolling along the beach with the Yank. Sure it's a grand picture now, lads, isn't it?"

Fallon, scanning the crowd, listened to the nervous laughter emanating from the group. Fallon was not unfamiliar with these types of situations and knew you had to take the measure of each man. He arranged them in his mind by size and ability, by their threat level. It did not take more than a moment.

"Megan girl," McGuire asked, "what are you doing with our American friend now? Are you slumming now?"

There was fire in Megan Clark's eyes as she stepped toward McGuire, her hands planted firmly on her hips. "Shut your mouth and be off with you, Sean McGuire, you and me are done and I want to have nothing to do with you."

As Megan leaned into McGuire, Fallon noticed she did an excellent job of maintaining her cool as clearly as she was angry. Beautiful and strong, Fallon thought and was more than impressed.

"You used to mean something to me, Megan," McGuire shot back, venom in his voice. "I guess you still do."

"Well, you can get over it because if Christ came down from the heavens and asked me to reconcile with you, I wouldn't."

At that, Fallon started to smile. This was a woman who was more than up to holding her own. McGuire, his eyes flashing, the anger evident in his face as his mates looked on, was bordering on rage.

"That mouth of yours is going to get you into trouble sometime, Megan," McGuire said acidly, his gaze turning to Fallon. "You are finding this amusing, Fallon? Maybe we can offer you something else to get a laugh out of you."

The crowd had tensed. They knew, as Fallon did, what was going to transpire. Fallon had most of them pegged as onlookers. He could tell they were fresh off a night of drinking and were along because they had nothing else to do. Most of them didn't have the stomach for what was happening, and as the drink wore off, Fallon could see that the majority of them were uncomfortable.

Cassidy, who was closest to Fallon, moved nearer. Fallon wasn't surprised it was him that made the first move. Fallon had the same sense of the man as he did that day in the bar. The difference this time being he was not about to walk away. And maybe despite his reluctance, despite his intentions, he really didn't want to. It was just going to be a matter of time; it might as well be now.

"So you're thinking all this is funny, Yank?" Cassidy wanted to know. Fallon could see that Cassidy was a big man. He judged him to about 250, 260, mostly big thick bone and heavy weight. As he spoke, Cassidy kept moving closer until he was about six feet from where Fallon stood. Fallon was braced.

"I like women who speak their minds," Fallon said agreeably. "I'm from America and we are used to strong-willed women." Fallon sensed Megan's appreciation of that remark. Cassidy narrowed his eyes and made himself bigger in the chest and arms. Fallon knew he wouldn't wait long. Glancing quickly at the crowd, Fallon could see the apprehension on their faces.

"Well, you're in Ireland now, Yank," Cassidy said.

"I don't want any trouble, Cassidy," Fallon said slowly, knowing it was falling on deaf ears. He looked at McGuire.

"Why don't you and your drunken friends just be on your way and be leaving us alone," Megan said to McGuire, but also to Cassidy. "John doesn't want any of your trouble and neither do I."

While Megan was speaking, Fallon had not taken his eyes off Cassidy. He knew that was where the trouble was going to come from.

McGuire uttered a brash laugh at Megan's retort. "Sure the man doesn't have the stomach to fight. He relies on his women to do his fighting for him. But I don't think that's going to happen today. Am I right, Cassidy?"

Fallon had been right; Cassidy was the one who was going to make the first move. If he had most of the crowd figured right, they were just here for the show. Fallon, bracing himself, was ready to go to work.

As Cassidy lunged wildly, arms flailing, Fallon sidestepped him, catching him in the throat full on with his elbow. Cassidy landed hard on the sand, his hand grasping his throat as he tried getting his breath back. Fallon stood over him and could see Cassidy's pain, the look of disbelief in his face. It was probably the first time Cassidy had ever been dropped that quickly before, never thinking it could be possible.

Casey, one of the other men who, along with Cassidy, had moved in quickly, swung wildly. Fallon, stepping to the side, caught Casey with a left hook that sent him crashing into the water, falling headfirst into the shallow water.

The crowd, including McGuire, had been shocked and stunned at what had transpired. Seeing Cassidy writhing on the sand and Casey had caught them all by surprise. It took a moment to register before Casey, pushing himself up on his knees, started forward.

"You son of a bitch," Casey roared as he took a run at Fallon.

Spinning away from Cassidy, Fallon kicked Casey in the groin, sending Casey to the ground, gasping in pain. Cassidy, shaking his head, climbed up from the sand, still with one hand on his throat. With the other, he stepped in back of Fallon and cracked him on the side of the jaw with a sledgehammer-like blow.

The others in the crowd hadn't budged. McGuire, smirking, was letting the drama unfold before him. Fallon, feeling as though he had been run over by a train, was up on one knee as Cassidy rushed him. Coming straight up from the ground, Fallon head-butted Cassidy in the nose. He could hear the bone crack as Cassidy's hands flew to his face, trying to stem the flow of blood that seeped between his fingers.

Not waiting, Fallon moved in. Stepping to the side, Fallon drove his fist into Cassidy's left side. Cassidy, with a grunt, let one of his hands drop, and Fallon without hesitation brought the next one up from the ground, breaking Cassidy's jaw as he sent him sprawling into the water. Fallon turned quickly.

"Stop it!" Megan screamed frantically as she rushed toward Fallon.

"Hold her." McGuire signaled to two of his men who grabbed Megan and pulled her back. Staring at Fallon, Cassidy was still down from Fallon's beating. He shouted over the crashing waves, "Okay, boys, take him!"

Two of the men, one of them Collins, the other one from the bar, moved in. As Collins reached to grab Fallon, Fallon dipped low, sending a fist crashing into Collins's ribs. Collins grunted, grabbing his side as his knees buckled. The other man caught Fallon on the side of the jaw, rocking him back. Moving in on Fallon, the man caught him with another shot to the side of the head.

Fallon, trying to clear his eyes, clutched the man, hoping to buy some time. Cassidy and Casey were back on their feet, closing in on Fallon. Fallon knew it was just a matter of time before they overwhelmed him. Bringing his knee up into the stomach of the man he was holding, Fallon braced for the others. Cassidy rushed forward, driving his head into Fallon's stomach, sending him backward.

Fallon could hear Megan screaming and then McGuire's voice telling her to be quiet. Just as Fallon landed one on Casey, he saw McGuire slap Megan hard across the face. Filled with rage, disregarding the blows from the others, Fallon managed to reach McGuire. Before McGuire could react, Fallon was on him. Blood streaming from his eye, barely able to make McGuire out, Fallon began to methodically pummel him unmercifully.

"Get him, you bastards!" McGuire screamed as Fallon's blows sent him to the ground, Fallon raining blow after blow on him.

They were all over Fallon now. Fists, feet, knees, they dragged Fallon off McGuire. Fallon, groping blindly, head-butted one of the men, hearing his jaw crack as he slumped to the ground. Not waiting to admire his handiwork, Fallon rolled to the side, kicking wildly as he caught the pressure point on the side of one of the men's legs, making him unable to stand or support his weight. He dropped easily.

They had Fallon overpowered now. Pulling him away from McGuire, Cassidy grabbed Fallon by the shirt and flung him toward the water. The shirt was torn from his body as he barely could stand up. His body aching from the beating, blood flowing freely from his eyes and mouth, Fallon climbed to his feet. With what little strength he had left, Fallon began moving in a tight circle, preparing himself.

Circling, keeping the men in his sight, Fallon knew he was down, but convinced he was going to take some of them with him. Waiting for the onslaught, Fallon, weary now, kept McGuire in his line of vision. McGuire and the others stood frozen, looking strangely at Fallon as the water from the ocean rolled across his feet.

"Jesus Christ," Cassidy uttered, a look of disbelief on his face. "Would you be looking at that now?"

"Christ, what a mess," Collins said, stunned.

Fallon, still standing in the surf, water crashing against his legs, was ticking the seconds off in his head, waiting for the inevitable. It never came. Even Sean McGuire was transfixed at the sight of Fallon, his shirt dangling around his waist, fists clenched at his side. Then it dawned on Fallon what they were looking at. He knew what had stopped the beating he was waiting to happen. His eyes shot toward Megan, who, like the others, was standing quietly, a look of sadness on her face.

Megan slowly moved through the crowd that was now eerily silent, their eyes focused on Fallon. Reaching Fallon, Megan's hand went to his face tenderly. When she spoke, it was barely above a whisper.

"What have they done to you?" Megan asked.

Fallon's back and chest were covered with scars from knife wounds, cigarette burns, seven bullet wounds (five of them exits), numerous surgeries to repair those wounds, and other internal injuries and broken bones, marks and permanent bruises.

Fallon's body, used as it had been for years of violent purpose, was ugly and enough to turn the stomach of most men. And to stop them in their tracks. Not unlike these Irish bullies who considered themselves tough, but not tough enough. Not tough enough because they had not seen it all.

"Now what the hell do we have here," McGuire asked, stepping forward. His crew of men was still licking their wounds, and Fallon noticed that most of the fight had been taken out of them. But there were the diehards. That included Cassidy, Collins, and Casey. Fallon still considered them cowards.

Fallon stood his ground. "Are we finished here?" he asked an astonished McGuire in a voice that sent chills up McGuire's spine.

McGuire was stunned for a moment before he regained his voice. "Are we finished, he asks." Smiling, he turned to look at his men. Turning back to Fallon, he continued. "You look pretty much done in, Yank. I doubt if there is much fight left in you. I can also see that someone put it to you before."

Fallon knew McGuire was referring to the scars. He wasn't about to give him the edge. "I'll keep going until just one of us is standing, McGuire. And that goes for your crew of daisies too."

McGuire tensed, as Cassidy and the other two looked bewildered. Looking to McGuire, waiting to see if he gave them the okay to continue, the bloodied trio waited silently. McGuire, hesitating, looked at Fallon and tried to decide. He knew his men were just waiting for the word, but like Fallon, McGuire felt they had enough of Fallon and were looking to call it quits. McGuire made his decision.

"You're a mess, Yank, and I don't know why but I'm feeling generous. We'll leave it like it is for today," McGuire said. "This isn't over by a long shot though. We'll be seeing you again. Now take the girl and go."

Fallon, without hesitation, completely ignoring the looks he was getting from the four of them, walked past them to where Megan was standing, holding his tattered shirt. Taking it, Fallon slipped it on as best as he could, noticing the horrified look on Megan's face. He had seen that look before. That was okay. He would probably always experience that and had long been comfortable with that thought.

Taking her hand, Fallon whispered softly, smiling. "Let's go, Megan." Megan nodded and they started walking back up the beach. The clouds had darkened the sky. The sea was raging now, and it wouldn't be long before the storm rolled in.

Fallon heard movement behind him and knew that McGuire and his cronies were watching them. Fallon stopped and turned around.

"McGuire," Fallon called out. McGuire, his face impassive as he tried to assist Cassidy who was still holding his throat, looked at Fallon.

"What do you want now, Yank?"

"If I ever catch you slapping another woman, I'm going to make you one miserable son of a bitch," he said coldly.

McGuire, frowning, turned back to Cassidy, trying to ignore the remark.

Fallon and Megan walked away.

FIVE

"Dan, it's good to see you. How long has it been?" Childers sat behind his desk and smiled heartily at Dan Morehead.

"Not long enough," Morehead said to Childers who stared back in return.

Getting up from his chair, Childers excused himself. "Make yourself comfortable, Dan. I just remembered something I wanted my secretary to get for me. As soon as I get back, we can catch up."

Watching Childers exit the room, Morehead got up and walked over to the window overlooking the city below. Letting himself drift back in time, he tried remembering how many times he had been in Childers's office, planning, scheming, working on some top-secret project that eventually caught up to him, forcing him to turn in his resignation because he couldn't stand it anymore.

Before arriving for his meeting with Childers, Morehead had contacted some old friends in the agency and had gotten the lowdown on what was going on and why he was being called in. Johnny must have reached that point in his career that Morehead had. It was time to get out, and he just up and disappeared. Childers was unaware that he knew what was going on. The self-centered son of a bitch was sure he had a handle on everyone and everything.

The haze that had settled over the city was beginning to turn the coal black snow into mush. Unlike his home and neighborhood, Dan Morehead had always found the snow soothing. It was clean and quiet where he lived, and for four years, Dan Morehead had enjoyed his life. Now it was coming to an end.

He was being drawn back in, and the worst part of it was that Johnny Fallon was the target. Johnny had been like a son to him. From the time he was recruited, Dan had been his mentor. Of all the people he had worked with, John Fallon had been the quickest study and the most knowledgeable recruit he had ever worked with.

Over the years, it had become more than a working relationship; it had developed into a true friendship. That was up until the day John Childers pulled Fallon into his devious and cunning world. Childers, a pompous ass and self-absorbed as he may have been, was not stupid and had seen the potential in Fallon. After that, Dan Morehead and John Fallon saw less and less of each other. But not entirely. Morehead heard the door open, and Childers was back, taking his seat behind his desk. Childers gestured to Morehead to be seated. Taking the seat across from Childers, Morehead sat and waited.

"Now where were we, Dan?" Childers began.

"You were telling me how much you missed me," Morehead answered sarcastically.

Seemingly ignoring the sarcasm, though the crimson color that covered his face didn't do him justice, Childers smilingly responded, "Dan. I have missed that sense of humor around here. You don't know how good it is to see you. We have been friends for a long time, Dan. What's wrong with wanting to renew old friendships?"

Dan Morehead, pushing himself up slowly from his chair, placing his hands on Childers's desk, leaned forward. "Childers, listen up and listen good. You and I are not and have never been friends. I thought you were an asshole the first day I met you, and you have done nothing since I've known you to change my mind."

It was like a slap in the face as Childers went ice cold across the desk. The room was so silent the ticking of the clock sounded like drums. The sun was fighting its way through the window and not making much headway. Morehead, though the expression on his face did not change, felt a deep level of satisfaction in seeing that high-level face go rigid. Leaning back in his chair, Dan Morehead was satisfied he had established the ground rules early. This would eliminate any bullshit from Childers.

"Who the hell do you think you're talking to?" Childers asked stonily as he tried unsuccessfully to regain his composure.

"You, Childers," Morehead replied. "I'm talking to you." Childers, visibly shaken, was half up and half down in his chair. He was trying to make up his mind when Morehead's voice cut through the air. "If you're going to make a move, Childers, make it. I won't wait too long before I take a run at you."

The two men stared at each other across the uncluttered desk. Childers hesitated too long, and Morehead knew it, relaxing in his seat. Childers dropped slowly back into his. He shrugged and smiled a thin-lipped smile and said, "Okay, Dan. I'll spare you the old friend's bullshit and get right down to it."

"Smart move," Morehead said.

"Raven has disappeared," Childers told Morehead. "And that is the problem."

Moorhead forced himself to show a modicum of surprise. He was not about to show his hand this early in the game. It was to his benefit that Childers was unaware of his knowledge about Johnny.

"I'm retired, Childers. Why tell me? It's none of my affair what goes on around here anymore. Get some of your flat-bellied suits to get off their dead asses and earn their money. I can't be of any help to you. Like I said the first time, Childers, I'm retired."

Childers barked a piece of laughter. "Nobody retires from this agency, Dan. There's only two ways to leave it, and only one of them is natural."

Dan Morehead looked away from Childers and out the window at the city, with the sounds of the traffic, the tall buildings that smothered the pavement, and the ever-present shadows they bestowed on the people below. The din of a vibrant, exciting, and fascinating city that never sleeps. A lifetime of living in it, Morehead could hear it and feel it move. He had lived his life in this city, the city that very few people really knew about. It was necessary, and dangerous, and also in the end it could break your heart. But it was Dan Moorhead's city, and he would have it no other way.

As much as he hated to admit it, what Childers said was true. You never left the organization known as World Wide Shipping, not feet first anyway. It was a truth you never signed your name to, it was truth borne out of the absolute secrecy and treachery the organization lived under.

You didn't know that at the front end. Clever marketing and a desire to help the world worked against you. Dan Morehead, like those before him, entered this mysterious and dangerous world under the mistaken belief that what they were doing was noble and courageous. It wasn't long before it dawned on you that all you were were killers for hire.

Coming in, you were excited to be part of something so important and dangerous when you were accepted into the organization, that you accepted the unspoken rules blindly and without hesitation. And there were many of them, rules that crawled inside your guts and made you sick. You realized the number of scumbags and politicians and mentally unstable mercenaries that made up your life's work. Then all you wanted was out. If you were sane or had a conscious or any scruples, you wanted out. And that's when the pressure really started.

Childers watched Dan Morehead with some degree of intuition. It didn't take a rocket scientist to know what he was thinking; he was thinking of the past. Childers was not unaware of Morehead's disdain for some of the tougher, more unpleasant aspects of the work they shared over the years. It was work Morehead had himself been responsible for. Putting his dislike for Dan Morehead and what he considered his sanctimonious outlook of the work they did aside, he knew that at this moment he was the only man who could accomplish what Childers thought was needed.

He did not care one way or the other what Morehead thought of him or the organization. Over the years, Childers had developed a hard shell around himself, a protective wall that kept him aloof and, in his eyes, above those who worked under him. Even the agents who had been killed did not dent that wall, and though Childers had never worked in the field, he felt he had a firmer grasp and understanding of what had to be done in any situation.

Personal issues never interfered in the job Childers did. This work had other loftier meaning for him. So as he pompously sat watching Morehead fighting his personal demons or whatever else he was considering, Childers just sat back and waited.

Finally, Morehead turned and faced him.

"All right, Childers," Morehead started. "Just so we understand each other. I'm in, but I'm out. I don't know if your peanut brain understands that, but those are my terms. If you can't live with that, color me gone."

"Can we do so without the smart remarks?" Childers replied coldly.

"I said I would listen to you but I'm not making any promises." Morehead hesitated, wanting to collect his thoughts. "My interest at World Wide is at an all-time low, and I'm getting too old to find energy without desire."

Childers nodded his head and frowned. "That's a nice speech, Dan, but I'm not all that impressed with how you feel about World Wide."

Morehead came out of his chair and started in Childers's direction. Childers smiled but was unable to hide the fear that passed through him. He raised his hand disarmingly. "Okay, okay. Bad joke. I know how you feel, Dan, I mean that. I understand you might be tired, and when I hit your age, I probably will be too."

Morehead said nothing and waited. He couldn't hide a smile since about two years separated him from Childers in age.

"Okay, here it is in a nutshell," Childers continued. "Bottom line, Raven has gone under. Disappeared."

"You have a lot of men working for you," Morehead said. "Why haven't you gotten them out looking for him?"

"I'm asking who I need to, don't worry," Childers answered too quickly. "But, Dan, I need you. No one knows Raven like you do."

Morehead knew the answer why long before Childers spoke it. No matter where you stood in the chain of command in the organization, there was always someone you answered to. Again he let Childers sweat.

"The man upstairs requested it," Childers continued. Morehead knew that was bullshit. It was no request; it was do it or else. "Raven was one of your bunnies. You trained him and you trained the men who trained him. Everyone in the company knows you took Raven under your wing, he was like the son you never had, all that psychologically relevant bullshit that we like to notice around here. If anyone can reach out to him and drag him back, it's most likely going to be you."

Morehead regrettably knew this to be true. The duck eggs that Childers had working for him couldn't find their ass with both hands. He knew what his reluctance was. Not just that he did look on Johnny Fallon like his son, but he could almost sense also why he had dropped out in the first place.

Something had gone wrong. Something about what he had been doing added up. The weight had become too offensive, too squalid, and too fulsome. Johnny had hit the wall and walked away. But what could he do? He had been retired for almost four years now. He was too removed from the action. Too many changes since he was last in the field, and at best, he was reluctant in going in.

"Childers, you know yourself, Raven was the best," Morehead offered weakly. "If he doesn't want to be found, he won't be."

Childers fixed his stare on Morehead. If it was to intimidate, Childers found out quickly that it wasn't working. He tried the back door approach. "Dan, if anyone can get him back in the fold, it's you."

"Without the gingerbread, Childers," Morehead said nastily. "I know you too long to believe anything you say."

Childers face reddened as he stared back at Morehead. Dan Morehead was enjoying watching Childers squirm. If he was going to be drawn into this fiasco, he might as well derive some pleasure out of it.

"All right, Dan," Childers said through clenched teeth, having a difficult time speaking to Morehead. What frustrated Childers the most was that everyone else who worked for him were either intimidated or frightened of him. He had never been able to wield that kind of power over Dan Morehead. Childers didn't like that. "You have made it perfectly clear how you feel about me. Let's get down to what we are going to do about Raven."

"Right from jump, I do have one question," Morehead said.

"What's that?"

"What if I do locate him? What then?" Morehead asked, his eyes narrowing.

Childers hesitated, but it was his eyes that gave him away. Too many years reading people, having to place his life on the line making split decisions, shooting from the hip, told Morehead immediately that no matter what Childers said, it was a lie. Morehead sat silently in his chair as he watched the wheels turning in Childers's head.

"Dan, cards on the table," Childers began. "Let's put our feelings aside and do what's best for the company. We have to pull Raven back if for no other reason than the fact that he is privy to knowledge that you know could take the company down like a deck of cards. This is nothing personal, but right now, Raven's a loose cannon."

As much as he would like to dispute what Childers had said, he knew he was right. Raven, if he decided to turn over, knew things about what transpired within the company that would have far-reaching circumstances. Even though Morehead knew he would never divulge anything, they didn't, and that was the kicker. But Morehead wasn't about to sit by and watch them take Johnny out.

"You still haven't answered my question," Morehead said quietly.

The frustrated look on Childers's face told Morehead he was not happy about being put on the spot. "I know what you are thinking, Dan, and that's the furthest thing from the truth. We are not looking to terminate Raven, he is too valuable. What I want to do is get him back in the fold and talk to him. If I can't convince him to stay, then he is free to walk. What I want, and I am sure you can understand my position, is Raven's assurance that any knowledge he has about the company will not be revealed. Does that satisfy you?"

From his past dealings with Childers and his chronic dislike for the man, Dan Morehead had no reason to trust Childers. But there wasn't much he could do about it either. Again he had to give Childers the benefit of the doubt. What he said made sense. But then why was the hair on his neck standing up?

"Okay, Childers, I'll see what I can do," Morehead said and heard the tired sound of his own voice. "But just so we are clear on this and you aren't being straight with me, beware of the consequences. If I find out you are using me to set Raven up and you take him out, old man or not, I'll be coming back here to get you personally."

Childers smiled at Morehead, a large genuine smile as though Dan Morehead had not just threatened his life. "That's the reason I thought of you, Dan, when this problem presented itself. You're the right man for the job."

Morehead nodded his head and stood up to leave.

Childers, still smiling, said, "That's why I thought of you, Dan. You're just the man for the job."

Morehead had all he could do not to reach across the desk and smack the arrogant smile off Childers's face. Nodding, Dan Morehead started for the door. Turning back to Childers, coldness crept into his voice that sent shivers through Childers.

"Just remember what I said, Childers. It's not just an idle threat. You try and get cute with me and you won't be around to give any more orders."

As the door closed softly behind Morehead, a bead of sweat started to form on Childers's lip. Shaking, he reached for the phone.

In another building ten blocks from where Childers operated from, Jack Harris sat in Al Reynolds's office while Reynolds worked his laptop. The phone call from Childers had sent Reynolds scrambling into his computer and was now scanning for an opening into Raven's disappearance. With Dan Morehead in the picture now, this ballgame had taken on a whole new perspective.

Reynolds knew Morehead and was not about to doubt the tenacity, the skill, and knowledge he brought to the table. He was a man to be feared, and even at his advanced age, Reynolds knew he was not one to be underestimated. The other thing that was nagging at Reynolds was the fact that Childers felt Harris and himself were not up to fulfilling this mission. Shoving his pride aside, Reynolds went back to work.

Darfur was beginning to look like a dead end. Their counterpart in Sudan had gotten several layers up the government hierarchy, all the way to an aide to the vice president of that country. The aide also had contacts within the army itself. From all appearances, the army had not been responsible for ordering the hit. At least they were saying all the right things and were denying any responsibility. Reynolds, old pro that he was, took everything with a cynical and cautious eye on everyone.

What nagged at Reynolds was the fact that they were not only opting out of any responsibility for the killing, but they were being very laissez-faire about it—unless it was the vice president himself or one of his cronies that ordered the hit, which was entirely possible.

So what did that leave? A freelance mercenary working on his own? Reynolds dismissed that as an unlikely scenario. There would have to be money, payments, something. Something would have leaked out. What else? A psychopath on the loose in Darfur? It could be one of many and not politically connected. A Jack the Ripper scenario? Not likely. For Reynolds, that would be reaching.

While Harris was occupying himself on the computer, randomly searching for other alternatives, Reynolds was reading an e-mail from one of his operatives right now, and it wasn't saying much. He had come up with the half-ass suggestion that the next viable step would be to infiltrate the rebels, the Arab radical factions, the neighborhood of the poor, or the wealthy, and do extensive groundwork. The question from the operative in the e-mail that spanned three sentences was, "How deep should I go?" Shaking his head in frustration, Reynolds wondered, "Where did we get these guys?"

Reynolds gestured to Harris to come look at the e-mails. Standing behind Harris as he scanned them, Reynolds lashed out angrily. "Sometimes I think Childers is an asshole. I just wish he had spent time in the field and get a firsthand look at what type of clowns we are relying on."

"You know, Al," Harris said, turning to Reynolds, "what he is asking is not too farfetched. It could be someone in the seat of power."

"Jack," Reynolds started patiently, "listen to me. We are operating on a timetable, and the clock is running. We don't have time to begin chasing conspiracy theories or start an investigation that could take months. We have to rein Raven in as of yesterday. Childers, as clueless as he is, wants this done immediately. So let's forget about 'how high up it goes.' Right now that doesn't matter."

Harris, reddening and feeling chagrined, got up from the computer and headed back to his desk. Sitting down, he said to Reynolds, "Even if it's not Raven, Al, isn't it something we want to know?"

"The question, Jack, is, Is it something World Wide should be spending money, resources, and time on?" Reynolds asked. Frowning as he reached for a cigarette, Reynolds continued, shaking his head. "And that decision is not up to you and me."

"What's your take on it, Al?"

"My feeling is they are approaching this in the wrong way," Reynolds said. "I know Raven, and tap dancing around all areas of what-ifs, I would concentrate my efforts in one direction."

"And what direction is that?"

"Go directly after him. Raven is not one to get mixed up in politics, use other people to accomplish his mission," Reynolds continued passionately. "Raven is a loner. He operates on his own and by his own rules."

"But if we go to Childers with an empty blanket, he might take us off the contract," Harris said with some justified worry. Harris, though only with the company for a short time, knew Childers to be a mean and vindictive son of a bitch with a lot of tools and ammunition at his disposal. He was known to hold a grudge and, when the opportunity presented itself, dropped on you like a house. He wouldn't have you killed for failing; of course, that was not Childers's way. But it was not farfetched to find yourself up against some incredibly tough odds one day, say, in Egypt or Saudi Arabia because you no longer were considered a high priority. Harris was not delighted with the options.

Failure was not rewarded. At World Wide, it wasn't even recognized because ultimately, it never happened. Someone else was always there to take your place.

Reynolds sat staring at his laptop and did not bother to answer Harris's question. Reynolds was lost deep in thought, and contrary to what Harris believed, he was not about to lose this contract. Some of the reasons were personal, and he was not about to share them with Harris.

This contract meant a lot to him.

He started typing instead and formed his e-mail response.

"Yes or no," Harris persisted.

"This is not Raven's work," Reynolds answered, placing the laptop on the desk and turning to give his full attention to Harris. "The hit was too soon. The place was too hot. Raven would have to have been working hard to establish contacts there, and I don't think he had the time." Looking hard at Harris, remembering what it was like when he was young with World Wide and full of piss and vinegar, he stretched his patience and shrugged. "That's my guess anyway. Are you okay with that?"

Harris looked hard at Reynolds. "I'll trust your gut on this. This time anyway."

"Good." Reynolds checked the message one more time and hit the Send button.

"What did you tell our man?" Harris asked.

"Vacation cancelled. Maybe later. Take care."

"I couldn't stand to live in the deserts of Africa," Harris said by way of conclusion. "The heat and boredom would get to me."

"You could stand it if you were African," Reynolds told him. "One way of avoiding that kind of duty is don't fuck up."

"Now what?" Harris asked.

"Now we get back to work," Reynolds said and stood up. Harris stood up with him.

Major James Neville sat behind his desk skimming through reports from the various counties located throughout Ireland. His mind was a thousand miles away and finding it difficult to concentrate. With a frustrated gesture, he shoved the reports to one side, several of them ending up on the floor.

They were the usual mundane hardness of life in Ireland. Beatings and murders, some taking place right inside the homes of the victims. There was the constant complaint from the shopkeepers, farmers, travelers and tourists of thefts, some of them of a violent nature. There was the ever-present sniveling and whining from the clergy. For Major Neville, these were the most distasteful and one he had no patience for.

Everyone wanted everyone else to believe just as they did. There were the Catholics who constantly complained about the way they were treated in Northern Ireland. The Protestants wanted the Catholics to get out of their part of the country and had no qualms about how they went about it. Everybody hated everybody else. They wanted the other either out or dead or converted. It made for an ugly life, but Neville didn't mind. It justified the harsh methods he used in keeping everyone in their place. Except for the one common enemy they had. The British.

Nothing warmed Neville's heart more than to shove the British troops down the throats of those that hated them. He knew they were all talk and most of them got their courage at the local pubs. He was the type of man who searched for order in the world and by any means necessary, and that suited him very well. He would spend his life seeking closure. It was instinct. The only thing Neville didn't like was that after all these years, every day was the same one running into the other. Nothing different. Here and there, maybe a little progress but not enough to satisfy a man like Major Neville.

Agitated now, Neville got up from his desk and walked over to the window overlooking the courtyard below. Men were training in different parts of the yard. The high wall that surrounded the compound kept them free from prying eyes. It was moments like this that Major Neville felt like a soldier, not some warden in an institution looking after the rabble they dealt with on a daily basis.

Neville was a career army man. He had been a good soldier. He could feel the anger coursing through his body as he thought back to the circumstances that landed him in a country that he felt was beneath him and populated by people inferior to him. He cursed the day he let his hair-trigger temper get the better of him. Why couldn't his superiors have seen that it was just one lapse in judgment?

It had been back in London two years before. Major Neville was commanding a troop of new recruits. It was his job to get them battle ready. He had already been warned about the sadistic streak that had followed him throughout his career. Weak sisters, he called them. At one point, he had almost been cashiered out of the army, but fortunately, his commanding officer at the time had been killed in a freak accident. Neville had shed no tears.

The troop that had been assigned to him was the bottom of the barrel. He would have to have been a magician to get them whipped into any kind of shape for battle. As the days wore on, his frustration only increased until finally one day he snapped. It was raining and they had been out on a ten-mile hike in full pack. Neville wasn't satisfied. He informed them they were heading back out and would continue to do so until they had it right. He knew that when the time came, it would be Craig Roberts.

Roberts had been a thorn in his side since joining up. He had given him several warnings, but the arrogant bastard had done all but laugh in his face. He was a tall handsome man, and the out-and-out leader of the troop. Roberts refused to go back out. Neville was glad it was him. Neville braced him and punched him in front of the troop. Unfortunately, Roberts slipped on the wet ground, his head hitting the ground in a sickening thud. He didn't move and was rushed to the base hospital where he stayed in critical condition for nearly a week.

Neville had been restricted to his barracks while he waited for a board of inquiry to be formed to hear his case. They waited until they had the results on Roberts to see what the final charges would be. Fortunately for Neville, Roberts recovered and left the hospital with only a slight scar to show for his encounter with Neville. He was back on duty in less than a month.

Major Neville appeared before the board. He was at the lowest point in his career, figuring he would be cashiered out of the army. One thing Neville had going for him was the fact that he had learned to play the game. The vicious, unfeeling soldier that was displayed in front of his troops was not the man his superiors witnessed. Neville had managed to build a fairly successful, though not outstanding, career, which enabled him to walk away with a reprimand. Unfortunately, it had taken him away from his duties, landing him in Ireland where he could only envision himself as a warden.

Moving away from the window, Neville sat back down at his desk and tried getting through the monotonous paperwork that never seemed to end. It was useless, he thought as he leaned back in his chair. Even as he was organizing someone's death, as the plan rumbled around in his head, it seemed mundane and not all that exciting. Just planning. Just paperwork. A meeting or two.

When there was a knock on the door and Sergeant Wilson walked in, Neville turned to him with some relief. Relief from the boredom he was feeling. He looked at Wilson standing rigidly at attention. Wilson was his kind of soldier. He was short, stocky, and built like a fire hydrant. A scar ran down the side of his cheek where one of his men tried to kill him. His short hair sat on top of an oversized head, and in his eyes was the gleam of a man who enjoyed inflicting pain. Yes, Wilson was proving very useful to him.

"Well, Sergeant, is everything ready?" Neville asked. "I'm assuming everything is moving according to plan. Ours and theirs," Neville added ironically to humor himself, if not Wilson.

"We put the word out on the street that the prisoners were being moved at nine a.m. The real transfer takes off at eight a.m. But we still have the route lined with as many men as we can spare," Wilson told him and smiled brutishly. "Just in case."

"Which will be the case more than likely. But unfortunately with this rabble, we must do what we can." Neville sighed, then leaned back in his chair and began stroking his mustache. Wilson could feel the wheels turning in Neville's head.

"Just make sure all the precautions have been taken. The last thing we need now is some gang of suicidal Irish rebels storming the prison not giving a damn who gets killed, including us. I'm not looking to make martyrs out of these swine, Wilson, all for the cause," Neville said dryly. "I'd rather not spend the next week reading about it in the papers."

"I don't think we have to worry, sir," Wilson said.

"Why is that?" Neville asked him.

"We have picked up nothing on their grapevine, which is nothing more than a joke. If there is anything going down, everyone in the bloody town is aware of it. The IRA is just a small faction in this area of the country. And of course," Wilson said with confidence, "our combat troops are better men. They are better trained to crack troops, really." Wilson smirked proudly at Neville.

Neville stroked his mustache. "I know our troops are more than adequate, Sergeant. But when you are dealing with fanatics, you learn to expect the unexpected and hope the worst doesn't happen, but you know it will," Neville said. "This is why there is a contingency plan for tomorrow. Do we have it in place?"

"Yes, sir," Wilson answered.

"And your informant?"

Wilson hesitated just long enough for Neville to feel he was unsure of what to say. "I could get nothing out of him. He claims they are planning something. That's what makes me suspicious, sir."

"What is that?" Neville asked cautiously.

"They are always planning something. He said he doesn't know what or where or when. I feel he's playing it too close to the vest."

"Did you apply appropriate pressure, Sergeant?" Neville asked.

After a moment, Wilson replied, "Yes, sir," and left it at that.

Satisfied, Neville nodded his head. "Then we will proceed as planned. Sergeant, keep a keen eye out for McGuire and his boys. This is no time to let our guard down. Be prepared for any and all surprises."

"I hope they do try something, Major," Wilson said with brutal relish. "I would like nothing better than burying them in this beloved land."

Neville frowned and turned away and began stroking his mustache again. "Well, you may get your chance, Sergeant. You may just get your chance."

Donohue, the barman and owner of the Three Oaks Pub, watched as his wife made supper in the kitchen.

His wife had gained weight in the last ten years, and it bothered him. He had always been heavy, so she knew what she had been getting into. He, on the other hand, was still surprised. When they had gotten married, she was a slim, comely lass with long flowing red hair, and half of the men in Offaly had their eyes on her. Why she had chosen him he had no idea. He took no pleasure from her body anymore, and he had never taken pleasure from her food.

Donohue had to get his mind off things like this. It was not time to let his mind wander into territory that could lead to his getting killed. The situation was getting sticky, and he would have to keep his wits about him. Looking at his wife's back, the only thing that satisfied him was her Protestant affiliations. That, now, was the thing that sustained him.

The phone rang, and he picked it up.

"Donohue." He listened and when he heard who it was, he walked the phone away from the kitchen.

Donohue's voice was shrill and agitated when he spoke. "I told you, all I know is tomorrow morning. Guns, but no bombs," Donohue said, working to maintain his calm under pressure. "No, I heard it myself . . . sure enough, but that's all I heard. It's to be a quick hit-and-run operation. They'll be waiting, so expect it early as I said."

Then remembering something he felt was important, Donohue added, "Five men are coming from the north too. That's all I know." Donohue listened some more. "Well, it isn't quite anything. But it's all I can get when these men play it close and quiet. They are keeping it low-key."

Donohue could hear his wife setting the table. Though she knew he worked for the Loyalist cause, he did not like her knowing or hearing when an operation was happening. When all was said and done, Donohue knew that he still loved his wife very much and did not want her harmed in any way. Though Donohue knew that could never be guaranteed in these troubled times in Ireland.

"I am doing what I can," Donohue continued, the stress obvious in his voice. Sweat began to form on his temples.

"Pat," his wife called loudly from over the stove where she was preparing dinner.

"Yes," he said both out loud and into the receiver. Donohue dropped the phone back in its cradle without saying goodbye.

Six

McGuire stood in one of the safe houses supplied by the IRA, reviewing the famous weapons that the British and Loyalists wanted turned in order to reach peace in Ireland and which the IRA refused to deliver. There would never be peace in Ireland until the British bastards left the country.

McGuire, along with the others of his band, stood before the weapons that no one who fought for Ireland would ever give up, stop buying, or live without. They would take their weapons to their death, literally, if need be. They had fought too long and hard to give in now, and the feeling of power McGuire was experiencing now, he was not about to relinquish it. He was too close to the leaders.

It was what McGuire had always wanted. He had always felt on the outside of the battles they were waging for the freedom of Ireland. McGuire had always resented the fact that he was relegated to the small not-too-important town of Offaly. He had willed the men who served with him to make a name for them. And they had.

Sean McGuire was an ambitious man, and being parked in Offaly had stifled his growth in the movement. He cursed his parents for having been born in this small town, wishing it had been closer to the North where McGuire had always felt. If given the chance, he would be able to distinguish himself. This upcoming operation had him edgy. This was the one, if they pulled it off, would put him at the forefront of the higher-ups. He was not about to let his guard down and let any of his men fuck it up.

The small band that McGuire led had staged numerous guerilla raids, sometimes venturing boldly into the northern counties, and it had caught the eyes of the leaders. They saw McGuire as one of their future leaders and had assured him that should this raid go off successfully, McGuire would be admitted to the inner circle. McGuire was going to make sure it went well, even if it meant the death of his men.

Cassidy and the others stood with McGuire before a table of handguns and automatic rifles that had been spread out on the tables. There were also numerous rounds of bullets and the delicate but useful Semtex explosives.

There were about twenty-five automatic rifles, roughly twenty handguns, and two sawed-off shotguns to choose from. They had been promised more weapons if the need arose. McGuire felt what they had on hand would be plenty for the operation they were about to pull off. McGuire saw it as a fast hit-and-run affair. The secret would be to catch the Brits off-guard and get in and get out fast.

Each man had a gleam of something like madness in their eyes as they looked over the weapons. A table of dull black objects that carried with them the power of life and death. McGuire watched as his men caressed the weapons like a woman.

The man who had delivered the weapons was from the North. He had taken a position on the far wall and was intent on watching the men as they chose their weapons. The same look that was in their eyes was in his.

The look of power, the look of greed, somehow, the look of death.

Something snapped outside the farmhouse, loud and close, causing the group to swing their attention to the door. They were all frozen in place.

McGuire, nearest to the table, snatched a Walther handgun off the table and quickly pointed it toward the front door. McGuire turned and silently nodded his head at Cassidy who was standing closest to the door. Cassidy reached out blindly, grabbing the nearest gun he got his hands on. Cassidy slipped out noiselessly for such a big man, disappearing into the darkness that had engulfed the farmhouse.

The other men went to the table and began snatching handguns from the table. There were Walthers, Brownings, Berettas scattered about. None of the men knew what they had picked up. They just picked by instinct, and if they didn't like the feel of it in their hand, they put it down and chose another.

By the time Cassidy returned, every man had a gun hanging restlessly in their hand. Some had the look of fear on their faces.

"Nothing," Cassidy announced, stepping back into the room.

"Or no one?" McGuire said, frowning.

Doubt crept into Cassidy's eyes as he came further into the room. Instinctively, Cassidy turned back to look at the door.

"Sure it doesn't matter. We have enough weapons now to kill an army," Casey said and laughed. "Look at us."

All the men looked around at one another. Sizing up his band of raiders, McGuire observed twelve men with guns standing near a table full of automatic rifles and even more handguns. Glancing over at the man who brought them, they both nodded, pleased with what they were witnessing.

McGuire took a moment to inspect his men. They all looked ready. McGuire allowed himself a moment to be pleased.

"You do look good, boys," he told them and felt the excitement he always felt before he set out to kill the British scum. He knew he was obsessed with the Brits, and in his own warped way of thinking, he knew that what he was doing was right. They had taken over his country, and by God, he was going to do everything in his power to rid Ireland of their presence.

"You just need some automatic rifles, and two apiece should do it. Then we'll be ready for the day," McGuire continued and laughed. "Just keep in mind that what we are doing is for Mother Ireland, and you lads will all do fine."

"Twelve handguns and twenty-four rifles," the man who had traveled with the weapons to Offaly counted. "It appears you have quite a morning coming your way then. Good luck to you all."

"Just another day in Ireland, friend," McGuire said. "You have to be prepared for anything. It's like going to church."

McGuire shouldered his AK rifle, let the feel of it sink in. The others all watched him, feeling humbled as though McGuire had an aura about him. He looked like a man ready to kill or die. Each and every man admired what they saw.

The rest of the men followed suit, choosing the weapon of their choice. For the next ten minutes, the only sounds that could be heard in the farmhouse were those of the men cocking, sliding bolts, making sure their weapons wouldn't jam at the wrong time.

"Now what?" Collins asked, a rifle in each hand and a gun tucked in behind his back in his belt.

"Sleep if you can. Otherwise, coffee if you can't," McGuire said and looked at the men with his hard eyes. "Myself, I believe I'll be getting some sleep. It's going to be a busy day tomorrow and I want to be at me best." Turning to take each one of them in, McGuire spoke very slowly and in a low voice that sent chills up the spine of every man in the room. Even the stranger looked uncomfortable.

"Every one of you is committed to the cause, and by God tomorrow if anyone of you fails to hold up his end of the job, you'll answer to me." When McGuire continued, he couldn't keep the venom out of his voice. "If I catch anyone of you with a drink tonight, you won't live to see tomorrow."

As McGuire turned and left the room, all eyes followed him as he went through the door into the bedroom. Silence followed.

Fallon sat with Kit after the sun had gone down. Fallon had spent most of the day just walking the fields, thinking, lost in the netherworld that separated right from wrong. What bothered Fallon the most now was not the altercation he had with McGuire and his cronies, but the fact that he may have to leave Ireland. These were the thoughts that saddened him as he watched the sun dropping in the west.

Fallon had burned his bridges behind him, and even if he hadn't, there was no way he was going back to World Wide operating as a killer for hire. Those days were behind him. As he started for the farm, his heart was heavy.

All his plans of coming home and living a simple life seemed to be fading in the distance like some puff of smoke. Fallon knew he could disappear, and they would never find him. But it was Ireland and Kit that he wanted. Kit was the only family he had, and it would kill him to lose her again.

Then there was Megan. Megan had not been in his plans when he left the States. The thought of meeting someone like Megan and falling in love was the furthest thing from his mind. But against all his training, being careful of making attachments, letting himself be vulnerable, it had. He knew he loved Megan and that she loved him back. He tried pushing her from his mind but found it almost impossible.

Arriving at the Fallon farm just as darkness fell, he could see Kit in the kitchen working at the stove. At that moment, he could not have loved his sister more. Fallon was determined now more than ever that he would find a solution to his problem and remain in Ireland. Stepping inside, Kit turned to greet him.

"John," Kit said, smiling, "sit down and I'll fix us a nice cup of tea. Dinner will be ready soon." So Fallon sat in the kitchen with his sister making small talk and continued getting supper ready. After dinner, Fallon helped Kit with the dishes. After cleaning up the kitchen, it was Kit who suggested sitting outside.

"It's a nice soft night, John," Kit said. "If you listen closely, you can hear the sound of the surf off in the distance. Some nights after a particularly hard day at school, I come out here just to enjoy the silence."

"I don't know how you do it, Kit," Fallon said. "It has to be difficult running the farm and being principal of the school."

"Ah, sure it's not that bad. I have a man who comes in twice a week and more if I need him," Kit answered. "He does most of the hard work. I just can't imagine ever giving the farm up. It's our home, John."

They were silent for a time as Fallon and Kit sat outside after the sun had gone down. When she broached the subject of what had happened on the beach, he tried playing it down as simply as possible. He had not told her much about the incident on the beach and was right now considering whether it was worth it or not to tell her more of the truth. He had kept it simple and brief. A run-in with McGuire and his boys, McGuire slapped Megan, and Fallon had intervened. He knew how gossip was and Kit would find out soon enough, but right now he had decided to keep it nondescript.

Kit had had a hard day on the farm and at school. Fallon did not feel that one more worry would make it any easier for her. And he knew that's all it would be. Fallon did not relish the thought of adding any more problems to Kit's life. And that's all it would be.

Kit had frowned through the story Fallon told her, and he could tell she knew he was keeping the worst from her. Kit nodded her head solemnly when Fallon had finished and thanked him for being there for Megan. She hoped for Megan's sake that this was the last time she would have to have any more dealings with Sean McGuire.

For Fallon, the incident left no fear, only another problem to solve. Was this going to be his future in Ireland? Was this the real face of Ireland? If anyone believed how the media reported on conditions in Ireland, especially in the States, Fallon knew they would be getting a distorted and biased opinion of his country.

What Fallon had to face up to now, a problem he was looking to explore and dissect, was to try and figure out how he could stay and live the life he had dreamed about and planned for when he disappeared from World Wide. He knew the one thing he had going for him was the fact at World Wide that they didn't know he was from Ireland.

He had come from Ireland at such an early age, and with his aunt and uncle having adopted him so quickly, the only record of him started in the States. He had never given World Wide any reason to think otherwise, and with no paper trail, Fallon was not concerned about being safe in Ireland. He had been a loner most of his life and had never shared with anyone anything about his past. He had that going for him.

What he had to do now was figure out a plan for staying. This was his country, his land, and his sister, and Fallon was not about to give that up. He was sure most people would let him fit in right away. The ones he was going to have to deal with were the hard men with guns; the rebels would keep standing in his way. Join or be branded a coward. That escapade on the beach with McGuire and his men was not about to help.

Off in the distance, Fallon could hear the roar of the ocean. In his mind, he pictured the whitecaps as they danced across the sandy beach, shimmering in the moonlight. Fallon knew his best chance was to play a dead hand and keep a low-key profile. He did not want to bring notice to himself. World Wide was a far more pressing problem than a local IRA assassination gang. Them he could handle.

Men who blew up churches and pubs, going into houses and killing women and children, had nothing on what the men of World Wide could do. And were still doing every day. Any attention he brought on would not only be bad for himself, but for Kit as well.

Kit sat quietly, watching her brother. There was sadness in her eyes, eyes that seemed to understand the pain he was feeling, and she knew he was off in that world now. Thoughtful, watchful, but respectful. Kit wouldn't ask; she could only wait.

Fallon felt Kit's eyes on him. He turned and smiled at her. "Kit, you do the work of three people around the farm. How do you find the time and energy what with running the school and the farm?"

"Three people," Kit replied, smiling. "Sure I never noticed that before." Kit then looked at Fallon and winked. "You get used to it, John. And after while you stop noticing or even thinking about it. After a time, you will see for yourself. And when you do get tired and feel it's too much work, what sustains you is the fact that it's your land, and a beautiful land it is."

Fallon knew by the look on Kit's face how true this was for her. He couldn't help but wonder, Could this also be true for him?

"Ireland is a beautiful country, Kit," Fallon answered. "Many's the time I missed it. Even as a child, I remembered when we were children and how we enjoyed the land. Then as the years passed, it became harder and harder to conjure it up in my mind and I began to forget."

A wistful look crossed Fallon's face as he continued. "Now that I am back, Kit, all the beauty that I had carried with me over the years came back. Kit, I missed Ireland almost as much as I missed you."

They sat quietly looking out across the vast expanse of land, and it was as if they were both thinking the same thing. The land was stunning to stand on and smell and be near of. It gave a little bit back when you stopped to take it all in.

"It is indeed," Kit responded, picking up the conversation again. "Now if we could only stop this senseless fighting, peace would only make it more beautiful, John. Isn't it sad how people don't see this and try to live in harmony with one another?"

"I agree, Kit. Peace is worth working for," Fallon said.

"Peace is already there, John. It's the people that get in the way. God knows it seems we have been at war forever."

That was true enough. More than true. Fallon didn't even answer, continuing to look off in the distance at some unknown picture that floated around in his head. Even living in America, Fallon had never lost track of what was happening in his country. Shaking himself out of his reverie and seeing that the conversation was getting too serious, Fallon changed the subject.

"What is the day like for you tomorrow, Kit?" Fallon asked.

"I'm meeting Megan in town for early tea and then we have some shopping to do," Kit answered. "You're welcome to join us if you want."

"Thanks, Kit. I'll think about it."

"I know Megan would be glad for your company," Kit added, mischievously looking at her brother to see how he would react.

Kit was a little more than curious about the relationship between her brother and Megan. But she remained respectful. Fallon smiled knowingly at her and nodded his head.

"When are you meeting Megan?" he asked.

"Early. Early early, in fact. We want to finish before the big commotion starts," Kit told him. Kit pushed herself up from the chair, yawning as she prepared to go back into the farmhouse.

"Then it's back to the quiet of the farm and the never-ending chores," Fallon said.

Kit looked lovingly at Fallon. The feelings they had for each other since childhood could still be seen in Kit's eyes. No one could ever replace the deep love the two had for each other and would withstand the test of time.

"Maybe you and Megan can stay in town and see what you're getting yourself into," Kit said slyly. "The town, I mean," she added and winked.

"Kit, forgive me for being suspicious," Fallon asked, not unkindly. "Are you taking up a new profession? Matchmaker?"

"Certainly not," Kit said, properly chagrined.

"Then maybe I will let Megan give me a tour of the countryside," Fallon said. "It has really changed since I was a kid."

"When I leave tomorrow, I won't wake you," Kit responded, her hand on the door. "But just on the chance we get to see you, there's a tea shop in the center of town. You can't miss it. It's straight up the street from the jail, of all places," Kit continued with some sadness in her voice. "But the rest of the town is pretty. You'll see."

Fallon stood up, and together they entered the house. They turned the lights off and made their way to their rooms.

"Good night, John, and God bless you," Kit said softly.

"Good night, Kit," Fallon answered.

In the small room that was his bedroom, a room for the child that Kit never had since entering the sisterhood, Fallon lay in bed and thought about Ireland. Thought about Kit. The thoughts he had about Megan Clark that kept pushing their way into his conscious mind he had a more difficult time letting go of. Fallon knew in his gut that he was courting a recipe for disaster. His background had left no room for commitments, yet Megan Clark was constantly in his thoughts.

And before he fell asleep, he told himself he couldn't avoid the town forever. And he had to hope that World Wide, as deep as it reached, did not reach into every tea shop in Ireland. That would be like reaching into every tea shop in the world.

It was just not possible.

The following morning, a warm gray day, British troops lined the sidewalk outside the jail where the Irish prisoners were being held. It was a calm, soft morning, but many people, seen and unseen, were watching.

A few blocks from the jail, Kit Fallon and Megan Clark were sitting in one of the shops that dotted the main street of Offaly, drinking tea at a table by one of the windows in sight of but not part of the machinations of insurgency and counterinsurgency that appeared to be brewing just down the street.

The streets were bustling with activity. The pubs and other shops were doing business as usual. But there was a difference this day as a pall of anxiety and uncertainty hung over the town. Even the farmers who had come in with their livestock, setting up for a day of haggling and bargaining, were uneasy as their eyes darted in all directions. The tension in town could be cut with a knife.

Megan and Kit were both assumed to be loyal to the cause in the eyes of the British contingent. But that was a complicated thing in reality. The cause for peace was extending into the cause for war. But in the end, the two women were innocent of any crimes. To Megan and Kit, they viewed the war as senseless and saw it as Irish killing Irish with no end in sight. But both of them knew they were victims by association.

Not that they weren't watched by both sides. Everybody was watched. But today it was different. Men with two rifles and a handgun tucked into their waistbands were sitting and waiting for the right moment as the British Army prepared to walk several prisoners to a van tucked away on the side of the jail. They were being transported to a larger tougher place. Kit Fallon and Megan Clark were in no way involved in the planning of the massacre that was to descend on the town that day.

But then again, both women knew that simply living in Ireland made them a part of it too. Megan and Kit were victims of their time, their struggles, their own people, and the philosophies of war. These were the feelings both women kept buried inside them and lived with on a daily basis.

It was in their lives. It was in their dreams. It was in their conversations.

Kit turned her eyes away from the jail and back to Megan. The sight of the British troops made Kit sad at what was happening to her country. "You know, Megan, it seems that every day I see more and more reasons to be unhappy about the way we live. And it's because every day I see on our streets, right in front of our eyes, a reminder of the violence that is always just beneath the surface. I can't seem to get through a day without that feeling."

"Aye, Kit, it is sad what is happening. But it goes both ways, you know," Megan told her. "There are men in those uniforms that would love nothing better than to kill some of our lads. Deserving or not."

Kit shook her head sadly. "It is a shame, Megan. But deep in my heart, I still believe that most of our people want peace."

"And it seems that all humanity will kill itself to get it," Megan added wisely.

They both went silent after that, each looking out the shop window, lost in their own thoughts as the British troops warily patrolled the street. Then Megan caught Kit's eye and saw what was coming in Megan's. It made her smile.

"Kit, what can you tell me about this brother of yours?" Megan asked shyly, feeling the scarlet glow on her cheeks.

"What would you like to know, Megan?" Kit asked.

"That day I ran into him down on the beach," Megan started hesitantly, "I still can't believe how he handled Sean and the others."

"I only know what little you have told me, Megan. John said nothing last night except he had a run-in with McGuire and his gang," Kit said. "And that if McGuire ever laid another hand on you again, he would be sorry."

"That's true, Kit, John did have a run-in with McGuire and his cronies," Megan answered, glancing out the shop window upon hearing some men shouting. Realizing it was just one of the officers shouting at some of his men, Megan turned her attention back to Kit. "He took care of Sean and the rest of them too."

"That's a Fallon for you," Kit answered, trying to keep the conversation light.

"But it's the way he did it, Kit." Megan did not want to let it go. "I can't get that picture out of my mind," Megan told her seriously. "I mean, I just can't believe what I saw John do to them. It was frightening."

"What did you see?" Kit asked.

"The way John, who appeared cold and detached, did it as though he had done this all his life," Megan said slowly, not wanting to hurt Kit's feelings. "Kit, he was like a machine."

"A machine?" Kit asked. "What kind of machine?"

"I don't know, Kit," Megan responded, sounding frustrated. "I can't explain it. Sean and the others came at him one at a time, three at a time, and he took them out one by one. He disabled them, Kit, is what seemed like. It was as though everything he did was done intentionally and methodically. I've seen men fighting since I was a child, but I have never seen anyone fight like that. How does he know how to fight like that?" Megan asked, with even a little bit of alarm creeping into her voice.

Megan could sense Kit stiffening up, and the look on her face told Megan she was choosing her words very carefully as though there were things she would not disclose. When she did speak, Kit spoke softly and carefully. Shaking her head, Kit said to Megan, "I have no idea, Megan. I don't know what John knows."

"Then when they ripped his shirt off, dear God, Kit, I have never seen anything like that in my life either."

The scars Kit knew about. It was not something John had ever discussed with her, and she had respected that. The only reason Kit knew about them was that Fallon worked on the farm with his shirt off and they had been seen by Kit. She never let on. "Ah, the scars," she said to Megan. "You've seen them then?"

"Yes," Megan said. "The scars. Kit, what happened to John to cause something like that? You must know."

"I have no idea," Kit told Megan and shook her head.

"And you have never asked him?"

"Megan," Kit began, leaning forward on the table. "John has never spoken about it and I have left it at that. You have to understand, Megan, John is a private man and I have to respect that. Knowing him, he'll tell me when he feels the time is right. But I have to assume that if I had a history like that on my body, I wouldn't be so keen on sharing it with anyone. I think it might be something I would have a hard time talking about. Don't you?"

Megan, taken aback by Kit's attitude toward John, feeling confused and frustrated, could only look at Kit and shake her head.

Kit smiled and nodded her head in understanding. Looking at her watch, Kit got up from the table. It was almost 9:00 a.m.

"I had better get my shopping done," she told Megan. "I also have to stop at the school and pick up some papers. John said he would meet us here and then head back to work at the farm. I shouldn't keep the help waiting," Kit said and gave Megan a wink.

Megan laughed.

"Do you mind waiting here for John until I get back, darling?" Kit asked.

"I don't mind at all," Megan said and smiled.

Kit laughed and touched Megan's arm good-naturedly. Then she turned and left the tea shop. Megan watched her walk down the street in the direction of the jail.

The prison was a dark ominous-looking structure with its high brick walls that stretched completely around the street. The barbed wire that was laid across the top of the walls like some venomous snake deterred anyone from thinking about an assault or escape over the top of the obscene structure.

Located at the four corners of the prison were four guard towers that were manned twenty-four hours a day. Men with high-powered machine guns patrolled from above. It was a veritable fortress giving the British troops who lived within it a feeling of security. They knew outside these walls were people who hated their guts.

The prisoners were led out the back door of the prison surrounded by British troops. There were five of them, all in blue prison uniforms.

This being Ireland and the fact that these men were even in prison uniforms at all was more than significant. To the Irish, this was a slap in the face, seeing their countrymen treated like common criminals. In the eyes of the Irish, the IRA in particular, these men were soldiers and should be treated as such. It was something else they were going to fight for.

IRA prisoners were being forced to wear the uniforms of the ordinary criminal. They were also forced to integrate with Loyalist prisoners. Before Britain changed the law, IRA prisoners had been treated differently. They were given special-category status and were treated as political prisoners.

But special-category status had been taken away from political prisoners in 1976. Another slight for the Irish to bite on. England needed to change the rules to suit their political needs. Under the new British ruling, people convicted of political crimes were treated as ordinary criminals. Prior to that, political prisoners had had different rights.

They were not forced to wear prison uniforms; they wore what they liked or what was brought to them by their families on the outside. They now had to work like ordinary criminals whereas in the past they were treated differently. They were allowed to have more visitors and better cells, and more parcels were allowed them than the other prisoners.

They had lived in separate compounds to serve out their sentences, away from the enemy. They had been treated like prisoners of war to some extent because that was what they were. At least in their minds, the mind of the IRA. They would never assume they were ordinary criminals, and definitely not terrorists.

When the British changed the rule in 1976 and undid the special-category status, they forced the political prisoners to wear the uniforms that were issued to the other prisoners. These were the thieves, crooks, muggers, even murderers waiting to be moved to maximum security prisons. They also required them to do the work of ordinary criminals and then the protests began in earnest, inside and outside the prison.

The first protest that began in the prison that was once called Long Kesh started with men going on the blanket. The men refused to wear the prison uniforms that were issued to them, discarding all clothes entirely, and spent their days wrapped in their own prison cell blankets, sleeping on the floor.

When the blanket protest failed to get the British to change the rules for political prisoners, the IRA prisoners of Long Kesh began the dirty protest and smeared their cells with their own excrement and lived with the terrible smell and filth day after day.

This too did not correct their circumstances, even when the British used beatings and other unsavory means to counteract their protest. They were ignored, and it was considered just another British insult added to the many they had endured over the years.

In 1981, ten men, starting with Bobby Sands and ending with Michael Devine, went on hunger strikes to protest the latest round of insults. To them it was the complete injustice. They demanded their special-category status be returned to all IRA prisoners and all the rights that entailed. It was another revolutionary movement in the H-blocks of Long Kesh, a prison that had seen many. Daily, in fact, and for years and maybe for its entire existence.

It takes about sixty days for a man to die from hunger. The first hunger striker, Bobby Sands, died on May 5, 1981. The tenth and last hunger striker, Michael Devine, died on August 20, 1981. Eight more IRA soldiers died in the days in between. And though these ten men died for their cause, nothing changed inside the jails. If anything, conditions only worsened.

But everything changed inside the Irish people. The movement to free themselves from Britain grew stronger. The IRA attracted more angry men. And more angry women. There were men and women now who would never have thought of joining forces with the IRA who gladly were ready to give their lives.

The fight went on. Even stronger. The fight went on every day.

Today it went on down the block from the tea shop Megan Clark sat in drinking her tea, waiting for John Fallon and staring idly out the window.

As the five blue-suited prisoners were moved toward the waiting van, a nondescript car parked on the west side of the street slowly pulled away from the curb. With all the activity going on at the jail, no one noticed the car moving out.

Another car parked east of the jail pulled away from where it was parked a moment later. They were headed in the same direction. Toward the jail.

Sergeant Wilson, his stocky body and the rigid set of his face, walked beside the troops, escorting the prisoners from the prison to the waiting van. There was a rifle strapped to his shoulder. Each of the British troops was carrying automatic rifles, and they looked grim and determined.

Inside his office on the second floor of the prison, Major Neville stood stroking his mustache looking down on the scene below.

Megan, sitting at the window drinking her tea, watched everything that was happening. At first, none of it registered with her.

The two cars both started moving toward the jail at about the same time. As they approached the van, they began to accelerate. Another car, a third car that had been parked just up the street from where Megan was sitting, began to pull slowly away from the curb toward the jail from the south. It was a much larger car than the other two, yet on the quiet street in Offaly, it was not even noticed.

The accelerations of the cars became more than normal. The squealing of the wheels brought several of the shop owners onto the street to see what the commotion was. It was Wilson, beside his troops, who were the first to understand what was transpiring. He immediately began shouting orders to his men to get ready.

The car from the east and the car from the south were heading for the police van at ever-increasing speeds. Wilson, after barking out some orders to his men, unslung his rifle and brought it up to the ready.

The car from the west hit the van first. The metal tore and shrieked, and the men inside the car yelled something that nobody understood or heard clearly. The troops inside the van were thrown to the side and battered the walls with their heads and bodies. Small drops of blood could be seen splattering against the side of the van.

They immediately began to recover, caught by surprise by the shock of how violently the van was hit. Grasping to get hold of something to steady themselves and prepare to respond to the attack, the car from the east rammed the van a moment later and sent the men flying again against the wall. Metal from the van and car was sheared off like shrapnel.

The men in the cars that rammed the vans scrambled out and began firing on the British troops immediately after the crash. The British had already begun spraying bullets at the two cars even before Wilson yelled to return fire.

Screaming could be heard coming from women who were in town for their shopping, scrambling wildly to find a safe place away from the bedlam. Shopkeepers ran back into their shops, closing their doors behind them. There were already several bodies on the street, mostly civilians.

As soon as the first car hit, the five men who were being marched out in prison jumpsuits dropped to the ground. When they came up after the second car hit, they were firing British army rifles. They too sprayed bullets at the men in the cars. The five prisoners were crack British troops who had exited the jail dressed as prisoners. The five IRA gunmen had been moved quietly several days earlier.

There were four IRA gunmen in each of the two cars that had rammed the van. Wilson had fifteen British troops, hard-core and battle-trained, along with the five men who had pretended to be prisoners who had set the trap that sprung like a vise on the gunmen. The IRA was no match for them.

It was a bloodbath on the streets outside the jail.

Major Neville's contingency plan had been a success.

The third car that had been coming somewhat slower from the south and seeing what had transpired jammed on its brakes, spun around, and roared away in the opposite direction out of town. Wilson, barking orders frantically now, running out into the street and firing wildly at the car as it disappeared, was joined by the remaining men who had stemmed the assault on the prison as the others finished off the remaining IRA gunmen.

"Open fire!" Wilson shouted as the disciplined British troops dropping to their knees emptied their automatic weapons at the last car as it roared out of town.

Megan and the other people in the tea shop had jumped low to the floor of the shop. Rising slowly, peering out the window, Megan was shocked and horrified at the spectacle that had transpired in front of her eyes.

The gunfight had exploded dramatically on the street as the heavily armed troops methodically cut the IRA men to pieces. Innocent people walking and working in town had been caught unaware, and the collateral damage was horrifying. The number of innocent people that had been caught in the crossfire was staggering.

After less than a minute of the constant beat of guns and almost as if pulled by a switch, the explosion of guns diminished until it was just the British that were firing at the car that had disappeared over the small bridge at the edge of town. Then came the sound of silence as the troops exhausted their ammunition and all was quiet.

The eight men in the two cars had been neutralized. The British soldiers tapered off, satisfied that they had accomplished their mission. Wilson, looking around the killing ground, called out to his men, "Cease fire!" The situation appeared to be resolved.

After the last shot had been fired, there was a moment of silence unlike any other. It was eerie and surreal. It was a silence filled with smoke and hot blood and death that could only follow something as permanent and horrific as war.

Wilson stood up in this unique silence and began cautiously walking toward the two cars that had carried the IRA gunmen. The troops in the van came out to view the damage and treat their wounds.

The British troops that had fought beside Wilson either took up secure positions or went over to the wrecked cars with Wilson. Two British soldiers lay dead on the ground. Another one lay crying uncontrollably with a bloody leg and shoulder. Neville came out of the jail and began walking slowly toward the carnage. Wilson, his face etched like stone, was the first to reach the cars the IRA men had used in their botched attempt at rescuing the prisoners. Cautiously, with his rifle at the ready, Wilson looked inside both cars. From what he surmised, all eight of the Irishmen were dead. If they weren't, they were going to be, Wilson judged. Each of the bodies was riddled with bullet holes and covered with blood.

The silence after the stunning violence was replaced by the stiff sound of troop movements and shouted orders from Wilson. Off to the side viewing the debacle, a pleased look on his face, Major Neville calmly waited, ignoring the heated voices around him.

An Irish voice from the crowd cried out, "Jesus! You've killed them."

That was followed by a chorus of angry voices from the people who had ducked for cover and were slowly making their way into the street. "British bastards!"

Major Neville, seemingly oblivious to the rage surrounding him, joined Wilson near the slain IRA gunmen in the car.

"Here we go," Neville said in Wilson's ear. "We were the ones attacked and they still think we're in the wrong."

Wilson was about to agree, but something on the street caught his eye. People were running down the street toward a small group that was forming. But strangely the crowd wasn't forming in front of the scene of the ambush. Wilson, his soldier's instinct coming into play, knew something was amiss.

People were yelling, running toward the crowd and away, across the street, and a few doorways down from the intersection where the ambush took place. Several of the shop windows had been blown out from gunfire that had gotten wildly out of hand. British troops, many of them new recruits, had fired blindly at anything that had been moving. The area people were running to now was nowhere near the jail.

Wilson was staring stoically at the gathering crowd. Neville followed Wilson's look. "What the bloody hell now?"

Several of the troops began to move slowly toward that part of the street. Their rifles, which were held at their sides, were cocked and ready.

Megan Clark was one of the people who were running down the street in the direction of the crowd. You could hear the wails of some of the women. Megan's face was stricken. Her eyes were wide with disbelief and fright. She forced her way through the first ring of people to the bodies that lay obscenely in the street.

She had seen them fall. From her seat in the shop where she was having tea and waiting for John Fallon, Megan had seen the three of them, and they almost fell at once, shot by British gunfire. Staring disbelievingly, the anguish and shock on her face, tears streaming down her cheek, she saw what she hoped was not true. One of the bodies lying on the street was that of Kit Fallon.

Megan rushed to her side and bent down close to her body. Kit's face and chest were covered in blood.

Fallon had just turned the corner to meet Kit and Megan when the assault erupted. Fallon, his experienced instinct kicking into gear, dropped low and took cover beside the building he was near of. He witnessed the two main strikes by the Irish and then the British response that was quick and precise.

At first, he had been alarmed about the Irish prisoners caught in the crossfire. But when he saw them come up shooting automatic weapons, he was not surprised.

What Fallon was watching seemed surreal to him. All the years, the killings, all the time he had spent with World Wide had not prepared him for this. Frozen in place, Fallon's entire past moved quickly before his eyes in a heartbeat. It couldn't be happening, he thought, not now. Shaking himself out of his reverie, Fallon, still shocked, appraised the situation.

He saw instinctively and immediately that the British would dominate this situation. The British not only had the better advantage, the IRA's plan was also slipshod and easy to see that they had planned and executed it from the seat of their pants. It was doomed to fail before it even began. It is almost impossible to succeed in an assault that depends on hope and luck and two cars on the run against an army.

The one car that had avoided the assault and had disappeared into the countryside, the one Fallon figured was to be the third car in this debacle, had seen it was futile and abandoned their fellow gunmen.

Fallon knew without thinking that even three cars strategically placed and planned differently would still not have been enough to pull off a stunt like this. Five cars, some people placed on the surrounding rooftops with the right kind of firepower, might have stood a chance, slim at best. The other edge they would have needed was to have operators on the inside feeding them the necessary information.

Either all those things in place or one person with a lot of skills, a lot of training, and a massive amount of firepower might have done a better job. But that type of man costs a lot of money to develop, and there is not many of them out there.

Fallon was one of them.

Fallon watched as the Irish futilely fired at the British and the British, methodical and battle trained, fired back. It was a slaughter. It was at that moment the situation hit Fallon like a right cross to the jaw. Until that moment, he was just another bystander witnessing a scene he had seen played over and over in other parts of the world, not feeling any emotion or involvement in what was transpiring before his very eyes. Then it happened.

He watched as his beloved sister Kit pitched forward obscenely, clutching the air as she fell to the ground, a stray round of bullets slamming into her.

He saw her chest explode before she fell.

He saw the whole thing.

When the massacre ended, Fallon, moving as though in a trance, started moving in the direction where his sister had been hit, never taking his eyes off her. He didn't even notice Megan Clark as she ran toward the fallen civilians. When Megan cut through the crowd, she spotted Kit Fallon lying on the ground. Stunned, Megan, hesitating momentarily, dropped down beside Kit. Fallon was two steps away.

Megan looked down at Kit with fear and confusion, her eyes wet from the tears. Fallon dropped down next to her and put his head against Kit's chest to see if there was a heartbeat, his hand touching the artery in the side of her neck. The muscles in Fallon's jaw tightened, his hand gently letting Kit Fallon's head drop softly to the ground.

Megan looked shocked to see Fallon, but recovered her composure quickly.

"John," Megan asked, unable to keep the anguish from her face, her voice a whisper. "Is she . . . ?"

Fallon held his hand up to stop her. He had to concentrate, to listen with his ear. His face was stoic, his eyes betraying nothing. He looked at Kit's face. It was drained of blood. Her eyes were closed.

Fallon closed his own eyes. He tried to listen, drowning out the chaotic sounds that were playing all around him. He listened very closely.

There was nothing. His sister was dead.

Fallon took a moment to digest this terrible fact; he had drifted into that faraway land that had always been there for him in the past. But it wouldn't work for him this time. He was unable to escape the moment. He had to confront it. Fallon didn't try to deny the feelings that were welling up inside him this time; he just let them flow over him, and the anger that had taken over his entire being was like an old friend.

He then sat slowly back on his heels and looked over at Megan.

"She's dead," he told her. His voice was oddly lifeless.

Megan clutched her throat, gasping, unable to catch her breath. She turned and looked lovingly at Kit, reaching out to hold Kit's head.

Fallon stood up in the crowd and looked over toward the British. Several troops were pushing their way through the civilians. Fallon was oblivious to all of them. He was concentrating on finding one. There was always the one that would stand out. He was the one Fallon knew had ordered the killing.

Fallon ticked off each face as irrelevant until he came to Wilson's. The squat, brutish man was barking orders to his troops, many of them in disarray from the shock of what had happened. Wilson was viciously making sure they were carrying out their duties. Fallon took Wilson in, categorized him, assessed his worth and lack of it, and then passed him over for the man standing beside him. He was a tall man with a mustache.

Major Neville stood calmly next to Wilson surveying the damage, assessing the good and the bad. The arrogance and total disregard for the mayhem around him told Fallon all he needed to know.

This was the man responsible for the killings and the death of his beloved sister Kit.

Neville, as if sensing Fallon's hard stare, turned and immediately their eyes locked on each other.

A deep inexplicable cold feeling ran through Neville as he looked at the man watching him from the street. He felt a cold chill move down his spine as he stared up at Fallon. Deep down he felt as though death had walked across his grave.

Before he could register what was happening, the man disappeared into the crowd.

Then Neville was distracted by the arrival of news vans and reporters and cameramen who had appeared on the street. They seemed to be coming from all directions.

Neville hesitated a moment, then turned to Wilson.

"All right then, Sergeant. Let's get this mess cleaned up," Neville said. "There will be plenty more coming or way after this."

Wilson turned from Neville and started to clean up a disaster that could never be cleaned up.

Seven

Two days before, Reynolds and Harris and a few nameless, faceless World Wide employees had begun an Internet-linked records search through most of the computer systems on the face of the earth. They tapped into every airline, train station, luxury liner, cargo ship, and every other form of transport, legal and illegal, that had a computer and combed their files for names, pictures, ID numbers, fingerprints, photos, whatever they could think of regarding John Fallon and Fallon's known identities. And some assumed identities as well.

They accessed the intelligence databases of the countries they did business with, countries they paid a fee to. Those countries they didn't do business with they just slipped in and out of anyway after taking a look around at what they wanted.

They pulled up the top-secret files that were labeled "For your eyes only," scanning and thoroughly digging into past jobs Fallon had performed with World Wide. And though Fallon was a lone wolf, there had been times he was forced to interact with others in the company, usually on jobs that required outside assistance. These were few and far between. Fallon was not one to get close to anyone. They all came up blank.

The world of computers is a borderless landscape full of an enormous number of files and pieces of information, and World Wide had a considerable net web at their disposal so it was extensive and exhaustive work.

But that was to be expected.

That was why World Wide had recruited some of the best hackers in the world. They worked in secret across the globe designing programs, creating secret pathways, and orchestrating and concealing methods of conducting searches like the one they had put on Fallon. The hackers were in their element when it came to this type of work.

Interestingly enough, some of the best hackers on the planet, getting top wages at World Wide, were barely out of high school. All World Wide was interested in was the fact that they were good at what they were doing, and most of them were surprisingly ruthless.

As Reynolds and Harris expected, nothing came back on Fallon. They had expected him to go under without a trace, and Fallon had more than lived up to their expectations. From what the geniuses had pulled up, it was as though Fallon had never existed.

The next step would be ground-based operations. Harris and Reynolds, along with help from World Wide, would begin the tedious task they all dreaded—footwork. Contacts of operatives in the field who had dealings with Fallon, informants, government officials, moles, bribes, threats, contracts, business associates, anyone that had contact with Fallon in any capacity. They drew a blank.

It wouldn't take long, but it would take a lot.

Both Reynolds and Harris left World Wide well after midnight and they were exhausted. They had gone over the same ground so many times that they were bleary-eyed. They separated, each going to their separate homes and beds knowing that the work had only just begun. Sleep barely touched them where they needed to be touched. They were already preparing for the next day.

The next day came early.

Childers woke Reynolds with a phone call. Reynolds in turn woke Harris.

"Childers wants to see us," Reynolds mumbled into the telephone, his mood curt after being jarred out of bed by Childers's call.

"What," Harris slurred into the phone, not fully awake and nursing a hangover that wouldn't stop.

"I said Childers wants to see us," Reynolds retorted, unable to keep the agitation out of his voice. "They've located Fallon."

Harris, suddenly alert and rolling out of bed and heading for the shower, the cell phone clutched in his hand, shot back, "Where?"

"I don't know," Reynolds answered as patiently as he could. "Childers didn't say. I'm sure we'll find out when we see him."

After Reynolds ended the phone call with Harris, both men prepared for their meeting with Childers in the same way. They got out of bed, quietly showered and shaved, ate a very minimal breakfast, packed a black lightweight suitcase, and reviewed their individual situations as they drove to Manhattan and World Wide.

They looked like any two men driving into work in the early morning hours, except that they were both thinking the same thing. Would they be good enough to handle Fallon? What would it take? Was there anything in their set of skills or their psychological makeup that was missing? These and the many other thoughts that were running through their heads distinguished them from the average man headed to a job.

Childers was sitting behind his desk when his two operatives entered his office. Childers's secretary had not made it into work yet. Reynolds, having known Childers longer than Harris, was unnerved by the smile that was on Childers's face. To Reynolds, it was obscene and could only mean trouble.

Reynolds and Harris smiled back at Childers, more out of nervousness, waiting for him to drop the inevitable bomb Reynolds knew was behind the façade. Reynolds had been in the game too long to let his emotions show. Glancing at Harris, he could tell that he had read Childers wrong.

In the shadow world they lived and functioned in, Reynolds had no illusions. He had lost all beliefs and aspirations, the "I'm going to change the world for the better" replaced by a cynical, distrusting, and cold-blooded individual who was capable of killing without feeling. He sat and waited.

Reynolds had no noble beliefs that what lay ahead of them was for the "good" of the country. He had his reservations and was secure with them. They had put much work in trying to locate Fallon, but Reynolds knew the real work still lay ahead of them. And that would be much more difficult. Or at any rate, more dangerous. More life and limb. So Reynolds sat quietly, letting Childers revel in whatever he was about to disclose.

Leaning forward, elbows resting on the desk, Childers slid the newspaper that was in front of him across the desk for Reynolds and

Harris to look at. Satisfied, Childers leaned back in his chair, a smug look on his face as he shoved the pipe into his mouth.

"What do you think of the picture?" Childers asked.

Harris and Reynolds looked down at the paper Childers had shoved across to them, not bothering to correct Childers since Reynolds and Harris had both reviewed the newspaper report back at the office on their computer before coming to the meeting, letting Childers revel in what he thought was breaking news.

The story in the newspaper was of an aborted IRA attempt to free several IRA prisoners that were being held and were awaiting transfer to a maximum security facility at another undisclosed location. The British, however, had set a trap and trumped the move of the local IRA group. There was a brief but intense gun battle, spilling over into the streets, leaving eight IRA gunmen dead, as well as two British soldiers and three civilians who happened to be in the wrong place at the wrong time.

The newspapers, naturally gravitating to the blood and gore that sold papers, went on to say how there was public condemnation and outrage at the actions of the British troops. In a statement by the commanding officer, Major James Neville issued his sincerest apologies and abnegation.

It was plain to see that the British were in damage-control mode. They were seeking absolution, saying it was just an unfortunate mistake. Neville went on to say how they had been attacked and were forced to defend themselves in a fierce gun battle they could not control.

There was, as there should be, public condemnation and outrage, even with the British spewing apologies at a rapid rate and abnegation. The British were seeking absolution—it was just an unfortunate mistake, "we were attacked and had to defend ourselves in a fierce gun battle we could not control."

The Catholics of the North were seeking revenge. To them it was just another instance of the random assassination of Catholics by the Brits—"they don't care how many of us they kill, they just want us dead." The stories went on and on like that, each side blaming the other for the massacre.

Accompanying the stories of the attack was a picture of the aftermath of the massacre and tragedy that had occurred on the street. The papers pulled no punches, and the pictures were graphic and sickening.

British troops and Irish citizens were locked together in a furious knot. Two cars were crushed up against a battered transport van, its metal and windows blown to shreds like some discarded vehicle you would find in a deserted junkyard. Dead men were strewn bloody about haphazardly in the cars. Civilians were captured in pictures standing in the street around three dead Irish bodies.

In a matter of minutes, newspapers, along with a plethora of photographers, had arrived on the scene and were snapping pictures and scrambling for interviews. They captured Irish men and women in the act of grieving and confusion, yelling and cursing the stone-faced British troops trying to untangle the carnage that had descended upon them.

Off to the side standing stone-faced and silent was John Fallon. Oblivious to everyone around him, his focus never wavering as he stared at one person, not aware that he was being photographed, Fallon had started moving slowly toward the crowd that had increased quickly and angrily.

One photographer had managed to catch Fallon, who was unaware of it, standing alone, glancing back and forth from the crowd to the British soldiers. There was a cold and menacing look on his face.

In the list of the dead, Irish and British—in the game or out, as the case may be—was the name Catherine Fallon.

As cold as he was, Childers had been sad to see that. Not that it would bother his conscience all that much or cause him sleepless nights; he could always justify it as being "the fortunes of war."

Fallon was not the only family member to die in that bloody conflict that day in Ireland. Or in any of the countless other conflicts in the world, past and present; and though Fallon was the agent of many families' distress in the past, the sting of a loved one being shot dead on the street, and for a mistake, would be very intense. Maybe even unbearable for a while. For Fallon, this was not the case.

On the other hand, the arrogant persona that Childers presented to Reynolds and Harris was that of a happy one, seeing Fallon's hard, dark face in the crowd.

"I like it when fate or luck or Divine Providence extends its hand," Childers crowed to Reynolds and Harris. Childers was sitting back comfortably in his chair, the smoke from his pipe drifting upward toward the ceiling. He had the look of a man who had just won the lottery. "It makes me feel that everything we do is up for grabs."

"I was surprised to see it myself," Reynolds answered thoughtfully, his hand holding the paper. "I thought Fallon would be smarter than that. Never get caught in a crowd. Never get caught in a mistake."

"Like having his picture taken?" Childers asked.

"What's our next move?" Harris asked them both.

Turning slowly to face Harris, Childers's face lost its smile. It was replaced with a mild contempt for Harris. "What the hell do you think our next move should be, Mr. Harris?" Childers had all he could do to suppress the anger that was raging just below the surface.

"I know we're going over there to make contact," Harris said, almost for a moment stuttering. "What I was asking, sir, was when and what type of contact we are to make. Are we giving Fallon any options?"

Before Childers could explode, tearing Harris a new asshole, Reynolds jumped in. "I have already booked Jack and myself two flights out of Kennedy tonight for Shannon," Reynolds said quickly to Harris. "I have also contacted our agents in the area, and all the equipment we will need will be at our disposal."

"So then the issue of what type of contact you are going to make is really up to Raven," Childers stated simply, making his dislike for Harris painfully obvious by directing his comments to Reynolds. "I'm sure Raven will let you know in his inimitable manner," Childers added and smiled coldly at both of them.

Neither Reynolds nor Harris responded, though they both felt something cold run down their spines.

Settling comfortably into his chair, a smirk creasing his mouth, Childers nodded toward Reynolds. "Do you anticipate any problems, Mr. Reynolds?"

Hesitating momentarily, Reynolds looked across the desk at Childers. "I anticipate problems only to avoid them," Reynolds responded evenly.

The arrogant smile crossed Childers's face again as he reached for the ever-present pipe. Taking his time, making more of it than necessary, Childers watched as smoke drifted upward and dashed against the ceiling. When he spoke, there was insolence in his voice that didn't escape Reynolds's notice.

"Good, I'm glad to hear that, Mr. Reynolds. I'm assuming you have no problem with the direction this retrieval is taking," Childers asked him.

"No, I have no problem with it," Reynolds answered. Hesitating briefly, knowing he was entering dangerous territory, Reynolds asked, "I assume you have pulled Dan Morehead into this operation to find Fallon. Now that we know where he is located and Jack and I are headed there, we have no need for him anymore. Can we expect him to disengage and go back into retirement?"

Reynolds watched Childers closely to see if the expression on his faces changes. After all the years he has spent in the field, Reynolds has learned to read people not by what they say, but by their facial expressions and body language. For the first time, Reynolds spotted hesitancy in Childers. He filed that away for later use.

Childers, after pausing momentarily, thoughtfully nodded his head once. "Don't worry yourself about Morehead, Mr. Reynolds. I will take care of him personally."

Getting up from behind his desk, Childers glared at them both. Reynolds knew this to be a signal that the meeting was over. Reynolds and Harris stood up to leave.

"The next time I hear from you, Mr. Reynolds, I will expect you to inform me that Fallon is no longer a problem," Childers said, coming around to their side of the desk and placing his hand on the newspaper in front of them.

The three of them looked down at the photograph of John Fallon, holding the blood-soaked body of his sister in his arms, British troops and civilians in the back ground. When Childers looked at them, there was viciousness in his voice.

"Be sure to pass on a message to Mr. Fallon," Childers addressed them before they left. "Before you kill Fallon, let him know he is very photogenic," Childers said, laughing as Reynolds and Harris left the office.

Dan Morehead was standing in his kitchen when the phone call from Childers came. Now as he listened to Childers reiterating his meeting with Reynolds and Harris, Dan Morehead had all he could do not to throw up.

Reynolds and Harris were on the way to Ireland to engage John Fallon in a "friendly contact." Childers was babbling on how he was hopeful that Fallon would keep it that way. Lying through his teeth, Childers was sanctimoniously telling Dan Morehead how he could understand his wish to get out of the dark life.

Childers went on in elaborate detail how he was devising ways to bring Fallon back and keep him active without having to venture out into the field. Childers was rattling on about using him in recruitment and training. Childers told Morehead that with his experience, Fallon was too good to just let go.

Morehead, listening with indifference to Childers, said yes whenever it seemed appropriate, waiting for Childers to ask. Finally he did.

"What do you think, Dan? Does this sound like a scenario that would capture Fallon's fancy? What are our chances?" Childers asked him.

"John's an intelligent man. I'm sure he'll listen to what you have to say," Morehead told him, his voice never wavering. "One piece of advice—make sure the offer is right and don't try running one on him."

Childers shifted nervously in the chair. There had always been something about Dan Morehead and the way he addressed him that kept him off balance and never sure of where he stood. He was smart enough to know that he would be unable to bullshit Dan Morehead or even attempt to con him.

"I would never try to pull anything on Fallon, Dan, you know that," Childers answered too quickly, not convinced that Morehead even bought what he was saying. "What concerns me, Dan, is what do you think a good offer would be," Childers inquired, hoping he sounded truly concerned.

"Whatever John wants would be a good start," Morehead told him.

Childers, wanting this interview with Dan Morehead to end as quickly as possible, especially since he had already dispatched Reynolds and Harris to Ireland, cursed himself for jumping the gun and bringing Dan Morehead into the picture.

Childers made the obligatory sound of consideration. "I'm sure you're right, Dan. So we should just let Fallon describe how he foresees his future with the organization and then work together to create something specifically for him where we can utilize his numerous talents. How does that sound?"

"What else could you do?" Morehead asked solemnly.

"Yes," Childers said. "Good point. Fallon is an invaluable man."

Morehead listened as he could hear Childers moving objects nervously around on his desk. He had all he could do not to reach through the phone and rip his lying lungs out. Dan Morehead knew that Childers had never liked John Fallon. The reason being Morehead knew was that Childers feared him.

"So it's back to retirement for you then, Dan," Childers said, smiling, hoping that Dan Morehead had bought what he told him. "I'm sorry to have brought you all the way down here for nothing."

"You did the right thing," Morehead said with an impeccable degree of sincerity in his voice as he slowly cradled the phone, not listening to Childers finish.

"Thanks, Dan," Childers said, equally sincere, unaware that Dan Morehead had hung up on him and dismissed him like some snake that had crawled into his life.

When Dan Morehead got off the phone, after placing several calls, he made arrangements for the first flight out of Kennedy International Airport to Shannon Airport in Ireland. He then told his wife Alice he was leaving and when and where he was going. Morehead then went upstairs to pack.

Morehead moved about his bedroom steadily, thoughtfully, pulling out of his closet the items he would need for his trip. Placing them neatly in his suitcase, Alice Morehead entered the room. She stood in the doorway watching him.

"Dan, I still don't understand why you feel you should go to Ireland," Alice said to him. Alice was a professional at this and worked to keep the anger out of her voice. Mostly she succeeded, but this time she was frustrated and confused. Dan had been retired and out of the business that had taken most of their lives and put them on the back burner.

Pausing in his packing, Dan Morehead looked over to his wife Alice, who was still standing stiffly in the doorway. He could see the stress in her face and was not unaware of the struggle that was going on inside her, trying not to show her unhappiness. He smiled weakly, hoping to keep the conversation light.

"Alice, I can't explain it or put my finger on why I feel this way, but deep down, I know John is being set up," Morehead told his wife. "Knowing Childers and the way he operates, he wouldn't know the truth if he fell over it."

"What do you mean?" Alice asked.

"That song and dance he performed for me today was all gingerbread. My feelings are that John is going to need someone to help him negotiate," Morehead told his wife. "If I read Childers right, knowing the way he operates, John Fallon is about to be terminated."

"That can't be," Alice replied, a shocked look on her face.

"I believe John needs someone to negotiate on his behalf," Morehead told his wife as he closed his suitcase, placing it by the door. "He will need someone to be there when Reynolds and Harris brace him."

"But why you?" Alice asked, knowing the reason.

Morehead looked at his wife. A feeling of guilt passed through him as he thought back to all the years she had stood by him, the lonely nights, not sure if he was going to come home or get that dreaded phone call that he was dead. She deserved better. But John Fallon also deserved a fair shot, and Morehead knew he was not about to get that from Childers.

"Alice, I am just going over to meet with John," he said, smiling. "Just bounce some ideas off him when they make him their offer."

Alice knew he was lying to spare her any worry or anguish. To her credit, she did not contradict him. She had never met John Fallon, but knew that her husband Dan had been mentor and over the years, even after Dan had retired, John Fallon had always stayed in touch with him.

Alice knew that John Fallon meant a lot to her husband and for many reasons she would never know or ask to know. But Alice did believe she knew one of the reasons her husband felt the way he did about him. They had never had any children of their own, and after all the years Dan had groomed and worked with John Fallon, he had come to look upon him more as his own son than a counterpart.

Morehead, finishing off his packing, zipped his suitcase shut. Dropping the bag on the floor, he turned to face his wife. Bravely, Alice Morehead smiled at him, a tired but pretty smile. They had been through a lot in their long years of marriage. Dan Morehead and now more than anything appreciated her steadiness and kindness in moments like these. The moments when he was putting his life on the line one more time.

How many times had Alice Morehead watched her husband head out into the darkened night, never knowing if he would return alive? If only he had known how many times she had cried herself to sleep, terrified of that phone call that would let her know the one man who meant more to her than life itself, was not coming home. But Alice had learned never to share these feelings with Dan. She just buried them along with all the other fears she harbored.

Dan looked lovingly at his wife. What he saw was a tough as nails woman underneath that beautiful skin. A tough broad after all. Dan had been lucky when she let him marry her forty years ago. Dan Morehead smiled back at her in his easygoing, confident way.

"I love you, Dan," Alice said to him as he gathered her in his arms, pulling her close to him. It was more patient than passionate.

"I love you too, Alice."

They embraced again at the doorway of the bedroom, each one wanting the moment to linger, not wanting to part again. Dan stepped back. They looked each other in the eye; Dan could see the tears welling up in the corner of Alice's.

"Hey, don't worry about me," he said as lightly as possible, knowing she could read right through him. "I still have a few moves left in me, you know. I'm not over the hill yet, so don't write me off too quickly."

Alice knocked him on the arm and said, "Who knows that more than I?" A bright light of knowing showed in her eyes.

EIGHT

AFTER THE FUNERAL SERVICE AND all the guests had left, Megan and Fallon sat on the porch in front of the cottage. The wind was blowing in from the sea; trees were rustling nervously as they swayed back and forth. The soft night was silent, a bright moon shone from the sky, and for all intents and purposes, if not for the occasion, one would say it was a gentle Irish night.

Fallon sat staring into the darkness, his eyes not reflecting any emotion. Megan had tried instituting a conversation and after several futile attempts sat waiting, knowing Fallon would speak to her in his own time. Megan knew how much he loved his sister, and deep down, that pain was festering inside him like a scar. His silence worried her, but she knew that what he needed now was just for her to be there.

Deep down, Megan felt an uneasiness stirring within her ever since the carnage from the aborted attempt at freeing the Irish prisoners. There was an underlying anger and resentment hanging over the town of Offaly, and Megan knew that the killings were far from over. The British had brought more troops in from the North and were being used to stifle the unrest that hovered over Offaly like a black cloud.

Armed troops were roaming the town. People, shopkeepers, children, and others who had always managed to stay far removed from the violence were now whispering and talking about revenge. It was mostly confined to the pubs. Megan knew that Offaly was sitting on a time bomb ready to go off at a moment's notice. That wasn't what was on her mind right now.

Looking over at Fallon, still staring off into the darkness, Megan had a sense of foreboding she couldn't shake. After the death of Kit Fallon, Megan sensed that Fallon had merely gone through the motions of Kit's burial. He spoke very little to anyone, and Megan was beginning to feel that he was shutting her out as though he had moved into another dimension and whatever he was planning, John Fallon was confiding in no one.

Megan, after seeing Fallon in the fight with Cassidy and the others and from what Kit Fallon had told her, was a very dangerous man.

Megan Clark was in love with John Fallon. Her heart told her Fallon loved her also, but his past and the things he was involved in kept him from committing to her. Violence had always been a part of Fallon's life, and now after moving back to Ireland in the hope of starting over, his life had been shattered. Megan was witnessing Fallon's return to that very man he had tried to change. And all Megan could do was stand by and watch.

Taking Fallon's hand gently in hers, tears welling up in her eyes, Megan Clark sat silently with Fallon, staring off into the darkness. No words were spoken, but Megan knew there was trouble in the wind.

As they stared off into the darkness, the silence deafening, Megan and Fallon were each caught up in their own thoughts.

Inside the farmhouse located on the outskirts of Offaly, Sean McGuire stood against the fireplace, his hands in his pockets. The glow from the embers flowed through the room; the faces of the men gathered there were hard and tense. Their eyes darted from McGuire, glancing furtively from one to the other. They waited until McGuire spoke. Pushing himself away from the fireplace, McGuire strode to the table where the men were gathered.

"Just what the bloody hell we need!" McGuire shouted angrily, his fist crashing down on the table.

The men, six of them, were startled, the nervousness showing in their faces as they looked down at the newspapers strewn across the table. They were filled with the events of the unsuccessful attempt at freeing the IRA prisoners. But more importantly, they have focused in on the killings of the innocent civilians. Particularly one Sister Catherine Fallon.

The articles went on to condemn the British troops for overreacting and killing so many innocent people. The story in the newspaper mainly focused on Kit Fallon though. She was one of the most beloved residents of Offaly, and the anger that permeated through the county not only included the British, but spilled over to the actions of the IRA.

The stories went on to say that the men in the getaway car had not been apprehended. Major Neville, commandant of the British contingent attached to County Offaly, stated that though the killers had escaped, they had a good idea who they were and that they would be apprehended in a few days. McGuire and his men were not too concerned with what Neville had said to the papers. They were sure he was whistling in the dark and trying to pacify his superiors who were not happy with the notoriety they were getting around the globe.

McGuire, still staring at the papers, finally turned to address his men. He was angry and lashed at his men.

"You bloody fools," McGuire said, pointing down at the newspapers. "Now we not only have the Brits on our asses, but our own people are angry over the killings of innocent Irish civilians too. Especially this blasted nun Fallon."

The men shuffled uneasily, knowing that when McGuire went off like this he was capable of anything. None of them want to be the one singled out for his rage. McGuire would as soon put a bullet in someone's brain as look at him. They remained silent, hoping McGuire would calm down. He didn't.

"Look at you all standing there like horse asses," McGuire rasped. "None of you have any idea how this happened?"

Finally Cassidy, showing his nervousness, spoke up. "Sean, sure the blasted Brits were waiting for us. They knew we were going to try and free our men on that particular day."

"And how could they know that?" McGuire asked.

The men all looked at one another, each thinking the same thing, but none of them willing to say it. Finally Cassidy broke the silence.

"There had to have been an informer, Sean," Cassidy said cautiously.

McGuire's eyes narrowed, his gaze moving slowly from one man to the other. In his hand, he was cradling a handgun. Cocking the hammer, the sound echoing throughout the hollow farmhouse, McGuire remained silent, taking the measure of each of them.

Fear was etched on their faces, knowing that Sean McGuire was prone to fits of anger, making wild accusations and generally following through with a bullet. McGuire never worried about the consequences of his actions. This made him even more dangerous. The men couldn't take their eyes off the gun dangling at his side.

Casey moved toward McGuire. The nervousness was evident in his voice. "Jesus, Sean, surely you don't think it was one of us?"

"Sean, you trust us, don't you?" Cassidy chimed in.

"I don't trust anyone, Cassidy," McGuire snarled through clenched teeth. "It's one of the reasons I've stayed alive so long."

They all waited as knowing McGuire, his brow furrowed, was processing all that had transpired. They were sure that whatever he decided would be swift and deadly. McGuire made up his mind. Tucking the gun in his belt, he motioned for the men to take their seats. The relief that crossed their faces was evident as they sat down.

"Don't get too comfortable with the fact I have dismissed any of you as informers," McGuire said. "However, I am going to give you the benefit of the doubt. For now," he added. Continuing, McGuire placed his hands on the table, addressing his men.

"The first thing on our agenda is to find out if anyone in town spotted us in the getaway car," McGuire began. "The last thing we need is to get the townspeople up in arms against us. That would just add more fuel for the bloody Brits."

"The people were so caught up in the chaos surrounding the jail, Sean," Collins said. "I don't believe any of them even noticed the car."

"Aye, that's right," Casey added.

"That's all well and good," McGuire said. "But we can't leave anything to chance. We have two items on the table right now that we have to deal with. The first is to find out how we stand with the town. Cassidy, when you and the men leave here, drift into town separately and feel out the people we can depend on. Once we're sure we are in the clear, we can move on from there. Is that clear?"

"Aye, Sean. But you said there were two things we had to do. What is the other?" Cassidy asked.

McGuire's eyes narrowed, the vicious look that appeared on his face sending chills up the spines of the men seated around the table.

"If you do nothing else, I want you to find the fuckin' informer," McGuire shouted. "I don't care how you do it or how long it takes, find him. And bring him to me. Do you understand? That bastard cost us the lives of our comrades and gave the Brits something else to crow about. Now they feel they have us on the run."

"Sure, Sean," Collins answered quickly.

"We'll find him and kill the bloody bastard," Collins said.

"No," McGuire snapped. "I want him. I am going to take particular pleasure in making him die slowly. When I get through with him, it will be a long time before anyone will ever cross us again. Understood?"

They all nodded in agreement as they began talking among themselves. McGuire pushed away from the table, frustration showing on his face.

"Well, don't sit their yapping like fishwives. Get your asses out in the streets and start acting like men. You have a job to do, do it."

The men quickly began getting up from the table. As they started moving through the door, McGuire's voice broke the silence.

"Cassidy."

At the sound of McGuire's voice, Cassidy turned to face him. The others hesitated only momentarily, not wanting to be on the receiving end of McGuire's rage. After the door had closed on the rest of the men, McGuire gestured for Cassidy to join him at the table. Pulling a bottle off the shelf, McGuire poured two stiff drinks for them.

"Mike," McGuire began, "we have a problem."

"Don't worry, Sean," Cassidy breathed normally again after realizing that McGuire did not keep him behind to lace into him. "It may take some time, boyo, but we'll find the bloody informer. It will be a sad day for him."

"Not that, you bloody ass," McGuire angrily shot back.

"Then what is it, Sean?" Cassidy answered, properly chided.

"After that fiasco the other day, I'm worried that the heads of the organization are not going to take us seriously," McGuire said, a worried look on his face. "We have worked hard in Belmont establishing an IRA wing to be proud of. Now this."

"What do you think will happen?"

"I don't know. They have already summoned me to meet with them and I'm sure it's not to have tea with them," McGuire answered sarcastically. "One thing for sure, if I do convince them we can still operate effectively, they are going to want more than just talk."

"What do you plan to do, Sean?"

"First thing we have to do is find the man who told the Brits about what we were planning. Then we have to make an example of him." McGuire leaned back in his chair, his fingers stroking the now empty glass. Cassidy had learned at times like this that the best thing was to keep his mouth shut and wait. He didn't have to wait long.

"After we take care of that piece of business, I am going to ask the leadership to include us in on their next big operation," McGuire answered, on a roll now. "Cassidy, I don't want to feel like a second-class citizen anymore."

"Do you think you can convince them, Sean?" Cassidy asked, unable to keep the excitement out of his voice.

"If I can assure them it won't happen again. And by God it won't." Leaning toward Cassidy, McGuire, knowing how to stroke Cassidy's ego, continued. "Mike, you are the only one I can trust."

"You know you can depend on me, Sean," Cassidy responded cockily. "Just tell me what you want done."

"The men we have now are okay, but deep down I don't feel their hearts are in it like ours. We need men who are committed to getting the British bastards out of Ireland for good," McGuire said passionately. "Your job from now on is to find those men. Men who are loyal to the cause and willing to give their lives for it. Can you do that?"

"You know you can count on me," Cassidy said. "Sure I know how you feel about the crew we have been working with. Other than Collins and Casey, I wouldn't give you tinkers damn for the lot of them."

"Okay, we're agreed then. As soon as we have cleaned up the informer mess, get to work recruiting the men we will need. And don't be afraid to go outside Belmont. We only want the best." McGuire paused before continuing. "One more thing, Mike."

"What would that be, Sean?"

"Keep your eye on Collins and Casey."

Cassidy looked puzzled at McGuire. His face was impassive.

The Fallon farmhouse looked just the same. The furniture was still arranged as usual, the flowers that surrounded the outside of the house still blossomed, and the house was as neat as a pin. But there was something different about the surroundings. Catherine Fallon was no longer there.

John Fallon stepped back into the living room where Megan Clark was sitting on the couch. In his hands he held two mugs of tea. Handing one to Megan, Fallon sat down across from her. There was an awkward silence that was finally broken by Megan.

"John, what are you going to do now?" Megan asked.

"I'm not sure," Fallon answered quietly.

Fallon's face betrayed nothing. His eyes were focused on the window overlooking the lush green land that surrounded the Fallon farm. Megan could tell from his expression that John Fallon's mind was miles away. Only his eyes gave anything away, and Megan was not pleased with what she saw.

"John," Megan repeated. "Did you hear what I said?"

"I'm sorry, Megan. I guess my mind was elsewhere," Fallon responded. "What was it you said?"

"Do you have any idea what you are going to do now, darling?" Megan asked lovingly. "I know losing Kit is devastating to you, but my fear is you are going to leave Ireland and go back to America."

Fallon rose from his chair, moving silently to the window. Not answering Megan, Fallon stared off into the distance. Megan got up and came over to him, putting her arms around his waist.

"John, I love you," she said, the tears flowing freely. "I couldn't stand losing you now. Please talk to me."

Turning, taking Megan in his arms, Fallon kissed her tenderly. Megan buried her head in his shoulder. She was trembling, her hands digging into Fallon's arms. Holding her at arm's length, Fallon tried explaining how he felt.

"Megan, I love you too. You've known for a long time how I feel about you. That hasn't changed." Pausing, lifting Megan's head up, Fallon continued. "Right now I am not sure what I am going to do. Kit was all the family I had and since her death, and I would be lying to you if I told you it is over. But I can't."

"I loved Kit too, John," Megan said desperately.

"I know you did. But someone has to pay," Fallon said in a way that frightened Megan, looking at the coldness that clouded his eyes. It was a side of John Fallon that Megan had never seen. A chill ran up her spine, and she knew that no matter what she said, Fallon was going after the men who killed Kit Fallon.

"John," Megan began softly, her voice a whisper. "I know how you are feeling right now. The anger is evident in your face. But ask yourself, would Kit want you getting revenge? John, no matter what you do, even if it's finding out who is responsible, nothing will bring Kit back to us."

Fallon's expression didn't change as Megan passionately spoke to him. Megan could see that he was miles away and had no idea what thoughts were running through his mind. Fallon moved over to the window looking out at the fog that had drifted in from the sea, covering the land in a sea of mist.

"Megan," Fallon said, his eyes unchanging as he continued looking out over the land. When he spoke to her, it was as if he hadn't heard a word she said.

"Megan, I will be leaving here soon," Fallon offered, a slight tremor in his voice.

"Leaving? John, where will you be going?" Megan asked.

Fallon turned to look at her. "Megan, there are things I have to do and they can't be done here. You are going to have to trust me on this. And please, Megan, don't ask me to explain or even when I will be coming back."

"But, John, you said you had come back to Ireland to stay." Megan's voice was pleading as she reached out, taking his arms in hers.

"Things have changed, Megan. It's difficult to explain, but I need to get away for a while and sort things out." Taking Megan in his arms, Fallon smiled weakly. "Megan, this will only be for a little while and then I will be back."

"I'm never going to see you again," Megan said, stepping away from Fallon.

"Megan, please," Fallon began. "You are—"

"No. Don't say anything," Megan answered, a hard edge to her voice. "If you return, John, I'll be waiting. But please, don't make promises you may not be able to keep."

Megan kissed Fallon on the cheek and turned, starting for the door.

"Megan," Fallon began. But without turning, she opened the door and started down the path. Fallon, walking over to the open door, watched as Megan hurried toward town. The sound of silence was deafening as Fallon watched until he could no longer see her.

Darkness came quickly as Fallon sat on the porch looking out over the land he had come to love. The night had crept slowly upon him. The roar of the ocean in the distance beckoned, an eerie sound in the dark and lonely night. Looking out over the land, Fallon, sat unmoving, only his eyes darting across the sea green grass that covered the land.

It had been several hours since Megan left, and still Fallon had not moved from his chair on the porch. Taking a deep breath, Fallon pushed himself up, moving to the end of the porch. Looking once more over the Fallon land, thoughts of Kit swirled in his head. He remembered how much Kit loved this place. Now it felt empty and desolate. Swinging around quickly, Fallon entered the house.

Moving slowly through the house, absorbing the memories as he walked through each room, Fallon stood at the doorway leading into Kit's bedroom. His sister basically lived a spartan life. There were no signs of material possessions to clutter the room. Kit Fallon believed in living simply and sharing whatever she had with others. Being twins, Fallon and Kit shared a bond that would never be broken. Even in death.

"The time for grieving is over," Fallon said to himself.

Making his way to his room, Fallon picked up his suitcase, reaching for the can standing in the corner. Walking back to the front door, Fallon dropped his bag on the porch. Going back inside, Fallon began emptying the can throughout the house. His movements were quick and deliberate. When he was finished, Fallon stepped outside again.

Taking one last look, Fallon struck the match. The gasoline ignited immediately, dancing obscenely through the house. With one last look, Fallon stepped off the porch.

"Time to go to work," he said out loud to no one.

As Fallon disappeared into the darkness, the flames engulfed the house and lit up the sky. Fallon never looked back.

World Wide did not exist outside the office of the presidency; in fact, it was common knowledge that not even the president himself was aware of its existence. Nonetheless, Reynolds and Harris flew with Secret Service documentation and photo ID. There were certain registrations, technicalities, and preboarding procedures for most agents of the government who carried weapons. But they were null and void for the two World Wide operatives who could travel with their weapons that were standard-issue revolvers.

Both agents knew that when they made contact with Raven, they would need more than a handgun. Before leaving the States, Reynolds had contacted one of their equipment drops in Ireland. There they would be supplied with what they needed.

There was no debate on this issue, Reynolds and Harris both being on the same page. They got their weapons first and then checked into their hotel. After finishing dinner, Reynolds and Harris started to plan their approach to Raven.

Ireland was not a big country, and County Offaly was relatively small. The one problem they saw in that, being one of the smaller counties, they knew they would have to proceed carefully. In places such as Offaly, strangers stood out. They also were aware that contact with Raven could happen easily and unexpectedly. He could be just walking on the street, and Reynolds and Harris were not going to be unprepared.

Reynolds, playing it close to the vest and not sharing what he knew about Raven with Harris, knew the way Raven thought. After what had gone down in the aborted attempt at freeing the prisoners was one thing. The killing of Raven's sister fell into another category. There was no way someone was not going to pay.

After arriving at Shannon Airport, Reynolds and Harris had to find a map to locate the equipment drop. In all his years with World Wide, Ireland was one of the few places Reynolds had never been. Harris was with the company too short a time. Not wanting to tip their hand asking questions, they managed to find it without too much problems.

The Irishman at the equipment drop went by the name of Ciaran McManus. The red nose, stomach that hung over his belt, and the nervous twitch told Reynolds this was a drinker. He was not a World Wide employee. Just an arms dealer. World Wide dealt with numerous independents around the globe. No doubt McManus was not above supplying arms to the IRA and the provosts from the North.

It wasn't hard to figure that the house they stopped at was in a Catholic town. It could be seen in the poverty that encompassed the town. It was a brick house that stood in the middle of a low row of other brick houses, nondescript, unassuming, a house that could belong to anyone.

"Quaint," Harris remarked, a sardonic look on his face. Reynolds did not bother to respond. After checking the address, Reynolds and Harris knocked on the door and introduced themselves, not giving their right names, of course. Since McManus was expecting them, he quickly ushered them into his dank, dark living room.

After they had initially sized him up, they realized that McManus was a small intense man who chain-smoked. He eyed them warily, nervously, during the entire transaction. The entire meeting lasted about half an hour. McManus, cocky and arrogant since Reynolds and Harris did not dicker about the prices like the rebels, had visions of making some big money from these two naive Americans.

The selection they chose from was located in one of the small rooms upstairs.

"This is just an overview, understand," McManus said. "It's similar to the iceberg situation. If you are interested in more than what is here, just ask. I can lay my hands on any type of weapon you need. I also have cutlery," McManus added and shrugged humbly.

Neither man felt the need for knives. After quickly assessing the quality of the supply—an illegal supply, high quality, more than likely obtained from the United States—they chose AK rifles, Browning with silencer attachments, a long-range rifle with scope and infrared (just in case), shoulder and ankle holsters, and lots of ammunition.

"Explosives?" McManus asked, salesman's hope in his nervous voice.

"Not this time," Reynolds answered. "Maybe later."

Harris laughed at Reynolds's jokeless joke.

"Good man yourself," McManus said and looked at both men, nodding. "Is there anything else I can do for you?"

Reynolds and Harris, glancing at each other, shrugged. Reynolds answered, "No, I think we have all we will need right now, thank you."

McManus was feeling pretty good about himself and the vision of his weapons being used on the assholes who called themselves patriots. As far as he was concerned, both sides could wipe themselves off the map and he wouldn't lose a moment's sleep over it.

"I think we're finished here, Jack," Reynolds said, addressing Harris. "Just one more chore we have to do."

"What would that—" McManus never finished the sentence.

From Harris's pocket, a mean-looking thirty-eight with a silencer attached, jumped into his hands. McManus had time to begin opening his mouth when the first slug tore through his right eye. As he slumped to the floor, Harris deposited one more in his head. He was dead before he hit the floor.

Neither man gave McManus a second thought as they left the decrepit house. There were men like him all over the world, and they had used them often. Sometimes they let them live.

They placed the suitcases containing the arms in the trunk and drove away. People on the street barely noticed them.

In the town of Galway miles from the Fallon farm, Reynolds and Harris checked into a hotel. After arming themselves sufficiently with inconspicuous handguns, they placed the suitcases under their beds and went to a pub across the street from their hotel.

Nine

Megan Clark confronted Sean McGuire in his own home that morning. The usually placid, happy girl that saw only beauty in people and the world was livid. Her face, the one that easily blushed, was burning red with anger. She banged forcefully on McGuire's door, and McGuire opened it with force.

"What do you want?" he spit out. McGuire's eyes were dark, black, and his face hard.

He hadn't slept since the attack failed. He was wired with caffeine and nicotine and whisky. McGuire was in no mood to deal with a hysterical woman. He had other problems, the main one being he was being second-guessed by the leaders about his decision on attacking the jail. The last thing he needed was Megan Clark and having to listen to whatever her crap might be.

Megan glared at McGuire with hatred. "Your death," she shot back.

The vehemence in Megan's voice caused McGuire to recoil. He had known Megan Clark all his life and had never seen her in such a rage. There was a time McGuire had the ability to make Megan cower under his glare. He knew those days were gone. Still McGuire was dumbfounded.

"What?" McGuire finally managed to get out of his mouth. He stared at her, confused; had he started coming out of his fog planning revenge?

There was no stopping Megan. Rage and anger had taken over. "You, Sean, and everyone like you. You and your cronies are killing us all, you bastard."

"I don't know what you're talking about, girl," McGuire came back, trying hard to regain his composure. "I still believe you're out of your mind." He started to shut the door. Megan kicked it open. McGuire stared at her in grim surprise.

Megan continued berating McGuire. "You and the others killed Kit Fallon, you rotten bastard."

"Kit Fallon." McGuire was trying now to buy time to see if he could calm her down. "I wasn't even there."

"You're a liar."

McGuire knew Megan was aware he was one of the men in the car that had escaped. He wasn't sure how many others had seen him. That was the least of his worries now. He knew the papers had shown the bloodbath and the Fallon woman was one of the victims. McGuire was also sure the story was being carried in newspapers all over the world.

"Kit Fallon?" McGuire said. He had not seen the actual killing but was aware of it from the news and the papers. "The bloody Brits killed her, you dumb bitch," McGuire was on the defensive now.

"No," Megan said. "You did. You and your kind."

"I'm shutting the door on you, Megan, before I smash your face in," McGuire said, his hand on the door. Shoving McGuire aside, Megan pushed her way inside. Watching her in disbelief, McGuire stared at her with true shock on his face.

Turning to face McGuire after he reluctantly closed the door, Megan continued, her voice surprisingly soft now. "You killed her, Sean," Megan said again. "You're as much to blame as the Brits, if not more. You're nothing but a common criminal hiding behind the guise of patriotism. A good-for-nothing criminal. You and your kind—"

"Are fighting a war!" McGuire yelled at Megan, cutting her off. "We're fucking revolutionaries trying to free fuckin' Ireland. And you damn well should know that, Megan. You were one of us once."

"Not anymore, Sean," Megan, her voice taking on a sadness that ran deep. "Neither does Kit. I admit I was naive once, Sean. But now I see what you and the others stand for and it sickens me."

"We're risking our lives to save your ass and free Ireland. Even for ungrateful sluts like you too. As a matter of fact—"

Megan slapped McGuire in the mouth. Stunned, McGuire gaped at her. Then after a moment of staring and considering, McGuire slapped her back.

Then they stood in the middle of the living room glaring at each other.

"You're no revolutionary, Sean," Megan said, rubbing the side of her face. "You're a failure. You're shit."

"Close the door on your way out, Megan," McGuire snarled menacingly. "Or do you want me to hit you again?"

Megan was not deterred. What angered McGuire the most was the look of pity that showed on Megan Clark's face. "You killed Kit just as sure as if you pulled the trigger, not the British soldiers. You shouldn't have attacked them in broad daylight with all those innocent people around and you know it. You have no regard for human life, Sean, except for your own. You're careless and you're stupid."

Megan's anger had been replaced by her grief. The last remark had hit Sean McGuire like a kick to the stomach. Megan continued before McGuire could speak.

"You think you are fighting a cause. You're not. You're just too stupid and pathetic to appreciate life. Or let others try. I feel sorry for you."

"Yeah, yeah. Listen to you sing," McGuire sneered, trying not to let on how much Megan's word had stung. He wasn't too successful. "You're such a pretty bird. Only you forgot something and it's this—no one is free in Ireland until the British leave our soil. You're deluding yourself if you think there's ever a good day in this shithole."

McGuire was on a roll now. There was passion in his voice and desperation too. Megan listened as McGuire raved about conditions in Ireland, knowing McGuire actually believed what he was saying.

"Ireland is an occupied country. And as long as we can, we're going to do whatever we have to do to kill every British and Protestant bastard that stands in the way of us getting the right to determine our own future—"

"And general amnesty for all prisoners?" Megan finished sarcastically.

"And a thirty-two-county republic where Irish is the language of the people," McGuire added tauntingly.

"You pompous ass," Megan said, unable to keep the disgust out of her voice. "You don't even speak the Irish."

"Oh, but one day I will, girl," McGuire said laughingly. "That's after we kill enough Brits and Prots and whoever else stands in our way."

"Kit Fallon for one," Megan pushed.

"Those were Brit bullets, not Irish."

"You keep telling yourself that, Sean, and maybe someday you will come to believe it," Megan moved in relentlessly. "You're not only careless but someone who twists and lies, fool some of the people. But not all."

"Who is going to stop me?" McGuire asked.

"John Fallon."

Hearing Fallon's name for the first time from Megan brought McGuire up short. The look of fear that crossed his face and passed just as quickly did not escape Megan. McGuire worked at composing himself before he spoke.

"What about Fallon?"

"You don't think he is going to forget this, do you?" Megan said.

"Fallon doesn't bother me," McGuire answered, the false bravado not doing it. "I don't expect that cowardly Yank to do anything but put his tail between his legs and head back to America."

Megan just shook her head sadly.

"Besides," McGuire continued, "I'm sorry about Kit Fallon's death and that's truth." The viciousness in his voice when he spoke startled Megan. "But I would do it all over again if I had to. The next time, Megan, maybe you should watch your ass. You might not be so lucky."

"Myself and every other innocent bystander will have to watch ourselves if you're in the lead," Megan said, disgusted.

"Join us and we'll throw in a bulletproof vest for you," McGuire said and laughed.

"I'm going, Sean," Megan said, turning for the door.

"I'm sorry you came, Megan," McGuire answered.

Megan turned on him one more time. "You don't give a damn about Kit or the other innocent people that were killed in your senseless attack on the soldiers, do you?"

"We didn't kill her and I don't kill innocent people. We kill Brits and Prots. Remember?" Sean said.

Megan, shaking her head in dismay, left without replying or closing the door. McGuire, standing out front, watched Megan until she was no longer in sight. Then he shut the door as he would on every one of her kind. He kicked it shut, loud and hard.

Walking over to the phone, McGuire dialed Cassidy's number.

"We need to meet," he said when Cassidy picked up.

"What's up?" Cassidy asked.

"Revenge is what I'm after. And the sooner the better," McGuire said urgently and with the full force and power of hatred.

That same morning which was the day after the massacre that killed the three innocent people, including Kit Fallon, also the same day Megan Clark had braced Sean McGuire, Sergeant Wilson, the top-ranking NCO of the British troops stationed in Offaly, was sitting in Major Neville's office, planning their next move.

Neville, under the gun from the British high command, knew he had to get this mess straightened out and make sure the blame for the killings were linked to the IRA. The bad press had already put the British in a poor light, and Neville knew his career was on the line. He knew the best way was to nip it in the bud right away.

Neville was neither happy nor at ease. He had been continually pacing the room slowly stroking his mustache. Wilson was his usual hard, determined block of anger and force. Neville's pacing was getting on his nerves, but he kept that thought to himself.

"Major, I don't think the Irish bastards will try anything like that again for a while," Wilson said and believed it. Wilson was a firm believer that brute force was the only thing the IRA understood. "The cost was too high. And I think we sent them a message that said pretty clearly we know their games."

Neville had stopped by the window and was looking at the empty courtyard below. Ever since the incident, everyone in his command had been put on high alert. To the naked eye it looked as though the compound was empty. In essence, everyone was on round-the-clock surveillance. Neville had even bulked up the contingent around his office.

Neville turned back to Wilson, only half hearing what the sergeant had to say. He walked over to his desk and sat down.

"Knowing the mentality of those drunken sots, they'll have to retaliate to show they are men and not boys. We're dealing with revolutionaries after all, Sergeant," Neville said with deliberate sarcasm. "They have to be taken seriously."

"Oh, they're serious men all right, Major," Wilson said, a smirk lining his face. "Especially the dead ones." Wilson barked once for laughter.

Sometimes Sergeant Wilson grated on Neville's nerves. But he had been with Neville for years and was aware how well his vicious tactics were useful in these situations. He needed him now more than ever.

"Even though I think you may be right, Sergeant," Neville said, "I think whoever was behind this attack will lie low for a while. But let's not underestimate them just yet." Neville looked at Wilson with caution. "These boys like the fight, make no mistake about that. So keep the men ready. Let's not give them an easy target for revenge."

"Right, sir," Wilson answered, his eyes narrowing with relish.

"Now let's get down to who they were," Neville continued. "You're sure it was McGuire and his gang? We have to be certain."

"I'm sure it was McGuire himself that drove that third car away. The bloody coward," Wilson spit out.

"Well, if you're right, Sergeant, whatever you do, don't pick him up," Neville said. Wilson looked at him with surprise.

Holding his hand up, not giving Wilson a chance to protest, Neville continued. "I want you to get the word to your informer that we don't know who was responsible for the attack on the compound." Pausing, Neville began stroking his mustache again. Wilson knew he was plotting something. He remained silent.

"But let him know somehow that McGuire's name never came up. I want McGuire and the others to feel safe," Neville said and smiled coldly at Wilson and left it at that. Wilson didn't have to know everything. "One other reason I don't want to pick anyone up yet is to give the bloody rebels another martyr to rally behind. When we make our move, it will be swift and final."

Wilson, after a moment of thought, grinned at Neville in return. "I'll make sure my informant gets to work right away," he said. "And what about the American, sir? The one whose sister was the nun and was killed in the crossfire?"

"And you're sure the American was there?"

"That's what the locals are saying, sir."

"Is it true that he burned their house to the ground?"

"Yes, sir," Wilson replied. "From the information I have gathered, the American just poured gasoline throughout the house, torched it, and walked away. I have been out there, Major, and all that's left is a pile of ashes."

"And the American?" Neville asked.

"That's the strange part, sir," Wilson answered, a puzzled look on his face. "No one has seen or heard from him. It's as though he just disappeared. I have my informant working on finding out what he can."

"This American sounds like a bloody lunatic," Neville rasped. "Just what was the relationship between him and the nun?"

"They were twins, sir. Apparently the American was sent from Ireland and raised by relatives. He has only recently returned to Offaly."

The astonishment was apparent on Neville's face. He was trying to fathom what was going through Fallon's mind and what was the reason why he would burn his home and then disappear. It only helped confirm his belief that Americans were bloody fools. His disdain and hatred for them was known throughout the ranks of his troops.

"What should we do about the American, sir?" Wilson asked.

"Find out more about him. Right now he is a loose cannon and I am not thoroughly convinced he is just a coward and has turned tail and left."

Wilson, not responding, listened warily to Neville. He did not agree with his assessment of the American. In his gut, he felt there was more to the man than the rumors put out by the citizens of Offaly. To Wilson, Fallon was a dangerous man and one to be reckoned with.

"Sergeant, I don't want this whole mess to turn into a political circus. I want you to see what you can do to allay that. And it was a bloody mess, Sergeant," Neville added with distaste. "I do want to know for sure who was responsible as soon as possible. When I do make the move on McGuire and the others, I want no loopholes. Is that understood?" Neville ordered and looked away.

"Yes, sir," Wilson said and left it at that. He had been properly chided and did not see any advantage in pursuing it. "As for the American, no one seems to know anything about him. He came back to Ireland to live with his sister on the farm. He works the farm, appears to keep to himself, and as far as any information I can get about him, has had a run-in with

McGuire and some of the others. I feel we can discount him as a rebel sympathizer. He has not been in this country very long."

"Well, just the same, keep an eye on him," Neville said. He remembered the chilling feeling he had had looking at the man in the crowd. At that time, he didn't know he was brother of the dead nun. There was a coldness he felt and the way the man locked onto his eyes and then disappeared. He had wondered at the time who he was, but with all the chaos going on around him, he had chosen to dismiss the incident. His instinct now and the chill that ran down his spine told him to be careful.

"Keep him in mind. I don't want any surprises," Neville added vehemently.

"Yes, sir," Wilson said. Major Neville had turned away from him and was now staring out the window again. Wilson knew he had been dismissed.

On the way out, Neville's voice stopped him. Neville was still staring at the compound below.

"Something to keep in mind, Sergeant," Neville told Wilson without turning around. "The man that turned that third car around and got away may not be a coward. Just be careful. I wouldn't underestimate him. In fact, he could be a thinking man and that is always dangerous in an adversary."

Fallon and Megan sat in the kitchen of Megan's home. Megan was handling the affairs of Kit's death, the wake, the funeral, the burial plot. Fallon was a stranger in Ireland, and Megan who had loved Kit as much as he did sincerely wanted to help. It was an area that was foreign to Fallon.

Killing had been a part of Fallon's life for as long as he could remember. But he never had to get involved in the aftermath of any of those killings. Kit, he had loved her and the pain he felt now was just beginning to engulf him. He knew it would pass if he let it run its course. Then Fallon would move, not on his emotions, but cold, calculating, and totally without feeling. That was a must in Fallon's life.

Megan in just one day missed Kit more than she could ever imagine. She could not conceive spending the remainder of her life without her. Intellectually though, Megan knew that she had to get away from that thinking and move on with her life. Megan, like many women in Ireland, had seen many people put to earth for natural as well as unnatural causes.

But Kit's death was something Megan was having a hard time coming to grips with. It was senseless and sickening. Kit was the one person in Offaly who was the most giving and loving person in the county. For her to die in this manner by armed thugs and troops trying to kill one another was sad. For Megan, it was the hardest of all the killings that had taken place that day to get out of her mind. She had to try.

Right now she was trying to understand John Fallon who had showed up at her home last night. When he had arrived, Megan had no knowledge of the fire. Even now his explanation had seemed vague.

Fallon himself felt ice cold and ready for revenge. Sitting at Megan's table, his mind seemingly elsewhere, Fallon was beginning to tick through the options, the methods, and the technicalities. But to Megan, he seemed distant and sad as he sat at the table drinking his tea. She wanted to reach out and hold him. But Megan knew any move or explanation would have to come from Fallon. So she waited.

It had been on the tip of her tongue several times since John showed up at her home why he had burned the Fallon house. She never asked. What she concluded was that John Fallon, in his own way, had reached closure with the death of his sister, Kit Fallon. It had caused quite a stir in town, and the tongues were wagging that John Fallon was some sort of deranged individual. It didn't seem to bother John.

What concerned Megan now was, what were Fallon's plans? With the destruction of the Fallon home and the deserting of the land, Megan feared that she would lose Fallon. Megan loved John Fallon as she had never loved anyone before. The thought of losing him distressed her to the point of depression. Megan knew Fallon was his own man and deep down also knew he would not let Kit's death go unpunished. She felt disconnected and useless right now, not knowing what his next move would be. So she waited.

The night was closing in on them. The gray of the dawn was turning black, and the last of the sunlight was drifting beneath the sky. Both seemed not to notice enough to turn on a lamp. It was as though they were each lost in their own thoughts. The kitchen was graying and casting large loose shadows all around them. Perhaps they did not want to see.

To keep her mind occupied and dreading what she felt was coming, Megan was sifting through the different notes and paperwork she had accumulated in her death-related duties. Fallon had asked her if she would mind handling the details of Kit's funeral and burial. Fallon sat across from her, watching her quietly. Appreciatively.

It was a new feeling for Fallon, the one he was experiencing with Megan Clark, this stunningly beautiful woman who had moved into his heart and touched him in places he had long thought dead. He loved her. Fallon had come to this conclusion a long time ago and knew he could not lie to himself about his feelings for her.

Fallon also knew he was going to hurt her. For what he had to do would be impossible with any emotional ties. His instincts had kicked in, and he could feel he was back to where he had to be to accomplish what he had to do. Megan would pay the price.

Megan broke the uncomfortable silence. She did not want to broach the subject, but knew she had to.

"John, what are you going to do about the farm now?" Megan asked.

"What do you mean?"

"I know the fire destroyed the house and much of the land," Megan began. "But it is not anything that cannot be fixed."

"I guess I haven't given it much thought," Fallon answered quietly. "I guess you think it was rash what I did."

"I'm not one to judge, John," Megan said, a gentle, loving tone to her voice. "I know how much you loved Kit and how close you two were." Megan hesitated, not sure if she should pursue what she was thinking. Throwing caution to the wind, she plunged ahead.

"John, Kit confided in me over the years when she would go away on holiday where she was going," Megan said nervously. She watched Fallon tense up, a guarded expression covering his face as his eyes clouded over. Megan shivered at the ice-cold man who stood before her. It unnerved her.

"What did she say?" Fallon asked.

"Nothing, really," Megan continued. "John, Kit never told me where she was going, only that she was visiting her brother. When she left, it was always in high spirits. She was so happy on those trips. When she returned there was sadness about her. She would lose herself in her work. John, Kit loved you dearly."

Fallon had moved over to the window and was looking out at the darkening sky. His expression disclosed nothing. Megan waited.

"Thank you, Megan," Fallon said, turning back to face her. "It must have been a blessing for Kit to have you."

Megan could feel the love she had for Fallon like an ache in her heart. As she went through the different notes and paperwork she had accumulated in her death-related duties, a task she had taken on when Fallon had asked for her help. Fallon sat across from her, watching quietly. Appreciatively.

Megan was reluctant to speak to Fallon about what had been on her mind ever since the funeral. But she knew she had to.

"John," Megan began cautiously. "What are your plans for the future? Now that the farm has been destroyed, what next?" Megan dreaded asking, afraid of what Fallon might say. But there was no alternative.

Fallon smiled at her sadly, and Megan's heart took a little turn.

"I don't know, Megan," Fallon lied. He knew this was going to be hard, but figured he might as well meet it straight on now rather than prolong the inevitable. Fallon knew exactly what he was going to do. "As far as rebuilding the farm, without Kit, I don't think I could run it. I don't know all that much about farming anyway. Remember, Megan, I'm just a stranger in this country, really."

Megan took a moment before answering.

"How can you be a stranger in a land you were born in?" Megan said quietly. "The farm and house can be rebuilt and I know how to run a farm. I've lived here all my life." After Megan had crossed the line, having dropped her guard, she looked at Fallon's dark, intense eyes and then looked away, a blush forming on her cheeks.

"We can work the farm together," Megan told him softly. "Together I think we should make out all right."

Fallon looked at this beautiful young woman and tried not to feel what was surfacing in his heart. As much as Fallon loved her, he knew that now was not the time to let any kind of emotion cloud his thinking. For what Fallon had in mind, Megan would best not be a part of it. He knew deep down in his heart he was going to hurt Megan and it would begin by lying to her. It was the price he had to pay.

When Megan looked back at him, Fallon smiled at her. He knew from the look on her face, the moistness in her eyes, she did not believe his reasons. It didn't matter. Fallon was going to play it out his way.

"That's a kind offer, Megan," Fallon said. "I think I should know better where I stand in a few days. There are some things I have to figure out. That and getting over Kit's death have been difficult for me. Kit was the only family I had, and if you don't mind waiting, I am going to need some time." Like who was going to pay for Kit's death for starters. And when.

"John, I'll wait for you as long as I have to," Megan said, nodding her head. "I've waited my whole life for you and I have no intention of losing you now. Whatever it is that you have to do, if you tell me, maybe I can help."

Fallon smiled and shook his head. "I appreciate that, Megan, but what I have to do is something I have to do alone. Please don't think I'm shutting you out. It's just that this is one time I can't use any help."

The look on Megan's face was tearing Fallon up. He knew he wasn't fooling her and she was fighting a battle within herself not to ask. When she answered, her voice was calm and restrained.

"All right, John, I think I understand," Megan said, forcing a smile. "Kit always told me the Fallons were deep and dark thinkers. I can see that she was right." Megan added and looked into Fallon's eyes.

Then after a moment, Fallon watched her look away.

"Take as much time as you need, John," Megan offered. "I'm not going anywhere. I'll be waiting for you."

"Thank you," Fallon said, taking Megan in his arms. He kissed her long and hard, felt the passion between Megan and himself. He held her for a long time. Each one did not want to let the other go. Fallon stepped back.

"Will you be okay tonight?" Megan asked him quietly.

"I will," Fallon told her. "I've taken a room in a small bed-and-breakfast just outside of Offaly. There are some things I have to take care of."

Megan watched Fallon as he walked down the path toward town. She waited until he was out of sight, letting the emptiness and the fear she felt flow over her. Megan, taking one last look, walked back inside the cottage.

TEN

FALLON HATED LYING TO MEGAN, but figured the less she knew about what he was planning, the safer Megan would be. After making the necessary phone calls, preparing himself for what lay ahead, Fallon made his way out to the "safe house." Acting on instinct, Fallon had secured this place after first landing in Ireland.

Driving there now, Fallon's thoughts drifted back to his past life. Fallon could remember every man he had ever killed. Effortlessly. The names, the dates, the circumstances. Even the reason behind the contract. He remembered the faces of the men he had killed, before and after. He could also remember the coldness that came with it each and every time.

Fallon no longer wondered how every time it was the same feeling. To kill is to kill. It's the same act, regardless of the reason. He could feel the life leave the body, leave the room, the air. Something inside him was getting lost, and Fallon had no control over how to stop it. Whatever that was remained nameless. This was the life he had chosen, and with it came the consequences of remorse and guilt that he had to live with every day of his life. Fallon had never gotten used to the killing. He wasn't sure anyone ever really did.

He remembered a conversation he had with Megan. At the time they were discussing the killings and carnage brought about by the troubles. Fallon had never felt a part of their struggles, and when he had spoken to Megan, he felt far removed from it.

Megan was discussing the "troubles," as the Irish liked to refer to them. Fallon thought by saying that it absolved them from what they really were—killing. Justifying it by labeling it with some word did not diminish the fact that they were killers. Just as Fallon was. The only difference being he did not lie to himself about what he was.

"It's sad what has happened to Ireland," Megan said. "It seems ever since I have been a child we have been fighting and killing, innocent people mostly. I have a hard time remembering when there was peace in our country."

There was sadness in Megan's eyes when Fallon looked at her. His heart was saddened by the fact that this beautiful, gifted woman would eventually come to hate him as she hated all the others who had brought unhappiness to her land.

"My parents died when Kit and I were very young," Fallon started. "I don't really remember them and sometimes I feel like a bad son because I am unable to conjure up any feeling for them. I have lost friends, but, Megan, I would be lying to you if I said I have any feeling for what's happening in Ireland."

He could see the anger in her face as she tried controlling it. Fallon knew he was being harsh, but knew in the long run it would be for the best. Better to let her begin hating him now rather than later on.

"That's a terrible thing to say, John," Megan replied through clenched teeth. "Even after what happened to Kit? I don't know how you can say something like that."

"I'm sorry, Megan."

Starting for the door, Megan stopped and looked at him. Fallon had hurt her, but he knew she still felt the same way about him. Megan loved him unconditionally, and Fallon was going to have to live with that. Megan, moving toward him, squeezed his hand, turned, and left.

Fallon watched as she walked slowly down the path, the dark taking her at the end of the driveway. After Megan had gone, Fallon returned to the kitchen to make two phone calls. A contact inquiry and a location for an equipment drop.

Then taking Kit's car, Fallon drove into the dark Irish night to a city that believed in the legitimacy of the struggle. A perfect place to purchase an arsenal.

Dan Morehead landed at Shannon Airport at 8:00 a.m., having taken the Aer Lingus flight out of John F. Kennedy Airport the night before.

Weaponless, Dan Morehead walked casually through Shannon Airport. Morehead could easily have been taken for a tourist, a businessman, or another Irishman returning to visit his native Ireland.

He was just another gray-haired nondescript man carrying an overcoat. If one were to notice him, they would see an older man who moved with rare agility. But no one did. The bleary-eyed passengers were too busy making their way to baggage claim to take notice of anyone. Morehead was just another man moving through an airport at night, a carry-on suitcase in one hand, an Irish newspaper in the other.

Morehead was retired so his ID was not current, but that didn't matter to him. Morehead knew where to get the guns. This was not Morehead's first trip to Ireland, and he had enough contacts in the country that it would be no problem for him to get pointed in the right direction by any number of men familiar with those that handled arsenals.

He had been here before and had handled many contracts and retrievals for World Wide in Ireland, and he knew who to contact. Even if they had changed personnel, Dan Morehead was aware that the same system was in place. There would be a small box in the want ads of the paper that was a coded lead. It was standard procedure throughout the world.

This one read: "Laurel-be true to Yourself. Life offers the weapons of promise and wisdom. Use them for your advancement. Don't give up the fight.-Ben." It was a standard ad that World-Wide kept running in all papers in the countries they operated in.

Satisfied, Dan Morehead started out of the airport. He walked alone along the tarmac and made a covered cell phone call and waited until he received a blank response. Breathing the fresh air, feeling better being outside after the six-hour plane ride across the Atlantic, Dan Morehead stood his ground like a man waiting for a ride. It did not take more than twenty minutes.

His cell phone rang. After receiving the phone call, Dan Morehead rented a car and followed the same path away from Shannon Airport that Reynolds and Harris had followed, arriving in a poor Catholic neighborhood where no one paid any attention to the quiet dignified man who had the look of a tourist coming back to revisit the "old country." It was not a long drive, and Morehead did not have to use a map. It was a road he had traveled many times, and like most things in Ireland, nothing had changed.

Even though McManus had never outfitted four Americans in the space of two days before, he was unaware that he had just supplied three sides of a dangerous triangle. All of them, whether they knew it or not, were converging on themselves. All McManus was concerned with was they had the money to pay for the weapons.

Even if McManus had known, he would not have cared. Like all parasites and mercenaries, all McManus was concerned with was the fact that they paid cash. McManus would have had a good laugh and been pleased with himself had they known. In fact, McManus thought it was as it should be. This was the life he had chosen and knew from the people he dealt with that it was the life they had picked and he would have been correct.

All four of the Americans had been businesslike, knowledgeable, and well resourced when it came to money. McManus enjoyed doing business with them. It was a welcome change from the "radicals" and "fanatics" that made up the bulk of his business. The Americans were obviously professionals. Quiet. Watchful. Cold.

But the last American had been the coldest.

This would be the man to watch. This man was the one that was more than likely to cause the most harm. Or have the most harm come to him.

McManus wished he could be there to see it. For study's sake. McManus called it professional curiosity. Little did he know after the last visit he would be leaving this life and crossing over.

Later that evening, after making use of the equipment drop and bringing two suitcases full of automatic weapons back to the flat where he was staying, Fallon checked each weapon carefully. There were small arms and long-range rifles, holsters, blades, a weapon Fallon was not adverse to using cutlery when deemed necessary; he had stored the weapons in the closet in his bedroom.

Fallon had no fears about anyone discovering the cache of weapons. No one, not even Megan knew where he was staying. The isolated dismal dwelling located in a section of Ireland that was just about out-of-bounds for any self-respecting person suited Fallon to a T. Operating from there would be to his benefit.

Fallon, deep in thought, walked slowly toward town. The three miles did not bother him. He carried a Beretta in a holster that he held close to his left side.

His thoughts kept drifting back to Kit, realizing how deeply he missed and loved her. He knew that was a bad place to let himself go, so Fallon turned his thoughts away from Megan. He knew that now was the time to stay focused on what had to be done. What bothered him most was that he was not thinking about what he was about to do.

Fallon's thoughts kept drifting between Megan and Kit. He knew he had to shake them from his mind and concentrate on what he had to do.

There had never been any hesitation since the death of his sister Kit, and Fallon had never wavered in the face of what he was about to do. It was what he had been trained for, and he was good at what he did. What troubled Fallon, something that nagged at him, was the fact that his main reason for coming back home to Ireland was to put his past behind him and hopefully find some peace.

But here it was again. Waiting.

The moonless night hovered over him like a safety blanket as he made his way into town. There was no rush. When it was all over, and if he lived through it, Fallon knew he would be leaving Ireland forever. He didn't delude himself nor make up elaborate lies about what was about to transpire; there were scores to be settled. That was how the game was played. And if the players weren't aware of what was coming down, they soon would.

He made no distinction between the Irish and the British. They were equally on his mind, and despite their civil, or uncivil way, they were just targets to John Fallon. Justifiable targets that had to pay the price.

Thinking back to the operation in the coldness of his heart, the coldness that had served him well in the past, the Irish had been sloppy. They hatched and tried to pull off an escape plan that was doomed from the beginning. They got innocents killed. In his profession, that was a no-no. They were thoughtless and acted like animals. All for the kill and to hell with anybody or everybody. Their mistake was Kit.

Though it was British bullets that had killed Kit and the two other civilians, Fallon held the Irish just as responsible. If McGuire and his cronies wanted to make a move on the prison, it should have been planned more carefully, at a time when there were less innocent people on the streets.

The British had been under attack, which would have been acceptable, but they had orchestrated that attack. That was bad planning. That was their mistake. Fallon had seen his fair share of violence and then some. He envisioned the thinking of the British. They were not that particular where the bullets went when it was just the Irish on the streets. From what Fallon knew of Ireland, he could not say this was true. But just from his observations, the British considered the Irish expendable.

Then again what interested Fallon was that the British Army was not surprised or did not even seem concerned about the attack by the Irish rebels. They had known it was coming and were ready for it.

Fallon knew what that meant. It did not take a genius to know there was "a mouse in the house." An informer.

Thinking about that, mulling over who was the most likely person to have pulled the plug on the rebels, gave Fallon a boost. That and the fact he had narrowed the field down and was sure he had nailed who it was.

Fallon turned all these facts over in his head on this grim overcast day as he walked through the night into town, like an inevitably.

The Three Oaks Pub was almost empty and eerily quiet. The events of the previous few days were still on the minds and thoughts of the townspeople.

Cassidy, Collins, and Casey were seated at their usual corner table. McGuire, who usually occupied the head of the table, was absent, most likely meeting with the leaders of the resistance, trying to come up with some lame excuse for how the escape attempt went down. Donohue, the owner of the pub, was sitting at the end of the bar reading the newspaper.

The three men sitting at the table had survived the massacre outside the prison. They had been in the third car with Sean McGuire, the car that had turned tail and got away. The car that had left their comrades to die.

They were angry and still shaken by how close they had come to be one of the ones lying in the street with a bullet in their heads. They were also feeling pangs of guilt that none of them seemed able to shake.

"I'm tellin' you, lads, the bastards knew we were coming," Cassidy said strenuously, unsuccessfully trying to show pain and loss for the eight men killed. None of the other civilians had come up in their conversation.

Cassidy was bitter and working extra hard at trying to get drunk, hoping to block out how things had gone so sour. His voice rasped, still sore from where Fallon had punched him.

"The bastard Brits were just waiting to slaughter us, for god's sake," Cassidy continued. "And that's the bloody truth."

Cassidy and the others could not shake the thought from their minds, and they could not stop rehashing it. The more they pored over it, the more convinced they became that the British knew they were coming. They had known what they were going to do.

The silence in the bar was deafening. Donohue was reading the paper, the few men laboring over their drinks with little to say to one another, and the wind howling outside as it blew through the open doors gave the scene in the pub a surreal look.

"One thing we can be thankful for, lads," Collins said in a voice barely above a whisper, "we were damned lucky. It could have been us lying out there in the street. At least there are some of us left to carry on the fight."

"We're not finished with the lousy buggers yet," Cassidy added, eyes bugging wildly. "We are going to get our revenge."

After the boys toasted this remark, Cassidy let them know what he was thinking.

"All this horse dung we've been throwing around is all well and good," Cassidy said slowly bitterly. As he was speaking, his eyes scanned the room, letting them fall on Donohue and the few others that were oblivious to them, lost in the drinks that sat in front of them. Satisfied, Cassidy continued. "Keep in mind, lads, this wasn't because the Brits are smart and figured this out for themselves."

Collins and Casey looked at each other then fixed their puzzled gaze on Cassidy. He plunged ahead, neither of them knowing where he was going with all this. These were twp men who would never be mistaken for having brains. They were guns and muscle. That was what McGuire wanted, and in these two he had found it.

"We've got an informer in our ranks," Cassidy told them, the rage shimmering in his eyes. "It's the only way it could have happened." Cassidy looked at each of them one by one, locking onto their eyes.

Collins and Casey looked back with a mixture of confusion and surprise. Cassidy had dropped a bomb in their laps, and neither one knew how to react.

Donohue sat at the bar, contentedly reading the paper, moving only when one of the bar patrons signaled for another drink.

Cassidy, usually slow in grasping even the minor happenings, had pondered this problem for quite some time. It was the only conclusion he could come up with. Cassidy had a hard time believing there was an informer among them, even though in his gut he knew it had to be true. He had some prodding to do.

McGuire had said as much that day to Cassidy when they had met alone on the outskirts of town but who and how far past the two men sitting at the table with him. Cassidy had no doubts that Collins and Casey were both trusted men. After arguing with Cassidy, McGuire, who trusted no one including Cassidy, after considering them for a moment, begrudgingly had to agree with him. McGuire rejected the idea and moved on, and neither man was able to come up with a viable suspect.

Sitting here now in the Three Oaks Pub with Collins and Casey, Cassidy was still trying to comprehend an informer in their world. As much as Cassidy would have liked to have dismissed the idea, he reluctantly had to admit there was no other way the British could have been lying in wait like they were. Cassidy's hatred boiled at the mere prospect of it. So much so that he was unable to focus on anything else.

As did Casey and Collins. Both men looked at Cassidy apprehensive, anxiously, and hoping to see some sign that there was a plan in place. Their faces were red with anger and hatred, both hoping for the opportunity for confrontation.

Finally, Casey's voice broke the silence of the three men, who were lost in their own thoughts, each pining for a chance at revenge.

"An informer," Casey said angrily, his voice rising. "I can't believe there's a fuckin' informer in our midst. So help me Christ if I'm the one who finds out who it is, I'll put a bullet in his head." Casey pounded the table in frustration.

Cassidy, his brows furrowing at Casey's outburst, looked around the pub to see if anyone has noticed his display of anger. Silence greeted him. The only sound was that of Donohue flipping the pages of his paper.

"Easy, Casey, you stupid bastard," Cassidy hissed through clenched teeth. "Are you looking to bring attention to us?"

What McGuire, Cassidy, Casey, and Collins had never figured out was that everyone in Offaly knew who was behind the movement. Their egos were such that they were sure they were like shadows moving in the dark, unaware that they were known by all. Even the British knew who they were.

But his words fell on deaf ears as Collins chimed in. "That's the only way to handle a bastard like that," Collins affirmed, hitting Casey in the arm. Collins and Casey looked at each other, nodding their heads in approval.

Casey was about to say something boastful, feeling that braggadocio uplift that several drinks can bring on, when Cassidy hissed, "Shut up, Casey."

The two men seated at the table, both bleary-eyed from the sauce, looked sullenly at Cassidy. But Cassidy was not looking at either of them.

Cassidy, his face frozen, the look of fear having appeared in his eyes, was staring toward the door at the far end of the bar. His look caused Casey and Collins to frown and follow his gaze in the same direction.

Through the door, moving silently as a cat, John Fallon, eyes taking in the bar with one quick glance, moved slowly to the center of the bar. The few drinkers hadn't noticed him at first, Fallon having made no sound. When they did, they paused, not sure what to do. Looking at Fallon, their attention shifted to Cassidy and the others.

Donohue, placing his newspaper under the bar, straightened up, indecision marking his face. He looked more than stricken as Fallon turned to face him. When Fallon spoke, his voice was barely above a whisper.

"Would you let me have a whisky please." Which Donohue, fumbling with the bottle, silently placed in front of him.

The silence that permeated throughout the pub was deafening. Other than Fallon, who seemed oblivious to the tension he had stirred up, he appeared to be the only one not affected by his surroundings.

Dropping a bill on the bar, Fallon, whisky in hand, moved slowly to the table where Cassidy and the others are seated. Two of the patrons downed their drinks and made for the door. The other two couldn't seem to make up their minds. Donohue, feeling like he was standing in quicksand, watched silently.

"Good evening, gentlemen," Fallon said pleasantly.

Cassidy, voice trembling, tried to answer with bluster. "What is you want, Yank? We're having a private conversation here, so get yourself out of our faces."

Fallon, ignoring Cassidy's remark, pulled a chair over to their table. "Don't bother to stand up," Fallon said amiably. "I'm not fancy." Sitting down, Fallon continued. "I just thought it would be nice if we all had a little chat."

Collins and Casey both eyed Cassidy, waiting for him to give some indication of what he wanted to do next. Collins and Casey, both having enough to drink and sitting on that raw courage that comes with it, were ready for something.

Sitting quietly across from the three rebels, Fallon knew he had backed them into a corner. They could risk the embarrassment of letting Fallon come into their pub and brace them. The other options were to bluff it out and challenge Fallon.

All their bodies right now were sending out signals that they could go either way and were ready for both. Factor in the drinking, their blood surging and none of them would know the difference. It didn't make any difference to Fallon. He was in his World Wide mode, and his decision had been made for him.

Cassidy, sitting stoically, confusion on his face as he tried to read Fallon, made no indication to Collins and Casey what they were going to do. The two of them were vacillating between taking Fallon out and backing off.

Cassidy's great bulk was not yet readable to Fallon. His eyes were filled with hate, a hate that festered like a burning candle, waiting to unleash at any moment. But there was also a newfound respect, tinged with fear.

Fallon had seen that look on men's faces many times before. It was not a look he was unused to. Fallon expected it and even cultivated it. Cassidy, like so many men before him, was a man waiting, not sure what his next plan of action would be.

Cassidy was limited in his thinking. Like the sheep who followed, Cassidy had always been one of them. It took a McGuire or someone like him to his thinking for men. Men of brute force and strength knew only violence and needed the McGuires of the world to get him off the dime. Cassidy, like the other two, Collins and Casey, were waiting, not sure what to do. This stranger had entered their midst, and they had not figured out how to handle him.

"Well, Yank, I'll say this to you. You have the balls," Cassidy spit out coarsely, deciding to bluff it out and play the hard guy. His mind was racing, wishing McGuire was here. "Any one of us here tonight could put a bullet in you without blinking. We've had enough foreigners in our land and I'm not lying. Right, lads?"

Collins and Casey nodded their heads like puppets, not sure what else to do, still hoping Cassidy would lead the way.

Fallon looked at Collins and Casey. Then turning back to Cassidy, he smiled a smile that sent shivers down Cassidy's spine.

"You could put a bullet in me, Cassidy, but you won't," Fallon said, his eyes taking in the other two men at the table. "Putting the small talk aside, Cassidy, what I want I'll get before I leave this place." Fallon told them without raising his voice. They all picked up the thread of the threat that hung in his words.

Collins stirred in his chair. Sweat had formed on his lip, his hands moving nervously as though not knowing what to do with them. Casey remained seated stiffly in his chair, muscles coiled, ready to spring into action.

Fallon ignored them. The smile still in place, he gave all his attention to Cassidy, slowly sipping his Tullamore Dew whisky. The fire touched his belly with that whisky-tough sweetness. It was very good.

Continuing in that soft, almost lyrical, voice that was unnerving the three men at the table, Fallon said, "My sister Kit was killed because of you assholes and your half-ass organization. Your plans were half-baked and I was there to witness it. I watched it happen." Fallon eyed Cassidy coldly, but tiredly.

Realization began to set in for the three of them. They were dealing with a very dangerous man, a man capable of violence and murder. They could not only see the hatred in his eyes, they could feel it. McGuire had assured them that everyone in town were convinced that the British were responsible for all the killings. It dawned on them at that moment with John Fallon sitting across from them that that was not true.

"It was the damn Brits, Yank," Cassidy said with disgust, knowing his words were falling on deaf ears. "If you were there like you say you were, you must have seen that. Why are you talking to us? Shouldn't it be them you should be after?"

Wearily, Fallon leaned back in his chair, his eyes never wavering. Donohue and the rest of the people in the pub were mesmerized, watching them. Though they could not hear what was being said, they were all aware something was about to happen.

"What I saw, Cassidy, was you and your people started a war on the streets without regard for the safety of innocent civilians," Fallon said coldly. His practiced glance took in the remaining patrons in the pub. None of them had moved. Fallon continued. "The first rule of warfare is to protect the innocent. Otherwise you are nothing but amateurs. Nothing but guerillas. It appears that is the first thing you clowns forgot." Fallon, though speaking to the three of them, looked at Cassidy with distaste.

"Listen to the Yank," Casey said with sarcasm. He wasn't fooling anyone. The fear showed in his eyes, and his try at bravado fell on deaf ears.

"What makes you the professional in matters like this?" Cassidy asked, latching on to Casey's false courage.

Then the picture of Fallon's battered and ugly body flashed across his mind, a shiver sliding slowly up his spine. He remembered too the punch to the throat that dropped him like a bad memory and the violence Fallon reigned upon them. Deep down, Cassidy knew this was not an ordinary man and he could feel the specter of death dancing on his shoulder.

Fallon, his expression unchanging, leaned toward Cassidy in his chair. Cassidy squirmed noticeably now, his confidence shattered as sweat formed on his forehead. Fallon noted with little satisfaction, ignoring the big man's question.

Fallon, sitting loosely in his chair making sure he could keep the three of them in his field of vision, thought about that terrible day and the reason he was here now. The picture of Kit's bullet-riddled body lying grotesquely in the streets of Offaly was still fresh in his mind, the gentle, beautiful face that had never harmed anyone staring at nothing as the life drained from her body. Fallon felt himself twitch.

Open warfare on a quiet street, mayhem and massacre meshing together as one, all for the sake of trying to free animals that thought nothing of life and death. Ireland had an entire history of it, leading to the death of innocent men and women. Dead by the hands of their own not cared for by their own.

The stupidity, the recklessness, the complete disregard for the value of human life. The same men who sat in pubs, one another's houses, back alleys, the same men planning over pints and booze their next debacle, all under the guise of "the cause." We are only given one life and to have it taken away like so much blindness to "causes" made Fallon sick. He knew there was only one way to correct it.

Fallon knew about killing, the sickening aftermath, the remorse and guilt that you had taken a human life. Killing because that's what you were trained to do. Killing because you were convinced that there was a noble cause behind it.

Specific. Pinpoint. Killing and assassination. The killings were politically motivated and professionally orchestrated. You believed them and justified them because you were on the side of right. Fallon, thinking to himself how deadly accurate he had become, until that last job. Fallon knew what it was to kill an innocent man, knew it for what it was and how he felt. It was his fault and his alone.

Even though it was a World Wide hit with the usual preparations and intelligence, when he arrived there that night, he was well informed by World Wide that the information they had given him was false. It didn't matter. Fallon had pulled the trigger and watched the man's life explode out of his chest. There had been no rhyme or reason for it. Fallon justified it as just another job. This time it didn't wash. Fallon knew in his heart that it had been his fault entirely.

Just as the massacre that had taken the life of his beloved sister and others lay at the feet of those responsible.

Shaking himself free of the thoughts he couldn't let cloud his judgment or deter him from what he had to do, Fallon leaned across the table, locking eyes with Cassidy.

"This is what I want from you, Cassidy," Fallon spoke slowly, his voice barely above a whisper. "It's a message I want you to get to McGuire." Fallon held his hand up, cutting Cassidy short before he can reply. Collins and Casey were still in his line of sight. They were frozen in place.

"I am not interested in your war or the reasons behind it," Fallon began. "As far as I'm concerned, the bunch of you are just a collection of low-life drunks who get their courage out of a bottle and travel in packs. Alone, you are just sad excuses for men. You can't think for yourselves."

Cassidy, chewing the inside of his lip, nervously answered, "That's strong talk for a stranger, Yank."

Fallon smiled viciously. "Strong talk." Nodding his head toward Collins and Casey, barely acknowledging their presence, Fallon continued. "If this is any indication of what your organization is made up of, I could put together a crew of Girl Scouts that would handle themselves better. They are skells, just like McGuire and the rest of you who kill innocent people without any regard."

"We're in a life-and-death struggle with the Brits, Yank," Cassidy managed to get out, feeling a little more cocky since he thought that Fallon was only there to talk. "We didn't set out to hurt anyone other than our enemies. What happened with your sister and the others was an accident, it wasn't planned."

"You're a liar," Fallon hissed. "You kill because you like it. Having the British here only gives you a reason to do it under the guise you are fighting for a cause. I don't believe any of you even know what that cause is."

Fallon paused, letting what he had said sink in. He scanned the faces of the three of them, the hatred evident in their eyes. Collins and Casey were primed, waiting for Cassidy to give them the word. They were not sure why Cassidy was sitting there listening to Fallon talk to them like that. Cassidy knew. Fallon was goading them, and he wasn't sure how to react. He wished Sean McGuire was here to tell him what to do.

"The cause you rebels are constantly referring to," Fallon continues, "is just a sham and a farce. It gives you the opportunity to prance around wielding weapons that make you feel like big men. Though they don't talk about it, even your own people can't stomach you. One other thing before I finish with you clowns, I haven't forgotten about the British either. They are as much to blame as you."

That was as far as Fallon got. It was Collins who made the first move. Fallon heard his chair move. Out of the corner of his eye, Fallon saw Collins's hand dart inside his jacket.

"You bloody bastard," Collins barked. That was as far as he got.

Without taking his eyes off Cassidy, Fallon pulled his gun from his side, shooting Collins in the shoulder. The force of the bullet drove Collins out of his chair, sending him sprawling on the floor. His gun slid across the floor.

Before he could regain his footing, Collins tried staggering to his feet, the blood pouring profusely from his arm. On his face was that look of surprise men get when they realize their life was about to end. Fallon turned slightly, eyed Collins up quickly, and then pumped two into his heart, driving him back against the wall of the bar.

Collins staggered, leaving a trail of blood on the wall as he fell and was dead before he hit the ground.

Seeing his friend Collins lying in his own blood, Casey, still in shock, shoved his chair back and pulled his own gun on Fallon.

Fallon moved his gun half an inch and shot Casey between the eyes. The back of his head exploded.

While Casey's body fell to the floor, hard and fast, all life-force gone, Fallon turned his gun on Cassidy. Cassidy was frozen in his chair, unable to move as he stared down at his two companions lying dead on the floor. He pried his eyes away from Collins's and Casey's bodies, gaping at Fallon with a scared white face, a face drained of blood.

In the silence that followed, Fallon glanced quickly at the bar patrons, noticing that they had not moved. The disbelieving look on their faces as they stared at the dead men and the stranger that had come intro their midst had them speechless, unable to move.

Fallon heard Donohue's voice behind him. "Sweet Jesus."

Fallon smiled at Cassidy. It was an easy smile, professional and full of grim death at the same time.

Cassidy, sitting stunned and speechless, managed to close his gaping mouth. He swallowed hard, the terror evident in his face.

"I have no gun. Yank," Cassidy managed to tell Fallon, his voice quivering. "You just can't kill me in cold blood."

Fallon wasn't sure why not, but didn't bother to ask Cassidy. He shifted his position in his chair, making sure no one tried to leave the pub. He wasn't concerned with what everyone did after he had concluded his business. For now he didn't need anyone running to the police.

"Two things," Fallon said to Cassidy. "One I want and one I think you and your army of skells should be made aware of."

Cassidy, finding it difficult to speak, aware now that no one was going to come into the pub and get him out of this, just stared at Fallon and said nothing.

"The first thing and this is what we in America call a free ride," Fallon announced to Cassidy, enjoying Cassidy's discomfort. "You have to be idiots not to have known there was an informer in your midst. It was someone who knew you well and sold you out to the British which were one of the determining factors in the massacre at the prison." Fallon paused to let what he had just said sink in.

"Tell me something we don't know, Yank," Cassidy, though terrified, managed to spit out, showing some semblance of anger. Fallon assumed Cassidy was still trying to portray the tough guy or unable to disconnect from the anger he felt, knowing they had lived with the knowledge that there was an informer among them.

"Okay, I will," Fallon said almost nonchalantly. "The IRA structures their cells in such a way so as to make them impervious to infiltration by the British Army. We call them ASUs, whether you know that or not. Active service units," Fallon explained as Cassidy was staring dumbly at him.

Cassidy was staggered at how much the Yank knew about them. He knew for sure now that Fallon was no ordinary man looking to get revenge. Just the way he talked and killed, Cassidy was dealing with someone he had never faced before.

Fallon continued. "Now—and this is significant, Cassidy, so I want you to listen closely—the informer lives among you but is not in your group. No one in the group ever knows the operational details except the leader, and of course, the leader is almost never the informant in a revolutionary campaign. Particularly in a cell like I'm describing."

Fallon, calmly speaking, his voice never rising above a whisper, informed the bewildered Cassidy. He did not go in to the why, the which, though he knew it was obvious except to a clown like Cassidy. Fallon was convinced Cassidy did not have a clue about how operations went. He was simply muscle.

The pub was so quiet you could hear a pin drop. The only sound reverberating throughout the barroom was Fallon's voice that could barely be heard. Cassidy didn't breathe. Donohue was standing behind the stick, a terrified look in his eyes.

Fallon continued talking to Cassidy, his hand loosely holding the gun that was giving Cassidy nightmares. "So, given this environment, there is someone directly in your life that is with you and against you at the same time." Fallon paused to let what he said sink in. The slow-thinking Cassidy was having trouble digesting what Fallon was talking about.

"What's even more interesting is the fact that I know who that man happens to be," Fallon said to Cassidy.

"Really, Yank?" Cassidy asked, trying to sneer, hoping to keep up his veneer of bravado. There was disbelief in his voice, and he knew Fallon was waiting for a response. "And just how would you be aware of anything that happens around here?"

"Without giving you my résumé? Call it professional insight," Fallon said. Fallon sensed the tension in the pub, realizing no one had tried to leave. He knew curiosity had taken over. He continued. "And my guess, though really it isn't a guess at all, the man that turned against you and your comrades is the man behind the bar. Donohue."

Fallon said it loud enough for Donohue to hear and also the rest of the bar patrons. After dropping the bomb, Fallon settled back in his chair, waiting to see where this was going to. He knew it wouldn't be good for Donohue.

From behind the bar, a ragged voice screamed, "That's a bloody lie!" Donohue looked desperately around the pub, his eyes darting from one man to the other, and they came to rest on Cassidy. "Lads, you know me. I have always supported the cause. You can't believe this lying Yank."

Cassidy's eyes flicked slowly over at Donohue, as though seeing him for the first time. He narrowed them at Fallon, saying nothing.

Fallon continued. "Donohue had always been my first guess as to having a direct line to the British or the UDA, but I had to be sure. I knew whoever staged the prison transfer and shot your people and my sister up had to have had a man inside." Turning casually toward Donohue, Fallon nodded his head. "That's their man inside."

"Neville and Wilson set us up," Cassidy said, more to himself than Fallon. He wished McGuire were here. Cassidy was in over his head and couldn't grasp the ramifications of what Fallon was saying.

Fallon registered the names Cassidy had just dropped, retrieved them, and said nothing. People usually list names from the top down, Fallon knew. Therefore Neville was the ranking officer in the chain of command, probably Major Neville, then Sergeant Wilson, given what Fallon knew of the British Army and their units.

"You're telling me you think Donohue informed on us to the Brit bastards," Cassidy said to hear it and understand it himself. Also loud enough for Donohue to hear. "That's just talk, Yank. Do you have any proof?"

"Yes, I do," Fallon said coldly.

"Let's hear it."

"Your friend Donohue is not all that bright," Fallon said. "After closing one night, I followed him. He was confident enough in his belief that you and the others would never suspect him of being a collaborator. After all, he was privy to all your plans."

By this time, the others in the bar had turned their attention to Donohue. Though not part of the rebel band, they believed in what they were doing. Donohue, by now, was frozen in place. His lips were moving, but nothing was coming out.

"That night," Fallon continued, "Donohue, taking a roundabout way home, of course, met with Sergeant Wilson. It was about one week later that you and the others carried out your botched plan at the prison."

For some reason, though he said it with disdain and incredulity, Cassidy was beginning to believe the Yank. And it was beginning to show on his face. There was something frightening about the Yank that Cassidy could not fathom. One thing he knew though—the Yank was not one to be trifled with.

But Cassidy knew Donohue, and somehow what the Yank was saying made sense. Everybody knew Donohue's wife was a Protestant and hated the Catholics with a passion. That could put Donohue that much closer to Unionist sympathy. Since no one trusted Protestants, Cassidy did not dismiss Fallon's theory.

Fallon read Cassidy and could almost see the wheels spinning slowly in his head. He may have been just a gun, but Cassidy had the street smarts that made for good sheep. He would follow. Fallon knew that Cassidy believed him and was instinctively responding to the fact that Fallon was a leader and Cassidy was just a follower. He was used to being told what was happening and what to do by someone from above. Cassidy was a man not used to thinking things out on his own. The perfect man to have around.

"That's a lie," Donohue screeched again. His voice was loud but trembling now. The man was scared. Donohue had moved to one end of the bar, the one closest to the door. One of the drinkers in the pub had already moved from where he was seated and was between Donohue and the back door.

But there was something in Donohue's voice that told Fallon it was time to turn around quickly. Donohue had reached under the bar and was just beginning to bring up a large handgun when Fallon swirled in his chair and shot him in the kneecap. His kneecap exploded, and Donohue dropped to the floor screaming, the gun slipping from his hand and falling harmlessly to the floor.

Fallon swung back to Cassidy. Fear gripped Cassidy fully now, and staring into the cold eyes of Fallon, he was further confused by the pleasant look on Fallon's face.

"You can do what you want with him." Fallon gestured to where Donohue lay on the floor whimpering. Fallon stood up, his gun dangling by his side.

"What are you going to do now, Yank?" Cassidy asked, a big man frightened and convinced that he was about to die.

Fallon pointed the gun at Cassidy's head.

"Walk me to the door," Fallon told Cassidy. He winked at him congenially, meanwhile taking in the others who had just witnessed a scene they were not soon to forget. Donohue, surrounded by the others, looked up, a pleading in his eyes.

Cassidy stood up slowly, unable to take his eyes off Collins and Casey as they lay dead on the floor. He began to move, Fallon nudging him with his gun toward the front door of the pub. As they moved past the two bodies, Cassidy looked down at Donohue, writhing and crying on the floor, holding his shattered knee.

Fallon poked Cassidy in the back with his gun. Cassidy actually quivered with fear.

"I want you to do me a favor," Fallon told Cassidy.

"What might that be?" Cassidy asked suspiciously.

"Tell McGuire I'm coming for him," Fallon said. Then he smacked Cassidy in the side of the head with the Beretta. He didn't want to kill him, just to keep him incapacitated until Fallon slipped out of the Three Oaks Pub.

Cassidy doubled over and reeled back into the bar, his large body crashing to the floor like a downed tree.

Fallon slipped quietly out the door of the pub, just as Donohue's customers started to converge on Donohue. Donohue fainted before they reached him.

Eleven

Reynolds and Harris walked back to their hotel. It was a clear, crisp night, neither of them seeming to be in any rush to get there. They had sat by themselves in the Irish pub across the street from their hotel and drank several pints of beer while watching the locals.

The pub they were drinking in had Irish entertainment, and the locals didn't give them a second glance. They were used to seeing Americans, and Reynolds and Harris looked no different than any of the others that visited their town. They had talked quietly by themselves, when they talked at all. Then having enough of the leisure, they paid their bill and left the pub and the singers and dancers behind.

The moon hung high in the sky, a soft glow covering the town. The sound of the ocean could be heard in the distance. The streets were deserted with most of the inhabitants having settled down for the night. One young couple passed them, holding hands and laughing. They did not say hello.

Harris stopped and smelled the air.

"You know, I have been trying to place that smell since we arrived," Harris said to Reynolds. "For the life of me, I can't place it. What about you, Al?"

Reynolds had stopped. His expression didn't change. "I have been here enough times and it still smells like Ireland. What you are experiencing, Jack, is mist that moves in from the bogs. It takes a while to get used to it."

Reynolds turned from Harris and began moving toward their hotel. Harris, pausing momentarily, turned and followed Reynolds as they walked into the hotel.

They had a room with double beds overlooking the street below. It gave them a good vantage point to observe the comings and goings of the townspeople. They both stretched out on the beds, their guns still strapped to their sides. Harris and Reynolds both stared at the ceiling. They did not have to review plans; they were professionals. They had done this many times before.

Dan Morehead, having finished staking out his surroundings, stopped outside his hotel. He was hungry, not having had anything since breakfast, and the pub next door looked inviting. He took two steps toward the front door and stopped. Then like dark liquid, he faded back into the shadows of the hotel entrance.

Reynolds and Harris stood on the sidewalk outside their hotel. They were eyeing the terrain. They turned into the hotel after pausing to discuss something that did not seem all that relevant to Reynolds.

Morehead watched them closely. He was particularly interested in their body language. He could see they were playing a dead hand and not letting themselves become objects of curiosity. They were keeping a low-key profile, and unless you were in the business, you would not be able to distinguish them from any of the other tourists or businessmen that visited Ireland.

Dan Morehead was familiar with Al Reynolds, having worked on several assignments with him. Reynolds, he would not underestimate. He was good. The other man, Jack Harris, had come to the agency after Morehead had retired. Him he would have to pay particular attention to. He didn't want to get caught holding the short end of the stick.

Morehead watched them as a young couple exited the hotel, almost knocking him over. Morehead was sure they weren't even aware of him. Morehead watched as Harris and Reynolds entered their hotel. The last thing Morehead noted was the fact that they were both packing. He filed that away for later. Morehead kept his eyes glued on Reynolds and Harris. If anyone had noticed them, Morehead could see how they would be mistaken for just two businessmen or travelers passing through Ireland. No one would have pegged them for the assassins they were.

Morehead lingered in the shadows after Reynolds and Harris had entered the hotel. He was running a scenario through his mind about being as close to them as he was, having rooms in the hotel just across the street. He discounted that worry and shunned it from his mind, knowing that the last person they expected to see in Ireland was him. He was sure Childers had informed them he had been removed from the search for Raven.

Morehead, his eyes locked on the windows across the street, watched as the lights on the second floor came on. He waited. No one came to the window. Sure of themselves, Morehead calculated they had settled in for the night.

Morehead slipped silently out of the hotel doorway and walked quickly and quietly down the street, always keeping to the shadows. He decided to skip the pub that Reynolds and Harris had come from and moved on to the next one. The last thing he needed was for them to return and have one of the patrons mention another American that had dropped in. He found a nice quiet one just several blocks away.

There he would eat a good meal and drink a couple of pints of Irish beer and do exactly what Reynolds and Harris had done. He would prepare himself silently, without words, for the following day.

Morehead, nursing the last of his beer, went over the options in his head of what he would do and how he would handle the situation when he made contact with Fallon. With Morehead, it was a physical thing, more than a mental one. Finishing off the last of his beer, Morehead paid his tab and left the pub.

It was a soft, starless night as Morehead made his way slowly back to the hotel. He was in no hurry. Reynolds and Harris were going nowhere for the time being. And as long as he knew where they were situated, Dan Morehead felt he was sitting in the catbird seat.

From past experience and having trained Fallon himself, Morehead knew that whatever John Fallon decided to do, upon contact, it would be fast and surprising as hell. There was no need for any elaborate plans. The body just had to be ready. Pausing once to glance over at the hotel

Reynolds and Harris were staying in, Morehead stepped inside and went to his room.

The lights were out in their room.

The following morning, Fallon got up early. He quickly readied himself for the day, knowing he would be going to see Megan, maybe for the last time. It was a small town, and Fallon was hoping the killings that occurred early that morning had not reached the ears of Megan Clark.

Fallon had no illusions of where he stood now, and anything that was going to go down would have to be fast and decisive. He was a hunted man now. The killing of Casey and Collins would put him at the head of the list of all IRA rebels in the area and beyond. As to how the British would react, Fallon was unconcerned about that. He wanted them thinking that Fallon blamed the IRA for the death of his sister. It gave him an edge.

Checking carefully around the safe house, making sure everything was intact, Fallon stepped out into the early morning where the sun was just beginning to rise. He didn't know how long this place would be safe, but for now it was all he had. Fallon, pulling the collar of his coat up around his neck to ward off the morning chill, started down the path to Megan's house. He was on foot, and if everything went as planned, there would be no need for a car.

Knocking softly on Megan's door, Fallon felt a pang of sadness, feeling that his whole life was behind that door. Why couldn't things be different? He didn't have time to muse over what might have been, as Megan opened the door looking more beautiful than ever.

Stepping inside, Fallon took Megan in his arms, and they kissed long and passionately. Fallon gently moved Megan back, knowing this was not the time to let his love for her cloud his mind. He had to remain focused.

Megan, who had been preparing breakfast when Fallon came in, returned to the stove after pouring Fallon a cup of coffee.

"Sit down, John, and I'll get you something to eat."

"Don't go to any trouble over me, Megan," Fallon answered. "I can't stay long. I have several things to do and want to get them out of the way as soon as I can."

There was disappointment on Megan's face as she looked at him. "I was hoping we could spend the day together. There are some chores I have to finish on the farm and then I am free for the day."

"Maybe when I finish, Megan, I'll come back and we can go down to the beach."

"I would like that," Megan said, her face brightening. "Now you are going to have something to eat before you go anywhere."

They talked as Megan continued making breakfast. It was comfortable and the beginning of a new day. Fallon knew it would be just a matter of time before Megan heard about what happened at the Three Oaks. He did not want to put her in harm's way.

Fallon listened as Megan ticked off the things that needed to be done and Fallon listened and nodded his head. Whenever he could, he would snatch glimpses of her. Take her in. Her beauty. After breakfast and Megan had finished cleaning up the kitchen, they went outside to tackle the jobs necessary to keep the farm operating.

While he worked, Fallon thought about his next moves. Fallon did not fear a quick reaction from the IRA for what had transpired at the Three Oaks Pub. Not this morning anyway. From past experience, Fallon had found that after an incident like that, confusion usually took over and the parties involved had to take time to get their act together.

The other thing Fallon was banking on was that the British would evaluate what he had done and come to the conclusion that Fallon blamed the rebels for the death of his sister. Fallon was banking on that. So he worked steadily and with an easy mind.

Every so often he would stop what he was doing and look around at the lush green country that surrounded him, and a feeling of sorrow would pass over him. Even the smell of the sea that drifted up the hillside, the low hanging mist that covered the ground, looking like sparkling diamonds, touched his heart. One way or the other, no matter the outcome, Thai was part of Ireland, his home that Fallon would miss.

Looking over to where Megan was working, Fallon felt lucky and sad at the same time. He would catch her eye and a beautiful smile would crease her face, causing Fallon's heart to melt. Fallon loved her and knew that he was going to lose her. It would be just a matter of time before Megan found out about Three Oaks. By that time, Fallon would be gone.

He had charted his course, and like missions in the past, he would not be deterred.

Having developed a rhythm to his work gave Fallon time to calmly run through the situation he was in. It was important since it was developing around him. It would be just a matter of time when they started closing in.

Nobody but the people who were involved in the game had been a part of last night, which was of some benefit. Even so, Fallon knew that spending time with Megan, helping her on the farm, was growing short. There was momentum now, and the situation he was in was growing. Whatever happens was going to happen fast.

Two dead bodies and a shattered kneecap would more than likely need some cleaning up. That was assuming Donohue was not already dead and buried. Fallon knew that Cassidy was not about to keep Fallon's name in the dark. He had known people like Cassidy. Over the years, he had encountered many of them, and the one thing they had in common was the fact that they were cowards and followers.

But then again, Fallon did not think that Cassidy or McGuire would really want to bring any attention to themselves right now. Not after the debacle at the prison, what with an attack on the British leaving eight dead Irish agents, two dead British soldiers, and three dead civilians. Fallon was counting on that to buy him time. Fallon knew that when he unleashed what he had to do, he was on borrowed time.

So all that was left was local rumor, which Fallon did not think would be actionable.

Not yet anyway. That meant he had some time left to spend with Megan. Looking over at her now, working in the garden, Fallon experienced for the first time in his life the feeling of loneliness he would experience losing her. Fallon, other than his sister Kit, had never loved anyone like this before, the thought that made him happy as well as sad.

That same day, hurrying across the British compound that housed the military, head down, a scowl creasing his face, Sergeant Wilson was making his way to Major Neville's office to give his morning report. Wilson was experiencing two sets of emotions. The first he was somewhat pleased and amused with the news from the previous night.

The other was the uneasiness that he felt when trying to get a handle on the Yank. Heading up the stairs leading to Neville's office, he hesitated at the top. What was it about this Yank that troubled Wilson? And Major Neville. Wilson had noticed a subtle change in his attitude. Was Neville fearful of the Yank, or was he just being cautious? Wilson would wait and see.

"Two dead IRA scum and a missing informant. Too bad that had to happen, Donohue had proved useful to us. We needed him," Neville greeted Wilson with as soon as he entered the room. Neville gestured to one of the chairs in front of his desk for Wilson to be seated. As soon as he was, Neville continued his pacing.

"What the hell happened at that pub last night?" Neville asked, turning to face Wilson. Wilson cleared his throat before answering.

"No one is talking as you can guess, sir," Wilson said, a smirk on his face as though he found what was happening amusing. "It seems as though someone walked into the Three Oaks Pub and shot some rebels up."

"And no one including the swine who were drinking there will say who it was?" Neville wanted to know, sounding exasperated.

"No, they won't," Wilson said. "Seems they are not quite sure of who it was." Wilson smiled.

"But what do the locals say?" Neville pressed Wilson, more out of curiosity than anything else. As far as Neville was concerned, they could all kill one another off and it wouldn't bother him in the least.

"Ah well, that's another story," Wilson said with some feeling of satisfaction. "There are a number of people on the street who witnessed the Yank going into the pub and watched him leave not long after the festivities took place. But Cassidy, who would be McGuire's right-hand man, the only one the gunman left alive didn't think it was the Yank. He claims he didn't know who it was. We can bring him in for questioning, sir, if you want."

"No, don't bother," Neville answered. "We can reach out for him anytime we need to. It might be to our advantage to have him roaming around free."

"Yes, sir."

"So your theory is that the Yank casually walks into the pub, shoots three men, walks out, and no one tries to stop him? Instead they are covering for him? I find that difficult to believe, Sergeant," Neville said as he stroked his mustache thoughtfully. "If what you say is true, someone has to have heard if the Yank said anything before opening fire on that trash."

"You mean patrons or locals who were peering though the window?" Wilson asked, laughing brutishly.

"That's exactly what I'm asking, Sergeant," Neville said, coldly eyeing Wilson.

Wilson, nervously clearing his throat, continued. "Well, nobody is saying and so far no one has come forward. We have to remember, sir, the Yank's sister was one of the people killed in the attack on the prison." Wilson cleared his throat again. "It was caused by the crossfire in that attack. My feelings are the Yank blames the rebels for the death of his sister."

"If my recollection is complete, Sergeant, it was your men that did the shooting that killed the civilians," Neville answered, the distaste evident in his voice.

"Perhaps," Wilson said. "But it was the Irish that imitated the attack. As far as I can surmise, the Yank feels it was the rebels that did the killing."

"And this is what the locals think?"

"The locals are always thinking," Wilson answered and grinned.

"And Donohue was your man then?" Neville followed.

"Yes, sir."

"And I can assume there is no sign of him?" Neville asked.

"He seems to have disappeared," Wilson said with mixed feelings. "I'm not too concerned. There will always be another Donohue for the right price."

"And the American?"

Shrugging, Wilson answered, "Truthfully, we haven't really pursued it, sir. If it's the American, all I can say is he seems to be doing a very good job at getting rid of the Irish scum. I say let him keep up the good work."

Neville narrowed his eyes and glared at Wilson. As vicious a reputation as the one he had gained in Ireland, Neville was first and foremost an army man. He knew that someday he would be back doing the job he was trained for.

"I appreciate your candor, Sergeant," Neville said sarcastically. "But let's not forget we are British soldiers and remember to act like one. We are not going to lower ourselves to the gutter like the rebels are doing. Do I make myself clear?"

"Yes, sir," Wilson replied, properly chagrined.

"Now, Sergeant. What about the local authorities? What have they come up with?" Neville asked.

"No one is willing to talk, sir, as I've said," Wilson explained. "That includes the Irish authorities. I get the impression they are as afraid of the rebels as the locals."

In Ireland, a witness is an informant. No one, including the police, wants to be tagged with the mark of Cain.

After a moment, Neville, who has been digesting what Wilson was telling him, shook his head. "This is strange, Sergeant. I just don't understand these people. Something about this American makes me uncomfortable. If he is the one behind the shootings the other night, why don't the townspeople turn him in? At the very least, take some action themselves."

Wilson noted that Neville was just talking out loud, not really looking for an answer. Wilson kept his mouth shut. Neville continued.

"Let's keep a close eye on him, Sergeant," Neville said. "Not tight eyes, cut him some slack, but keep track of his movements. I want to know where he is, what he is doing, and if there is any sign of trouble, pick him up."

"Yes, sir."

"Don't get too distracted by the American, Sergeant," Wilson added. "I don't want you letting up on the rebels either. This is the type of atmosphere that develops unwanted situations. The last thing we need now is any surprises. I'm taking a lot of grief from the home office, and if we are going to get reassigned back to active duty away from these scum, we need to clear this mess up fast."

Wilson nodded his head in agreement.

Neville, getting up from behind his desk, dropped his pipe in the overflowing ashtray. Wilson got to his feet. They walk to the door together.

"From what I understand, the Yank has been spending quite a bit of time out at the farm that Clark girl owns. It might be a good idea if you and your men paid her farm a visit." Pausing, Neville turned to Wilson. "We don't want the Yank to get too comfortable and go around thinking he is not noticed."

Neville stared purposely at Wilson and stroked his mustache. Wilson nodded his big forceful head and smiled his crooked cruel smile.

Fallon, his hair damp from the rain that passed through Offaly, was standing on a hill far from the farmhouse watching the sheep graze on the emerald sea of grass. He heard the cars approach before he saw them. Instinct told him to seek cover. He walked quickly to the large wall of stone that ran along the hillside and bent downward.

A number of army vehicles were making the long approach to Megan Clark's farmhouse. This puzzled and bothered Fallon.

Keeping a keen eye, Fallon saw two soldiers and an officer exit the first vehicle. The other men jumped from the trucks and stationed themselves around the house.

His only concern was for Megan's safety.

After all the vehicles had stopped and the men got out and were stationed in their positions, three of the men walked toward the front door. Fallon watched them closely. The lieutenant looked like a young man who had not been in the army long. It was the squat, barrel-chested man who looked familiar.

Fallon's mind slipped back to that bloody day when Kit had been killed. It was the same sergeant who had given the orders to shoot. Fallon knew from the look on his face at that time that this was a man who enjoyed violence.

That was why he looked so familiar. Fallon had locked him in that special place in his brain, convinced, along with the major who had been on the scene, that he was the man responsible for the massacre of his sister Kit and the other civilians.

After they were out of sight, Fallon began to make his way cautiously down the hill, taking a position not far from the farmhouse, but out of view from the soldiers.

At the knock, Megan went to the door. The three men from the British Army stood on her doorstep.

"Who are you?" Megan asked defiantly.

"This is Lieutenant Warner," Wilson said, gesturing toward the pleasant-looking young man who was standing with a smile on his face. "I'm Sergeant Wilson," he said. He showed his ID, not giving Megan credit for noticing that they were all dressed in military garb—and, Megan noticed, armed to the teeth.

"May we come in?" the young lieutenant asked.

"Why would you want in?" Megan asked suspiciously.

"We have some questions we would like to ask you about the American stranger," he said pleasantly.

"You mean the man whose sister your men killed in cold blood, along with the other innocent people?" Megan said angrily, not giving ground.

"Sergeant," the lieutenant said to Wilson. Then he turned and walked back to one of the trucks.

"The very one," Wilson said, pushing the door open and walking inside. The other soldiers hesitated and then followed Wilson into the house.

"You can't just walk in here like you own the place," Megan said, placing herself in front of Wilson.

Wilson turned, pointed to the door. The other soldier had taken up a position at the entrance. "I just did," Wilson told Megan and sneered.

"All right, what do you want?" Megan demanded.

Wilson, a sardonic smile on his face, looked around the house, then turned back to Megan and took a second to take her in. He let his eyes slowly linger up her body, taking in her beautiful and angry Irish face.

Wilson actually smiled at her. "Is the American here?" he asked.

"No," Megan stated simply.

"Where is he?" Wilson's voice was taking on a menacing and threatening tone. It frustrated Wilson that it didn't appear to faze Megan.

"Out," she replied calmly.

Wilson laughed.

"Why do you want to know where John is?" Megan asked Wilson, ignoring the attempt Wilson made at trying to get her to react.

"John, is it?" Wilson said, raising his eyebrow, trying not to show the anger he felt at Megan for laughing at her.

Megan cursed herself silently.

"Well, it's John then that we are curious about. I'm sure you are aware of the trouble he has gotten himself into," Wilson told her.

"He has been in no trouble. I've seen him just about every night," Megan told him. "Why can't you people just leave him alone? Haven't you done enough to him already?"

"I'm sure you have seen him frequently, Ms. Clark," Wilson said, quietly smirking as he directed his men to search the house. Ignoring Megan's insistence they had no right to be doing that, Wilson continued. "As to us having done enough to your beloved American, I can think of nothing we did to him."

"You killed his sister," Megan said quietly.

Wilson, taken aback momentarily by Megan's bluntness, nodded his head. "That was an unfortunate accident, brought on by the vicious attack by your rebel friends. But that's not what we are here for."

"What is it then?"

"We believe your friend John," Wilson answered sarcastically, making the name sound like a dirty word, "may be caught up in some misguided cause. We believe he is the one behind the killings at the Three Oaks Pub."

Wilson waited while he let that remark sink in. Megan, staring at Wilson defiantly, said nothing.

Smart woman, Wilson thought.

"Some men were killed in that pub the other night," Wilson offered up.

"And you think John had something to do with that?" Megan asked incredulously. "That's impossible. John was here with me. Like all your kind, you're just looking for a scapegoat to blame a killing on just because he's from America."

Wilson lost it. Moving quickly, Wilson slapped Megan across the face. Stepping back, he watched as the blood trickled down the side of Megan's mouth. Megan smiled, refusing to even acknowledge the slap. Wilson tried pulling himself together. He realized that this was a woman was not easy to intimidate.

"Then you are saying the Yank was here with you all that night? Am I correct?" Wilson asked, trying to regain the edge.

"Yes," Megan lied.

"Well, be that as it may, your man Fallon was seen leaving the Three Oaks Pub after a killing. Irish men at that," Wilson added, a smirk of satisfaction crossing his face. "And if we are not mistaken, they were IRA boys."

"Why are you looking for John?" Megan asked again, clearly toying with Wilson, knowing she had gotten underneath his skin. Megan, refusing to wipe the caked blood off her lips, was enjoying watching Wilson squirm. "As far as the men who were killed were Irish, I don't know what that has to do with anything, seeing John was born and raised in Ireland."

"And the Irish don't kill the Irish," Wilson said weakly. "Anyway, we would like to talk to your John."

"Why?"

"Because we feel like he might be part of the movement, or whatever you Irish like to call it. 'Brits out of Ireland and all that rot,'" Wilson smiled viciously, trying to gain back the ground he had so clearly lost with Megan.

"You're pathetic. If John were part of the 'movement' which he isn't," Megan asked Wilson disdainfully, "why would he kill IRA men? Wouldn't it be more prudent to kill you?" Megan said with a veiled threat behind it and relishing the thought.

Wilson knew he was losing ground with Megan and all the threats in the world were not about to change her. He decided to change tactics. "You're an arrogant little twit, aren't you, Ms. Clark? If I thought it would do any good, I would take you down to headquarters. We have certain techniques we use to get information out of people like you."

"Sure, all I'm looking at is some thug who doesn't have the nerve to face up to a man," Megan answered defiantly. "You are good at killing innocent people and trying to intimidate others as long as you have all your men around to protect you. You want to take me into town? You go right ahead and do it."

Wilson knew he had lost his battle with Megan Clark. Any ideas he had about goading, harassing, or intimidating her about Fallon had long since dissipated. He was sitting on the short end of the stick and knew there was no way he was going to break her. His only hope now was to try to convince her that Fallon was the main suspect in their hunt. If anything, Wilson knew Megan's feelings for Fallon ran deeper than just being a friend.

"Ms. Clark, the way I read your friend Fallon," Wilson spoke softly now, working hard to control his anger. "The way I see it, he had a falling-out with his rebel friends over the death of his sister. He more than likely feels they are responsible for her death. Consequently he means to kill them."

"If you believe that, why are you after him?"

"Ms. Clark," Wilson answered sarcastically, "we British are not barbarians. The last thing we need is some loose cannon running around arbitrarily killing people. No, we can't have that. Even without your help, we'll find him."

"John is not part of the IRA," Megan said again. "He is not a murderer. And he's not one of the Protestant provincials either."

Wilson nodded his head. "The Americans are always confused," he seemed to agree. "Anyway, we would like to talk to him."

Wilson handed Megan his card.

"This is where I can be located. If you happen to see him, would you please ask him to stop by? Otherwise, Ms. Clark, you can expect us to keep stopping by to see you," Wilson told her and began moving toward the front door. "It would be a shame to have to keep trashing your house this way."

"If I see John," Megan said defiantly, "I'll tell him what you said. But I can tell you right now there isn't a chance in hell that he is a part of this." Megan hesitated, staring Wilson down before continuing. "I doubt very much if he will stop by."

"Even though he has burned his house down, we know where it is," Wilson reminded her mildly. "My feeling is he will not be too far away from that farm. And I don't mind the drive in getting there." Wilson smiled at Megan and started out the door.

"Sergeant."

Megan's voice stopped him. Wilson turned back to face her.

"Yes."

"I wouldn't worry too much about finding John."

"Why is that, Ms. Clark?"

"Because John will be coming to get you."

Wilson, a cold chill crawling up his back, stared at Megan, who was standing calmly smiling at him. Unnerved, Wilson wheeled and stormed out of the house.

Twelve

Outside, from behind the farmhouse, Fallon watched the British soldiers exit the house and climb into their vehicles. The last one to leave was the sergeant, the one Fallon recognized as leader of the attack that killed Kit. He climbed quickly into the vehicle. They turned around and drove slowly down the long dirt highway.

Fallon had heard the whole thing. The British were more suspicious than he thought they would be. He did find it rather amusing that they tied him into being a member of the IRA. It also meant they were scared. They hadn't gotten a lead on him yet, and Fallon was okay with that.

He stood beside Megan's farmhouse and considered his options until their vehicles were out of sight. Then he went inside. His first concern was Megan.

She had to know the truth.

On the outskirts of the village, McGuire and Cassidy sat inside a safe farmhouse smoking cigarettes. Cassidy looked anxious. McGuire not only looked tired but had taken to hitting the bottle hard. His eyes were bloodshot, his speech slurred. Both men, though tired and fearful, were angry.

Outside the farmhouse, several men hung loosely around the perimeter with the weapons the British and the Protestants insisted the Irish rebels give up before there can be any more talk of peace. It was an exercise in futility. These hard-core Irishmen would never surrender their weapons. The men who were stationed outside the farmhouse now were walking patrol with automatic rifles and sawed-off shotguns.

Ever since the killings at the Three Oaks Pub, McGuire had beefed up his protection. Fallon had them all jumpy, and it wouldn't take much to set these men off. Most of them were trigger-happy anyway.

Inside the farmhouse, McGuire and Cassidy were both also armed. Handguns were strapped to their sides, and automatic weapons were not far from them on the table.

"I'm telling you, Sean, the man's not human," Cassidy said again.

"You're repeating yourself," McGuire shot back disgustedly.

"Sean, he killed Collins and Casey without blinking an eye. Then he calmly turns and shoots Donohue in the knee. When he turns back to me, the look on his face is like someone who is out for a stroll in the park. That's how calm he was. Jesus, he must have eyes in the back of his head. There was no way he could have seen Donohue pulling a gun. I didn't and I was facing him," Cassidy said with disbelief in his rasping voice.

"Well, one good thing came from all this," McGuire said, his eyes narrowing. "He showed us who the traitor was. Now we know how the Brits have always been one step ahead of us, knowing what we are planning. The filthy scum."

"The Yank called it a freebie."

"He can it call it whatever the hell he wants," McGuire said angrily, taking a long drag on his cigarette. Cassidy frowned as he watched McGuire, the nervousness in his voice evident. McGuire continued. "And how far out is Donohue again?"

"Two miles out in the Irish Sea."

"That's far enough. And a good place for him too. Hopefully the sharks mistake him for one of their own since he wasn't one of ours," McGuire said with hatred. "So now it's next up, right? What do we do now?" McGuire asked himself.

"What the hell is happening, Sean," Cassidy asked, unable to keep the panic out of his voice. "The bloody Yank can't blame us for the death of his sister. Sure and that's crazy. The blasted Brits are thee ones who killed her. Sure and they killed our own along with her, didn't they?"

McGuire looked disgustedly at Cassidy. "You are stupid, Cassidy. There can be no other words for you."

"What did I say?" Cassidy whined.

"Do you really believe that the Yank gives a shit who killed his sister?" McGuire said. "It doesn't matter to him that it was a Brit bullet that did it, he wants his pound of flesh and he is looking to get it. Right now I haven't figured out what he is up to, but I intend to."

"Do you think Megan's a part of this?" Cassidy asked.

"This isn't about Megan and it isn't about that run-in you had with him on the beach. I haven't figured it out yet, but he's an American and you never know what they're about to do. Their sympathies lie all over the place," McGuire told Cassidy. "You never know where they stand because they don't know where they stand."

McGuire paused, letting what he had just said sink in. Cassidy remained silent, waiting for McGuire to continue.

"From what I have witnessed so far from his actions," McGuire continued, "the Yank is no stranger to violence. He knows how to handle himself. Cassidy, he is coming after me and if it's me he wants, he's going to do it. And don't delude yourself, that means all of us," McGuire emphasized, gesturing to the hulking Cassidy.

"Let him come, Sean," Cassidy said with grim bravado and assurance he didn't really feel. "And what he'll get is a taste of Irish justice."

McGuire, appearing agitated, got up, nervously pacing as he moved to one of the windows and looked out. Cassidy watched intently as McGuire made his way back to where Cassidy was seated. He was watchful, smoking his cigarette with shaking hands.

"There's something about this Yank, Sean, that I don't understand. Who is this guy? Or really, what the hell is he?"

"I don't know," McGuire answered bitterly. He didn't mention to Cassidy that question had been on his mind since the incident on the beach.

"Where the hell did someone like him come out of," Cassidy asked, a puzzled look on his face. "Is he with the British Army or one of them Ulster bastards? And what sort of game is he playing? This all can't be over the death of his sister. Jesus, he's running around the country just killing people."

McGuire looked disgustedly at Cassidy. "Stop being an idiot, Cassidy. This Yank has got something on his mind. He wants his pound of flesh."

"For what?"

"For his sister, you bloody fool," McGuire shouted impatiently at Cassidy. "If you haven't figured that out yet, then you're dumber than I give you credit for. We don't have to accept it, but by god we just need to prevent it from coming off our backs." McGuire stared hard at Cassidy. "Do you think we can do that?"

They both smoked their cigarettes silently after that, both of them lost in their own thoughts. McGuire was up and pacing the floor again. Cassidy continued to sit silently at the table trying to think.

"Well, the Yank is only one man," Cassidy offered finally. "Sean, we've got a small army. What can he do?"

"That may be the case about us having an army of men," McGuire said, coming back to the table. "But so far he appears to be able to do what he wants. What I think we need at this point is Megan Clark."

"Megan Clark," Cassidy asked, dumbfounded. "What good is she, Sean?"

"Cassidy, sometimes I don't think you have the sense of a one-year-old," McGuire answered sarcastically. "You can see the way the Yank feels about her. We grab her, we have something he wants."

Cassidy, after a moment, smiled. He began to understand.

Fallon knew he was pushing his luck. Sitting in the kitchen with Megan, Fallon knew that he shouldn't be here. He was running out of time and had to keep moving. Not only for himself but he was putting Megan in danger. But loving Megan the way he did, he had to try and get her to understand. Megan returned from the living room and sat down.

Looking across the table at her, Fallon realized he never believed he could love someone as much as he loved Megan Clark. Watching her, Fallon could see in her eyes that Megan feels the same way as he does. Megan broke the silence.

"What are you thinking, John?" Megan asked softly.

Fallon smiled lovingly. "How beautiful you are," Fallon answered.

Megan, blushing, reached across the table and took his hand. "Sure I must look a mess. After cleaning out the attic, I haven't had time to make myself presentable." Megan frowned, knowing there was more. "Something is troubling you, John. What is it?"

"It's about Kit," Fallon began. "Missing her funeral was unforgivable."

"John," Megan said, "I know you must have had a good reason. I know how much you loved her, and knowing Kit, I believe she would have forgiven you. Please don't feel guilty about it."

"But I do," Fallon continued. "Megan, what I am about to tell you is something I have never shared with anyone but Kit."

"John, you don't have to explain anything to me," Megan answered, squeezing Fallon's hands. "I love you, John. Nothing you tell me can change that. I know you are going to leave, that you feel you have something to do that will make Kit's killing all right."

"Megan," Fallon began, "this is hard for me to say. Over the years, Kit and I have seen each other many times. It has never been in Ireland and we have always kept that part of our life secret. We made a promise to each other that whoever died first, the other would stay away from the funeral."

"John, you don't have to—"

"Please let me finish, Megan," Fallon interrupted. "The reason for this was the work I did. I never wanted Kit to be connected in any way. It was for her safety, Megan. I guess we both felt that with the business I was in it would be natural for me to go first. Megan, the people I work for never knew about Kit. If they did, I don't know what they would do."

Fallon paused. Megan could see the anguish in his face. She waited, knowing Fallon wasn't finished.

"When I decided to walk away from it, Kit was the only one who was aware of my past. Megan, I'm not proud of what I did. But I can't change that. What I wanted to do when I came to Ireland, Kit was aware of this, was start with a clean slate." Fallon paused again, Megan knowing this was difficult to talk about. When Fallon continued, there was a look of sadness on his face.

"It's ironic. As much as I tried keeping Kit from having to be exposed to the life I led, Kit's the one who gets killed. My not going to her funeral was just my way of keeping her name clear of what is going to come."

"It's not over, is it, John?" Megan asked, knowing the answer before she asked.

"No, it isn't."

"John, going after the men who killed Kit means more killing. It still won't bring her back. Let's leave this place," Megan pleaded. "We can start over someplace else and make a life for ourselves. This place holds no ties for me anymore either."

Fallon, reconciled to what he has to do, knew this was going to be hard. He loved Megan Clark and was also aware that he may never see her again after tonight. Taking her in his arms, Fallon held her tight. Megan sensed what was coming; tears were streaming down her cheek. She stepped back.

"I'm never going to see you again, am I?"

"Never is a long time, Megan," Fallon answered, trying to keep the conversation light.

"You're going to kill the men who did this to Kit," Megan stated bluntly.

Fallon looked at Megan for a long time. He didn't answer. He walked over to the window looking out at the sea of green before him. Megan came up behind him, wrapping her arms around his waist. "I love you, John," she whispered softly.

Fallon continued looking off into the distance. The silence hung between them.

In the hotel room not far from the Clark farm or the safe house where McGuire and Cassidy were planning their next move, Reynolds and Harris sat waiting. Reynolds, adept and experienced in this part of the job, stared out the window at the street below. Lost in his thoughts, contemplating their next move, he waited.

Harris, antsy and hyper, lay on the bed reading the newspaper without much success. Unlike Reynolds, Harris was unable to stem the emotions that threatened to move him to make bad decisions. When he has had enough, Harris dropped the paper on the floor, pushing himself up off the bed. Harris was clearly frustrated.

He looked over at Reynolds, clearly agitated. "How long are we just going to sit here, Al? Don't you feel it's time to make some kind of move?"

"What do you suggest, Jack?"

Harris, unable to come up with an answer, looked at Reynolds. Pouting, he dropped into one of the chairs facing Reynolds.

Seeing he was not going to get a response from Harris, Reynolds resumed his vigil at the window. "We wait as long as it takes."

It was the green misty countryside that had Al Reynolds's attention. He found that he actually liked it.

"Al, we've been here for three days and others have been going out to eat, all you have done is stare out that damn window. What are we waiting for?" Harris got to his feet as Reynolds turned to face him. "Fallon's killed two of the IRA rebels already. We know he's holed up on that broad's farm. We should just go over there and get it over with. That's what they are paying us for. Besides, I'm tired of this damn country."

"Fallon has just buried his sister," Reynolds said.

"So what?" Harris asked, confused.

"I owe him that," Reynolds answered without going into any detail. "Besides, he isn't going anywhere," Reynolds stated quietly.

There was a confused look on Harris's face. He could see that there was more to Reynolds's waiting than just the right time. "You sound like you give a shit about this guy, Al," Harris said, surprised. "And not just as a rep for World Wide either. What do you mean you owe him?"

"It's personal."

"Come on, Al," Harris pressed. "We're in this together. Christ, we have burned enough guys over the years that I can tell the difference. You actually seem to care. What is it, Al?" Harris did not sound pleased. That and the fact he was getting tired of watching Reynolds staring out the window.

Reynolds didn't answer right away. He continued staring out the window, his thoughts somewhere else. When he did answer Harris, it was in a matter-of-fact manner, catching Harris off balance.

"We served in Nam together. Fallon saved my life," Reynolds said, turning and looking at Harris. He resumed looking out the window. Rain had started to pelt the windows.

"Maybe it's guilt, I don't know. I just feel the least I can do is let the man finish what he started," Reynolds continued. "Knowing Fallon, I know he is not ready to leave just yet." Reynolds gestured to Harris, pointing out at the lush green countryside. "Al, all you have to do is look out the window and see how nice it is around here. Fallon, if I read him right, wants out. And what better place to retire to than here."

"Bullshit," Harris spat out. "I don't care what he thinks of this country. I just want to finish this job and get the hell out of here."

"Plus, if he has started something with the IRA, I assume they will want to take a run at him. I'm not sure what I feel about that just yet," Reynolds said with consideration. He wondered if they would have to do anything at all if the IRA was in the game.

Harris stared at the back of Reynolds. His look softened as he came to realize that what had happened between him and Fallon meant more to him than he thought. He asked Reynolds, with more respect in his voice, "How did this guy save your life, Al?"

Reynolds, hesitating at first, turned, deciding to tell Harris the story. He moved over to the table, sitting down in one of the chairs. His face looked distant, his thoughts somewhere in the past. Harris remained standing. Reynolds, after contemplating how far he should go, decided to tell Harris about his relationship with Fallon. When he turned to face Harris, his eyes were hard, his face set in stone.

"The company I was attached to in Nam was captured by the Cong after our Huey was shot down," Reynolds began. "We came down hard, and when we finally got it together enough to get out, we were surrounded. Two of our crew are dead. I didn't even fire one round. But then again, I could barely see straight." Reynolds let out a thoughtful, almost wistful, laugh at the memory.

"So they took us. There were seven of us that had survived the crash and the feeble firefight that ensued. They marched us about two miles to one of their villages not far from where we went down. They had constructed prison shacks just outside the village. They did this on the chance they would be discovered and there would be less chance of being bombed." Reynolds shook his head, knowing that never happened.

Continuing, Reynolds was speaking as though Harris was not even in the room and he was remembering yesterday.

"The first time I saw Fallon, he was tied to a bamboo pole in the middle of one of those rat-infested shacks they kept us in and the Cong were torturing him. They had formed a semicircle around him and the soldiers were taking turns beating him around the head. Not hard enough to kill him, which they didn't want to do. This was a game to them, and Fallon was the sport. Then they started putting cigarettes out on his body, and after tiring of having their fun, they drifted out slicing little nicks of flesh off his body. They did this so it would attract the bugs. It was like Nam television to them."

"Jesus Christ," Harris said. He looked away from Reynolds for a moment with that feeling of guilt that men who have never served in a war will have when they are around men who have. Especially men who served in Nam.

"You see, Jack," Reynolds continued, "they didn't want to kill him. It seems right from jump after they had captured him, Fallon had braced them every chance he got. No, they wanted him alive as an example to the rest of us."

Reynolds paused, moving over to the window and looking out. Harris waited, mesmerized by what Reynolds was telling him. Reynolds, turning back to Harris, continued. His voice was low, almost reverent.

"Jack, back then we were just kids. Hell, I was just twenty. Fallon, as bad a shape as he was in, looked even younger."

"You helped train him for World Wide, Al. You must have found out then."

"I never asked what his story or background was. Fallon had all the credentials needed for an operation like ours. If you remember, Jack, I never asked about your past either," Reynolds reminded Harris. Reynolds continued with his story. "Anyway, we weren't there too long before finding out their pattern with Fallon."

"Their pattern?" Harris asked, confused.

"They would take a run at Fallon for several days running, bringing him close to death. Then they would back off, take care of his wounds, and when he was somewhat manageable again, they would start over. The beatings, the burning, the cutting. We wondered how Fallon managed to stay alive. Toward the end, he didn't give a shit about anything anymore. Do you know what he used to do, Jack?"

"What?"

"He would spit in their eyes." Reynolds laughed at the memory. "Man, they brutalized him. We couldn't believe it. And we had to watch every day."

"You said he saved your life, Al," Harris asked.

A thoughtful look passed across Al Reynolds's face. "You know something, Jack? To this day, we are not sure how he pulled it off. One night after the guards were sleeping—they weren't too concerned about security at the camp since most of us were half dead anyway—Fallon's voice, barely audible, got my attention."

"Christ, from what you tell me, Al, I'm surprised he can even talk. What did he say to you?"

"First he produces a knife. How in the hell he ever got that I never knew," Reynolds continued. "Then he tells me to cut him down. Lying on the floor of the hut, Jack, he looked to be about a hundred pounds. His body wasn't even a body. I don't know where he even had the strength to talk. But the next words out of his mouth are, 'We're going.' I was dumbfounded, I stupidly asked where."

"Did he mean an escape?"

"That's exactly what he meant." Reynolds was on his feet again. "Most of the men were half dead, starving, suffering from malnutrition, and some had died off. There were about fifteen of us that were up to trying a break. I really believe that the men tried it because of Fallon."

"Why?"

"Because of what they had seen him go through, they believed he could actually pull it off. We waited until the guards in the camp had settled down for the night when we made our move. The Cong were so sure of themselves they only had one man guarding our hut. The first thing Fallon does is slit his throat. Fallon motioned for us to move out quietly and head for the jungle. He said he had some unfinished business to take care of."

"Unfinished business?" Harris asked incredulously. "What the hell would that be?"

"Jack," Reynolds answered, "that crazy son of a bitch sneaks into one of the tents and kills the commandant and two of his men. Where he got his strength I don't know. Next thing we know, Fallon is with us in the jungle."

"I heard this bastard can be brutal, Al," Harris said with some level of professional awe. And a fraction of fear.

"No question about it, Jack. He is as hard as any man I have ever met." Reynolds paused, remembering that time. "We spent five days trekking through that jungle, eating things you wouldn't give to a dog. To be honest, if it wasn't for Fallon, we would have given ourselves up. He wouldn't let us. I was sure we were all going to buy the farm. Somehow, as bad a shape as he was in, we all drew strength from him. Finally we hooked up with some friendlies and eventually made our way back to our company."

Reynolds paused again. Harris could tell he was back in that jungle. When he resumed talking, there was an element of melancholy in his voice.

"Fallon saved our lives, saved our asses," Reynolds said. "I guess there is a part of me that wishes we didn't have to go this route. If nothing else, it gives me the chance to put my memories in place. But don't worry, Jack. When the time comes, I'll be ready and I'll do what I have to do."

"I know that, Al."

Reynolds nodded and turned back to the window.

"Al, can I ask you a personal question?"

"What is it?"

"How did you two come to work for World Wide?" Harris asked.

Reynolds took a moment. "I came to work for them right off Nam," Reynolds answered. "They were a fairly new covert operation then, not the unknown entity we have become. One thing they were interested in was recruiting the best, most qualified people. That meant the kind that was not above handling the kinds of assignments that were not always above board. I knew Fallon had become a mercenary and was doing field work for the Sandinistas. He was selling himself out like a gun for hire. For the money as well as the principal. But mainly for the money."

"Not like us," Harris said, not without some sarcasm. Reynolds ignored it.

"I tracked him down. When I told him about World Wide, he was interested. And after checking his background, they were definitely interested in Fallon. At the time, Dan Morehead was heading our team."

"Dan Morehead?" Harris asked.

"Morehead was before your time, Jack. Morehead knew his stuff," Reynolds continued. "Fallon was too good to be a mercenary. But then again, most people try to do what they are good at. Morehead took Fallon under his wing and became his mentor. Right up until he retired, Fallon answered only to Dan Morehead."

"Can he really be that good?" Harris wondered. Harris had hear the rumors and seen the numbers, but he wanted to feel some level of safety given what was coming.

Reynolds didn't offer him much of that.

"Jack, you underestimate Fallon for a split second and they'll be carrying you out in a body bag. And one second is usually too long a space of time," Reynolds said.

"So in the meantime, we sit around this crummy hotel collecting bedbugs until after he buries his sister. Then what?"

Reynolds took a moment before he answered. When he did, it was with a sense of finality that sent shivers up Harris's spine.

"We find him. Then I kill him."

It was raining hard now, slashing against the windows of the low-profile hotel directly across the street from where Reynolds and Harris were staying. Dan Morehead stood at the window with a small set of binoculars, looking down at them. Reynolds looked pensive to Morehead, and that was a good sign, Morehead thought.

It didn't take a genius to figure out what they were planning. Morehead knew Childers was going to send his top operatives after John, but it was a brilliant and dangerous move sending Reynolds.

Brilliant because Dan Morehead knew about the relationship between Reynolds and Fallon. Dangerous because Childers was rolling the dice that Reynolds would not get an attack of conscience when it came to taking Fallon out. From the looks of their animated conversation, Dan Morehead was sure that it would be the former.

Morehead's phone rang. "Yes," he said and listened. "No, don't bring it over. I'll come by and pick them up."

After hanging up, Dan Morehead returned to the window, taking one last glance at Reynolds and Harris. He could see where they were settling in for the night. That meant they were waiting to make their move on Fallon. Consequently, everything wasn't in place yet. It must mean they hadn't located Fallon yet or could be waiting for word from Childers.

Morehead, traveling light and under an assumed name, set about throwing his stuff together and cleaning up the room, making sure any trace of his having been there was erased. Fortunately, it was a small room and Morehead removed all evidence that he had even been there. Old habits die hard.

Morehead, leaving by the back way of the hotel, thought how strange it was that he was going to collect his weapons probably from the same source that Reynolds and Harris had used to get theirs. It would also prove interesting that sooner or later they might all be pointing the same weapons at each other.

Reaching the street, the rain having settled into a steady drizzle, Morehead cautiously moved away from the hotel. When he had retired, Dan Morehead was sure he left all this behind him. Unfortunately, it was not to be.

There has to be an easier way, he thought, as he ambled down the street until he was out of sight.

Thirteen

The moonless night hovered over British army headquarters. The fog that rolled in from the sea has blanketed the area, making it near impossible to see. The contingents of soldiers, still jumpy from the latest skirmish with the IRA, were nervous and nerves were frayed, making them more trigger-happy than usual.

These were the thoughts that were going through the mind of Sergeant Wilson as he made his way cautiously across the darkened compound. It wouldn't surprise him if he was shot by one of his own men who were jumping at shadows. So much for dealing with professional soldiers, something that was missing from this collection of misfits.

He considered himself a good soldier, a man who had seen action and handled himself well under fire. He blamed Major Neville, whom he had been serving under when his orders had come through; he had been relegated to being a prison guard in a country he despised. On top of that, the men who had been assigned to this detail were the bottom of the barrel. There was no way the British Army was going to assign hardened soldiers to serve in a country Wilson wouldn't give ten cents for.

Cursing Neville under his breath, Wilson could see the dim lights of the guards' shack as he neared the gate. Stopping at the sentry post, he stuck his head in to see who was on duty. Shaking his head he growled, shaking the sentry out of his reverie.

"What the hell are you doing, Martin?"

The soldier, dozing on the stool inside the shack, jumped to his feet. Grabbing his rifle, which was leaning against the wall, he snapped to attention.

"Sergeant Wilson," Martin stammered.

"You stupid bastard. What if those Irish bastards decided to attack? With clowns like you on duty, we might just as well hand the place over to them. If I wasn't short on men," Wilson said disgustedly, "I would put you on report."

"Sergeant Wilson," Martin said, stumbling over his words, "let me explain."

"Shut up. I don't want any of your lame excuses. Now get out here and try to give me some sort of report on how things are going."

Stepping quickly out of the gatehouse, Martin, getting himself together as best as he could, forgot the litany of excuses he was working on and tried to answer Wilson.

"It's been exceptionally quiet, Sergeant," Martin said, stumbling over the words. "Surprisingly, there doesn't appear to be much activity going on in town."

"The bloody cowards are probably hiding in their holes afraid to show their faces," Wilson growled. Wilson hesitated momentarily and then proceeded to give Martin a tongue-lashing about responsibility and always being on guard. Martin, deflated by Wilson's ranting, was properly chagrined.

"I'm leaving for a while, Martin," Wilson concluded. "When I return, if I find you or any of the other slackers sleeping at their post, you'll answer to me. Have I made myself clear?"

"Yes, Sergeant Wilson," Martin answered weakly. "My feeling, Sergeant, is that they won't be trying anything. We gave the bastards a bellyful the last time, didn't we?"

"On that point, I agree with you, Martin," Wilson answered, calmer now that he had vented. "They would be fools to try anything now. Especially so soon after fucking the last one up. But you know the top brass. The rebels are on the run, and the major still has the jitters."

"Sergeant, the one thing we all know is what the Irish are good for. And that is drinking and talking big. Without a pint in their hand, they haven't got an ounce of courage."

Wilson had to laugh at that. He was feeling better, and the dark mood he was carrying after his meeting with Neville had passed. He was looking forward to the night ahead.

"You're right about that, Martin. But let's keep the major happy. Stay on your toes and be prepared for the worst. I'll be gone until morning, Martin."

"It wouldn't be that blond wench you were out with the other night now, would it, Sergeant?" Martin said, feeling more confident.

Wilson laughingly gave Martin a playful punch in the arm. Smiling, Wilson wheeled around with a wave and started making his way into town. Heading out the gate, the dense fog made visibility almost impossible; he could hear the sound of his footsteps on the cobblestone street.

Not able to move too swiftly, the frustrated Wilson moved slowly toward the center of town. Rehashing his last meeting with Neville, the anger began to build again; Wilson couldn't help but feel he was treating him like a child. Ranting relentlessly, Wilson couldn't help but sense the fear in Neville's voice. He was going on endlessly about the Yank, calling him a loose cannon and saying that as long as he was free, he presented a danger to them. When Wilson pointed out that all he considered him was a low-level Irishman who blamed the IRA for the death of his sister, all this did was set off Neville again. Pointing his finger at Wilson and waving his arms frantically, he began berating him again. The meeting ended with Wilson being thrown out of Neville's office and told to find the Yank.

"To hell with Neville," Wilson said out loud. He was a good soldier, and the last thing he needed to do was be a nursemaid to a fucking officer who was ready to wet himself over one man. He let his mind drift back to the Irish tart he met several weeks ago. She wasn't the greatest to look at, but Wilson, in his brutish manner, found her satisfactory. For the rest of the night, as far as he was concerned, Neville could go screw himself.

Wilson stopped abruptly. His mind, which had been elsewhere, suddenly sensed someone else on the street. He glanced over his shoulder. There was no one there from what he could see in the fog. Shrugging it off, he continued walking. He proceeded a few more steps. A cold chill passed through him as he came to a halt. His hand dropped to the holstered gun.

"You'll never make it," a quiet voice came from the darkness.

Frozen from where he stood, Wilson saw no one. "Who is that? Damn it, man, show yourself. I demand to know who you are."

The footsteps were quick and sure. A powerful arm wrapped itself around Wilson's throat. Pulling him hard against his body, he dragged Wilson into the alley. There was terror in Wilson's eyes. He struggled but was unable to free himself from the man's grip.

He felt the cold steel of the blade as the knife was plunged into him. A feeling of disbelief crossed Wilson's face as he slumped to the pavement. The figure stepped out of the shadows and stood in front of him.

"It's you," Wilson gasped, already feeling the flow of blood oozing from his stomach.

"When you get to hell, tell them to reserve a spot for Neville."

Wilson felt the knife as it slid across his throat. His last memory was of John Fallon disappearing into the night.

A cold wind had blown in from the sea during the night. The sightless fog had dissipated, the sun slowly streaming through the sky. The police were fighting a seemingly fruitless battle with the townspeople who had encircled the bloody body that lay obscenely in the street.

Store owners were standing outside their shops and pubs, straining to see who had been killed. The people were talking nonstop among themselves, the stories varying from group to group.

Two early morning street cleaners had stumbled across Wilson's body as they pushed their brooms through the streets.

"Jesus, Mary, and Joseph!" one of them had shouted upon discovering Wilson.

"He's a fuckin' mess," said the other.

"I'll call the police."

By the time the police and ambulance arrived, word had spread and the people had already filled the streets. The police had all they could do just to get the ambulance near the body.

On the outskirts of the crowd, standing quietly, Reynolds and Harris watched as they began their cleanup campaign. The two men, looking like businessmen from anywhere, were talking among themselves. They waited until the man was loaded onto the ambulance. The police had restored some level of order and then disappeared with the crowd.

Sitting at a table in one of the restaurants, with a clear view to the happenings outside his window, Dan Morehead watched as Reynolds and

Harris drifted back in the direction of their hotel. He was in no rush. He knew where they would be. Waiting until they were out of sight, he paid his bill and left, moving in the same direction.

Major Neville's quarters were located off the base in a fortresslike compound located on the outskirts of the town. He had two floors with a balcony that overlooked a vast green stretch of Ireland that to anyone else's eye could only be described as beautiful. Not Major Neville, who hated the very sight of it.

Neville, in his arrogant way, saw himself as a military man, a good soldier, who was serving a sentence in a country he despised. As he stood on the balcony, a glass of scotch in his hand, Neville could feel the burning anger that lingered inside him like a disease. He finished his drink and moved back inside the house.

Neville splashed some more scotch in his glass and made his way into the bathroom to run his bath. He did not like Irish whisky for many reasons, one of which was political, the other was that he needed what he considered a more complicated taste for his palate, although he was also fond of American bourbon. A taste he picked up many years ago on one of his trips to the United States.

While he waited for his bath, Neville dropped into a chair and let his mind wander back to the events that had dropped him in this godforsaken country. One mistake. That's all it took. After almost twenty years of faithful duty to his country, he had been banished to a land that he despised. Doing a job that could only be described as a prison warden. Because that's what it was.

It was an accident that had happened on maneuvers. He was a training instructor then with a flawless record and in line for another promotion. Due the incompetence of one of his NCOs, Neville was held responsible for the deaths of six of his men. Damn higher-ups. So he had been drinking the night before, what the hell difference did that make. Even he was still suffering from a hangover when they went out on maneuvers and he placed his noncom in charge, he was held responsible for their deaths. What really frosted him was that the top brass never saw that they had saddled him with inexperienced men.

No, they wouldn't own up to that. Covering their own ass, they threw him, Major Neville, to the wolves. No promotion, no field command, and most humiliating of all, they took away six months' pay. Then the icing on the cake—banishment to this godforsaken country that he hated with a passion. And to top that off, with this last debacle, he was on the hot seat again with strict orders to clean the mess expeditiously.

Neville thought about the wife he had lost to cancer seven years ago. He had lived alone since that time. He did not mind the solitude; in fact, he preferred it to his marriage.

He lit his cigar and sipped scotch as he bathed. While he was feeling his body winding down from all the stress of the last couple of weeks, he considered the situation he was presently in. In actuality, it was his own country that had been put under a microscope. And his ass was sitting right there with it.

At least four dead Irish civilians and one of the blasted women had to have been a nun. The heat was a fire that was following him around. The high command was pressing for news, and they wanted answers. The problem was that he was supplying the answers that no one seemed to like. If they could do any better, let them get off their fat behinds and come over here and do it. Fat chance with that. He was the patsy and he better get used to it.

But beyond that was the situation with the local IRA. Even though they had been playing a dead hand for the time being, Neville was absolutely certain they were up to something. They always bloody were. And that was the tragedy for both sides. There would never be a thirty-two-county Irish republic. Neville knew it and everyone else knew it. And from what he could ascertain, most of the continent didn't want it.

Northern Catholics had British subsidies flowing freely into their pockets, and the Southern Catholics didn't want their taxes increased to make up the difference, as what would have to happen in Ireland if the island was to become an Irish free state without Britain to back up the coffers. Neville was starting to develop a headache.

That left Britain's government in the middle, and Neville felt sure that was the last place they wanted to be. Northern Ireland was just one big subsidy to them. And a headache worse than the one he was experiencing right now. The one thing he was sure of since his deployment here, Ireland was a land of bloodshed, and that wasn't going to end anytime soon. If ever.

The sad truth was that Northern Catholics had more in common historically and also on a day-to-day basis with Northern Protestants than they did with Southern Catholics down below. And the Northern Protestants had more in common with the Northern Irish than they did with the British.

Yet the Protestants blew up Catholic churches and pubs and had no compunction about killing innocent people in their homes. The Unionists did the same. He sighed, thinking these are the people he was sent to straighten out. In Neville's opinion, the only way to straighten out this country was to nuke it.

And the British army stood by and watched them both.

Neville knew the British had no plan. They were in the middle, leaning toward Ulster. But really, after years of futility, what they really wanted was an end to it. If some people saw that as being inconsistent and weak, the British saw it as being normal. If Britain backed the Unionists, they did so only to combat the IRA. The problem Britain had now was a PR problem. The bad press they were receiving throughout the world had come back to bite them in the ass.

This, of course, made the IRA stronger. This made Britain look weak. This made Neville's job and others like his harder. This made Neville harder and more cynical as to achieving success.

This at this moment made his scotch taste even better in the hot bath with a cigar.

Being a military man with a military mind, what he couldn't fathom was what made these people kill themselves for something that was never going to happen. Why fight and why stay? To Neville's way of thinking in war, there had to be clear-cut objectives. To Neville, everything was black and white. Neville sipped his scotch and pondered the unanswerable.

If it was up to him, he'd give the Irish what they wanted—let the two sides kill themselves or help themselves to their hearts' content.

But he wasn't being paid to make those decisions.

In the meantime, up until recently, for Neville and his men, all that was left was to put down the IRA as the IRA tried to put down the Ulster Unionists and the British army. It was long, slow, tough work. That is, until the Yank. As if he didn't have enough on his plate, he now had to contend with a psycho bent on revenge.

What the hell did he want? And why the killing of Wilson? Didn't the Yank realize it was the Irish that were responsible for the death of his sister? This crazy bastard was killing everyone. Neville had felt something that day he looked into the Yank's eyes. Neville considered himself a brave man, but that day, he felt a fear he had never known before. Now because of him, he had two of his men accompanying him wherever he went. That included his home where they were stationed outside in case he showed up here.

Neville ended his bath, toweled off, and in his robe, headed toward the living room for another glass of scotch. Two steps into the room, he felt a gun pressed against his neck. Dropping his empty glass, Neville stopped cold immediately.

The shadow of a man moved in front of him, the gun still pressed to his neck. It stayed that way until the man stepped out in front of him.

The man looked familiar, but by then he knew who it was, and even if he hadn't stepped out into the light, Neville could have placed him immediately. Even though he had only seen him for that brief moment that day on the street.

"Neville," the man said in an American accent. It was the Yank.

"What do you want?" Neville asked, still shaken, trying to maintain his composure but unable to free himself from the fear of the cold iron pressed against his neck? His mind was working quickly to think of the significance of the American in his room with a gun pressed against his neck.

"The first thing I want you to do is remain as calm as you can," Fallon said easily. "If you're wondering about your two men outside and hoping they will get you out of this, forget it. They bought the farm."

"You killed them?" Neville asked incredulously.

"Let's just say they are in a better place. Now do we understand about remaining calm and not trying anything stupid?"

"I'll do just that," Neville answered, glancing across the room to the night table where his gun was. It was still there.

Fallon pressed the gun deeper into Neville's neck. Gesturing with his other hand, Fallon pointed to one of the empty chairs near the table.

"Plant yourself in that seat," Fallon said, his voice never rising above a softness that unnerved Neville. Then Fallon walked Neville to a chair with his gun.

Neville moved readily and sat down. Fallon, positioning himself several feet from Neville, leveled the gun at his stomach. Neville could see that the gun had a silencer in place.

Sitting stiffly in a straight-backed chair, Neville, with typical arrogance, feeling he was going to get out of the situation he was in, looked coldly at the man who had invaded his home. No doubt about it. He remembered Fallon, that face with the cold eyes, which were staring back at him on that bloody day. Fallon saw the recognition in Neville's face and smiled.

"You remember who I am."

"I remember your face from the crowd," Neville answered evenly.

"And do you remember that day? Do you also remember what you and your men did that day?" Fallon asked.

"I did nothing that any other soldier would not have done," Neville answered pompously. Neville, feeling on surer ground now that he had Fallon talking, felt the odds were swinging in his favor. His bluster was back, and with it the confidence that he was going to emerge from this situation intact. He continued. "A good soldier sees his duty and carries it out to the best of his ability."

"And that includes killing my sister as well as other innocent people?" Fallon asked.

Stunned by the coldness and matter-of-fact tone in Fallon's voice, Neville was taken aback. "I regret that your sister was unfortunately killed in the attack. Let's not forget that the IRA instituted the attack."

"My sister and the others on the street were innocent. They were civilians," Fallon reminded him. "Is that what is referred to as collateral damage?"

"That was a tragic mistake."

"That was more than a tragic mistake," Fallon answered, the gun never wavering. He was speaking deliberately now as though he wanted Neville to understand everything clearly.

"That was a catastrophe that did not have to happen. Your soldiers are trained in combat and taught how to handle difficult situations. They don't kill innocent people. And if they do, it's the boss's fault. In this case,

Major Neville, the responsibility falls on you." Fallon looked at Neville with darkening eyes.

At this point, a sinking feeling started in the pit of Neville's stomach. He knew now what Fallon wanted to do in this grim situation. He began to run different scenarios in his head, in a worried way, how he was going to disarm Fallon.

"We were attacked by the bloody rebels," Neville said with some defensive anger in his voice. "The IRA attacked us. As soldiers, we could only react. And in the situation, we did the best we could."

"The best you could was not good enough."

"What about Sergeant Wilson?" Neville shot back.

"Collateral damage," Fallon answered, smiling. Then he continued. "You were lying in wait," Fallon reminded Neville. "You had set a trap for the IRA. That means you were expecting company. If you weren't, you should have been better prepared. You were in control of the situation. You should have done a better job. You also should have planned for it to happen in a place there were not a lot of civilians."

"They picked the killing ground," Neville blurted out. Then in a demanding voice, hoping to distract Fallon, the gun pointed at his torso now squarely on his mind, Neville asked, "How would you control a situation like that?"

Fallon did not answer the question.

Neville saw a deep coldness in the Yank's eyes, an unending darkness that clouded his face. It made him shiver.

"What is your name?" Neville asked, hoping to buy some time.

"Fallon. John Fallon."

"Well, Mr. Fallon, I deeply regret what happened to your sister and the other innocent civilians, if that's what they were, and I have been trying to get to the bottom of the incident since it happened. The investigation is ongoing, and whoever is responsible, if we find it was due to my men's negligence, will be dealt with accordingly. I promise you. Since it happened just a short time ago, you can't expect us to have answers already?"

"Executed you mean?" Fallon asked him.

"Executed?" Neville looked at Fallon, confused.

"The fitting end to what they have done," Fallon said casually. "They murdered innocent people in cold blood. They should be executed."

Continuing, Fallon said in a voice that unnerved Neville, "I'm sure you feel that way. Don't you?"

Neville felt he was being toyed with, and it made him angrier and more insecure.

"Soldiers don't get executed for doing their duty in time of war, Mr. Fallon." Neville was angry now, momentarily forgetting about the precarious position he was in. "Do we make mistakes? Yes we do. Look at your involvement in Vietnam," Neville told Fallon. Feeling more in control now, Neville began to stroke his mustache to ease his anxiety.

"Many of your American soldiers killed innocent Vietnamese civilians," Neville continued. "None of these soldiers were executed. It was war. Collateral damage is expected. And what about Iraq? I don't believe that all those good men and women that defend American interests who have accidentally harmed innocent men and women and children should be executed for doing their duty, do you?"

Fallon did not answer. He just continued to look in Neville's eyes.

Unnerving as it was having Fallon staring at him, Neville rushed on. "How many American soldiers fighting for your interests right now, even as we speak, would you put to death, Mr. Fallon?"

"None," Fallon answered.

"Because they were doing their best in time of war," Neville said, proudly feeling he had gotten his point across.

"No," Fallon replied gently. "Because they didn't kill my sister."

Fallon stared at Neville coldly and went silent. Neville, shocked, did not know how to reply. Like a bolt from the sky, it dawned on him. Fallon was not looking for justice in the moral sense. No, Fallon was unconcerned about politics, IRA, British troops, or any of the logical problems that could have caused this fiasco. He was interested in only one thing—revenge. Neville knew at that moment that trying to moralize with Fallon would prove useless.

Neville looked nervously at his gun on the table, but felt very little comfort. Though Neville had managed to shorten the distance by sliding slowly over, the gun was still several steps away. He had to come up with something. Something fast. Fallon meant to kill him. Of that he had no doubt,

"This isn't about who's right or wrong then. This is all about revenge," Neville said nervously, trying to feign a degree of indignity. He knew it came across as just whining. "I'm a British soldier trying to fight a war and you're just a man out to get revenge for the death of his sister. Isn't that a little bit cold-blooded?"

"Ask my sister. She's cold-blooded," Fallon said quietly. "She's dead."

Neville did not like that answer. Both for inappropriateness and its finality. Fallon was like an iceberg. He had to find a way to reach him, and time was running out. Neville began stroking his mustache anxiously, visibly concerned.

"We're in the middle of a civil war here, Mr. Fallon," Neville tried to reason. "You must consider we do the best we can."

"I don't think you do," Fallon said, cutting Neville off. "And you didn't that day. I was there and saw exactly how you handled it. You and your men didn't consider the entire situation beforehand, or you would have had a contingency plan."

The realization had sunk in that Fallon was not just a loose cannon out for revenge for his sister, but that he was an experienced professional; that made him even more dangerous.

"There were no snipers on the roof," Fallon continued in that quiet, easy voice that was driving Neville wild. "No blocking sight line with another vehicle. Your guards on the street did not even attempt to move civilians out of the way in case you lost control of the situation. There were no considerations of the dangers of setting a trap in a public place. No containment, Neville. Men arbitrarily opened up with automatic rifles and began spraying bullets all over the place."

"The IRA was to blame," Neville answered lamely.

"I hold them responsible also," Fallon said, pointing his gun at Neville's chest.

"You just can't kill me in cold blood," Neville's quivering voice spit out. "That would make you a killer, an assassin."

Fallon did not answer.

"I'm a major in the British Army for god's sake," Neville said pompously. "If you kill me, they'll hunt you down and kill you."

Fallon stared at Neville calmly, neutrally. Neville felt his emptiness.

"Good god, man," Neville, unable to hide the desperation in his voice, repeated himself. "They'll kill you."

"I'm not to too concerned with that." Fallon smiled. "Let's face it, Neville, everybody dies. But I will do this for you. I don't want you to think I'm just some cold-blooded killer. I'm going to give you a chance to go for your gun."

"What?" Neville asked alarmed.

"I can see the wheels turning from over here. Don't think I have missed you eyeballing the piece on the table. I'm just giving you a chance. The gun that's on the table. You can get it. Then I'll kill you."

Fallon, getting to his feet, the iron dangling by his side, stepped to the side, giving Neville a clear path. Neville stared at Fallon, too shocked to move.

Fallon waited in silence. Neville, sweat flowing freely now, looked at the gun with nervous back-and-forth movements of his eyes.

"This can't be happening," Neville said as much to himself as he did to Fallon. "What kind of chance is that?"

"Better than the one you gave my sister."

Neville was in full panic mode now. This cold-blooded killer sitting across from him meant to kill him. Neville knew there was no reaching him, no bargaining, no hope of finding any sense of humanity in the man. He knew he was going to have to do something, and it was going to have to be fast. He was only going to get one chance. Neville had to try one more time to get through to him.

"This isn't happening," Neville repeated, shifting slowly in his chair.

"That's what I said when I watched your men cutting down my sister on the street," Fallon told him.

"That was a tragic mistake."

"It was no mistake. It was poor planning by men with guns who didn't care."

"I'm telling you again," Neville reiterated, beyond the desperation point now. "I'm not lying."

"Like I said, I'm not worried."

"This all seems so pointless," Neville said, outwardly scared now. "Fallon, how will killing me bring back your sister?"

Fallon shrugged. "Like you say, it probably is pointless. And no, it won't bring Kit back. Like the war in Ireland. Like war in any country or on the face of the earth. There's a lot of pointlessness going on." Fallon continued speaking. Neville was sure he had a plan. "I'm not going to wait much longer, Neville. Fish or cut bait."

Neville stroked his mustache. His mind was racing rapidly now.

He considered his option, knowing if he didn't make his move; Fallon was going to gun him down. Neville took a deep breath, his hand darting to the lamp on the night table to his right, flinging it at Fallon. Neville dove for the floor, rolling in the direction of his pistol, grabbing the gun, fingering the trigger, and swinging it quickly on Fallon.

Fallon shot him dead before the British soldier could pull the trigger.

Then after making sure Neville was dead, Fallon slipped quietly back out the window, disappearing into the dark night.

The sun was just starting to set over Megan's house. The sea green grass was blowing gently in the night breeze from the sea. Megan, who had not slept since Fallon left, was standing vigil at the window. She was feeling the weight of what Fallon had told her and wondered what she could do to deter Fallon from following his path to sure death.

Walking away from the window, distracted by the many thoughts flooding through her mind, Megan moved about the house aimlessly. She was unaware of the car that has pulled into the driveway.

The door swung open. McGuire, gun in hand, stepped through the door followed by Cassidy. Cassidy swung a shotgun around the room.

"Check the other rooms," McGuire barked.

"Did you ever hear of knocking, Sean?" Megan angrily asked.

McGuire sneered, calling out to Cassidy, "Did you find him, Cassidy?"

Cassidy stepped back into the room, the shotgun held loosely in his hand. "The bastard isn't here. He has probably turned tail and run."

"Alert the boys outside, Cassidy. Make sure they stay alert and not fuck off," McGuire said. "Then you get back in here." McGuire turned his attention to Megan.

Megan was sitting stiffly in one of the chairs in the living room. Across from her, nervously moving around the house, his eyes darting frantically, she watched McGuire. When Cassidy walked back in, McGuire leveled his gun at him.

"Jesus, Sean," Cassidy said, a frightened look on his face. "Take it easy, will you? You scared the shit out of me."

"Shut up and get back in here," McGuire snarled. Cassidy shut the door and moved to the far side of the room. McGuire took the chair across from Megan.

"Look, Megan," McGuire began, "all we're asking you to do is help us. Help the cause, Megan, like a good Irish girl."

"Help you what?" Megan spat at McGuire. "You're actually asking me to help you kill John. You have to be insane."

"Are you crossing over to the other side now, Megan?"

"What side is that? The side of sanity?"

McGuire, nervously laughing, chided Megan. "Oh, I'm sane enough, darling. I can't stand by and watch my own people get killed and not give a damn. If you can, Megan, then you've slipped a long way."

"To hell with you," Megan said and stood up.

"Sit down, Megan, and stop this foolishness," McGuire hissed at her, his voice blistering with venom. "You know what situation we are in. We have the bloody Brits breathing down our necks and a psycho Yank running around killing people on a whim. So let's stop playing games and get to it."

Cassidy was about to put his hands on her shoulder and force her to sit down, but Megan sat down on her own, not giving him the satisfaction. Cassidy, a look of disappointment on his face, stepped back. She glared at McGuire and smiled viciously.

"You're just a weak little drunk and dumb as dirt, Sean," Megan said, staring at McGuire. "As for your stooge Mike Cassidy, he is nothing but a goon. Between the two of you, neither one of you has the sense God gave an ass."

"You'll shut your mouth, you bitch, or I'll be shutting it for you," Cassidy snarled, stepping toward Megan. "If you run your mouth off like that again, by god, what I will do to you will make you—"

"Or you'll what, you coward?" Megan interrupted Cassidy bitterly. "You will show us how tough you are? Sure, it's probably easier for someone like you to take on a woman. I'm probably just the right size for you."

Cassidy, moving quickly for a big man, moved to where Megan sitting, slapping her hard against the side of the head, sending her toppling out of the chair onto the floor. Lying on the floor looking up at Cassidy, Megan smiled. Blood was flowing freely from her mouth as she pushed herself up immediately.

McGuire stared angrily at her, but remained silent.

Cassidy, furious at Megan's reaction, began making another move to where she was standing. Megan, defiant, challenged him.

"Go on, Cassidy. Do it again, you coward. Use your gun the next time then, why don't you? It makes you a bigger man," Megan hissed sarcastically.

Cassidy was about to hit her again when McGuire, nervously laughing, stepped between, holding his hand up to stop Cassidy.

"Shut up, Megan. No one is going to shoot you," McGuire said shakily. Turning to Cassidy, his eyes blazing, McGuire shoved him back. "And you, Cassidy, if you touch her again, I might be the one that does some shooting and it won't be Megan I'll be pulling the trigger on. Do you understand?"

Cassidy hesitated and then slinked over to one of the chairs, slumping down, the gun resting on his lap. McGuire turned his attention back to Megan. "If I wanted to kill you, Megan, I would have done it myself the last time you gave me some of your lip. If that was what was on my mind, we wouldn't be sitting here asking for your help."

McGuire didn't miss the disgusted look on Megan's face as she gestured to the door. "You have three men sitting outside, all with weapons, waiting for John to show up. When they spot him, Sean, they are going to kill him. The only help you will get from me is if you are going to kill him then you'll kill me. Sean, I'm not stupid. You can't afford to leave any witnesses to murder. Please don't insult my intelligence."

McGuire glanced quickly at Cassidy. Cassidy's face was impassive. McGuire, unsure of himself, quickly addressed Megan. "There are no witnesses in Ireland, Megan, you know that. Only informants. All I want to do is talk to your John Fallon, try reasoning with him before anyone else gets hurt. We're not going to kill either of you."

"You're a liar," Megan said quietly.

McGuire leaned toward Megan, looking to make his case.

"Christ, Megan, the man is running around the countryside killing people. And you're afraid of me?" McGuire looked at her like she is crazy. "Your Yank friend is a menace, Megan. He is just loose cannon and needs to be sopped. I'm just hoping he will listen to reason. Megan, Fallon is running wild, and if you want to worry about who is going to kill him, then look to the Brits. He is killing them arbitrarily."

Megan stared at McGuire with a stone face.

McGuire, struggling to reach her, tried being reasonable. "Look, girl, all I want to do is talk to Fallon. He can pick the time and the place." McGuire was pleading now. "What could be fairer than that?"

"What about the men outside?"

"Those men outside are there in case he doesn't want to talk," Cassidy sneered.

"Shut up, Cassidy," McGuire snarled, turning to Cassidy. "Megan, all I am doing is asking for your help."

"I don't know where he is," Megan answered.

McGuire angrily scrambled to his feet. When he addressed Megan, there was fire in his eyes. "Dammit, Megan, I don't have time to play games with you. You're not good at them and you're not holding any of the good cards."

"Let me help her, the bloody bitch. Give me five minutes with her, Sean, and she'll tell us everything she knows," Cassidy threatened. "Sean, maybe Megan has become one of those British-loving bastards."

Before McGuire could answer, Megan turned to Cassidy. There was venom in her voice. "What is that supposed to mean, Cassidy?"

"It means you are willing to see your own kind killed by this bloody Yank. And not give a damn about them."

"Don't ever put me in the same category as you, you drunken sot. If you think John has any feelings for the British, you are dumber than I thought," Megan fired back

"Shut up, you bitch, or I'll—" Cassidy jumped up from his chair, starting across the room to get at Megan.

"Cassidy," McGuire's icy voice froze him. The gun in his hand pointed at Cassidy. "Don't make me warn you again."

Megan laughed at them both. "Big tough men," she spat at them. "And even though I'm telling you the truth, if I knew where John was, do you really believe I would tell you where he was?"

McGuire turned back to Megan, his teeth showing a sly smile. It was almost the kind of smile he used on her when they were dating. Megan was sickened to see it.

"I know you are a strong-minded girl, Megan, and it appears that you are going to want to do this the hard way," McGuire told her. "And you know me well enough that I don't mind doing it the hard way. But we loved each other once, Megan, and for the sake of that, we'll just sit here and wait. I'm sure your lover Fallon will show up sooner or later. The one thing we have on our side is time. In the meantime, Cassidy and I could use a cup of tea."

McGuire sneered. Cassidy eyed Megan angrily but said nothing.

"What will you do when John doesn't come?" Megan wanted to know. She did not move from her chair.

"He'll come," McGuire said and stood up and went toward the stove.

"How can you be so sure?" Megan asked, watching McGuire with distaste.

"Because of you, Megan," McGuire said. "Now that we have you, there is no way your lover isn't going to show up.

McGuire picked up the teapot and began filling it with water. Megan looked from McGuire, who moved easily around the familiar kitchen, to Cassidy who was still smarting from having been put down by McGuire. Her eyes darted to where the men were stationed outside her house. Megan could see the flame from one of the men's cigarettes. She wondered what they would do.

Megan felt the side of her head begin to pound blood through the bruise, but she did not make a move to show that she was in pain. She wiped the trickle of blood from the side of her mouth, her mind spinning, trying to come up with some way to warn John.

"I'll take a cup of that tea, Sean, since you're making it," Megan said, trying to sound like she wasn't scared.

But she did not feel safe any longer.

Fourteen

As Fallon made his way down the beach toward the back of Megan's house, the rain that had been mostly a gentle mist had settled into a steady, slashing rain that made visibility all but extinct. Fallon did not mind the hammering, blinding blackness that encompassed him. It would make what he had to do that much easier.

Crossing the field, Fallon started slowly over the hill. Stopping at the top, wiping his eyes, Fallon saw the lights from Megan's house in the distance. He also noticed the two cars that were parked off to the side of the house, apparently hoping not to be seen. Fallon knew immediately that McGuire and his cronies were inside.

Fallon went low to the ground, knowing he had to cover at least two hundred yards of open field. He was not too troubled, knowing the weather was on his side. Moving quickly and silently, Fallon, having decided that coming in from the far side of the house was the best way, started across the open field.

With the backpack slung across his shoulders, Fallon, barely able to see now, closed in on Megan's house. Coming to a halt, he dropped to the ground. Straining his eyes, he counted three men standing on the porch of Megan's home. He could not make out their faces. The men were unfamiliar to Fallon. He assumed that McGuire, along with Cassidy, were inside the house.

Fallon gave himself about five minutes, making sure he had not been spotted. The three men, intent on smoking their cigarettes and not wanting to venture off the porch into the rain, continued talking among themselves.

Fallon, soaked now through the skin, didn't move. He watched closely, watching their movements, trying to detect a pattern. It didn't take him long to see that one man steps off the porch every few minutes, hurriedly making a cursory turn around the house, then returns to join the other two on the porch. Fallon, taking advantage of their disinterest, began moving quickly toward the side of the house.

Moving cautiously now, he moved from where he was, keeping low to the ground. When he felt it was close enough, using the bushes in front of the house and hugging the house, he waited for an opening.

"Fuckin' miserable night," one of the men said. "I don't know what the hell Sean is worried about. There isn't a chance the Yank is going to show up here on a night like this. Especially here. He has to know we are waiting."

"Aye," the second man said, flipping his cigarette into the night. "We should all be tucked away in a nice warm pub having a pint. Well, me bladders about to burst. I'll take a turn around the house. At the same time, I'll take meself a leak."

"Make it quick, will you," the first man said.

Fallon slid slowly along the side of the house, making his way to the back. He had already determined that they were heavily armed and knew that he must even the odds. Crouching, he pulled the backpack off his shoulder. Reaching inside, he extracted the Uzi and forty-five from the bag. Draping the Uzi and putting the handgun fitted with a silencer inside the waist of his pants, he pulled the knife from his boot. He waited for the man.

Fallon heard his feet crunching on the path, the man cursing under his breath. Fallon waited until he leaned his weapon against the house. He had his back to him as Fallon, knife at the ready, stepped quickly up to him. Grabbing him around the throat, stifling any noise, he slit his throat. Letting him slip slowly to the ground, Fallon slid the knife back into the sheath in his boot and moved cautiously back to the front of the house.

Stopping under the window, Fallon chanced a glance inside the house. He saw McGuire and Cassidy talking animatedly. Fallon's muscles tightened as he saw Megan sitting proudly, dried blood having formed on her cheek, sitting silently watching them. There was a welt on the side of her face, and it was red and swollen. Straightening, Fallon moved to the front of the house.

The two men were still standing on the porch, smoking their cigarettes and staring into the darkness. They had hard looks on their faces and were both bored and angry. The guns they had were held loosely in their hands.

"Miserably fuckin' night," one of the men said.

"Aye," the other responded. "What the hell is taking Kelly so long to take a bloody piss? Did he get lost?"

"Maybe he can't find his dick."

They burst out laughing. Fallon moved closer to the two men. He was only twenty feet from where they were standing. His hand wrapped around the iron in his hand, he edged ever closer.

"Well, if Sean is right," one of the men said, "the sooner the Yank shows, the better. Then it's off to the pub for me."

"It's always the pub for you," the other said, smiling.

"Better than the whores you go to every night."

"What if this Yank doesn't show tonight? And I don't know why McGuire thinks he will. But if he doesn't come, how long are we supposed to hang out like this?"

"I guess we'll stay as long as Sean says to," the other said. Moving to the end of the porch, he looked off into the darkness. "Jesus. Now I'm beginning to worry about Kelly. If he isn't back soon, I'm going to go find him."

"Don't worry. He'll be back."

"You know, Frankie," the other one said, "Sean has to kill the Yank bastard, don't you understand that? The way he is going around killing people, it's just a matter of time before he comes looking for the rest of us."

"I know," the one called Frankie said.

Fallon, seeing that they were both distracted with their thoughts, sensed that this was the right time. Stepping lightly onto the porch, his voice low and deadly, Fallon said, "Don't even breathe. The first one of you that makes a sound, I'll blow your head off. Lay the guns down nice and easy."

Both men were stunned when they saw Fallon, the Uzi held confidently in Fallon's hand, pointed at them. Placing the guns on the floor of the porch, Fallon then gestured for them to lift their arms.

"Move off the porch," Fallon whispered. "Quietly. If you have any ideas about warning McGuire or Cassidy, forget them. Unless you want to meet your maker. Now start walking to the back of the house. And stay close together. You can hold hands if you want."

The two men stepped nervously off the porch. With Fallon walking behind them, they began walking around to the back of the house.

"What are you going to do to us?" the man called Frankie rasped.

"Just keep walking. I'll tell you when to stop."

"What happened to Kelly?"

Fallon didn't bother to answer. The rain was almost blinding now, lightning and thunder crackling across the sky. Fallon, looking once over his shoulder, saw that there was no movement from inside the house. Letting the Uzi dangle from his shoulder, he pulled out the automatic in his waistband.

The two men, their movements jerky and nervous, terrified expressions on their faces, continued. Stumbling from the blinding rain, one of the men bolted for the woods on the left. Without a word, Fallon pumped two bullets into his back. The muffled sound of the silencer, along with the rain, was barely audible.

The man called Frankie, seeing his companion lying facedown in the mud, panicked, turning around to face Fallon. "You've killed him. Please. I haven't done anything to you. Let me go, I won't—"

He never finished. The first bullet caught him between the eyes, sending him tumbling backward. Before he hit the ground, Fallon's next shot hit him squarely in the chest. Walking over to where he was lying, Fallon looked down. Moving to where the first man was, Fallon made sure he was dead. Satisfied, Fallon headed back to the house.

Standing on the porch now, Fallon reloaded his weapon. He was not sure if McGuire or Cassidy checked on the men periodically. He couldn't take any chances.

Moving closer to the living room window, Fallon looked inside. He could see Cassidy's back. He was in the doorway to the kitchen. He couldn't see McGuire or Megan, but he knew they were in there.

Through the rain he could hear muffled voices. Fallon knew he didn't have much time. He had to move fast. Checking his weapons, Fallon, wiping his eyes as best as he could, decided that the best way into the house is through the side door. He started in that direction.

Reaching his position, Fallon girded himself, knowing he has to make sure of his move and keep Megan out of harm's way. He tested the door. It was not locked. Pushing the automatic back into his waistband, he stepped quietly into Megan's house.

"The purpose of our cause is to give the people of Ireland a right to determine their own destinies," McGuire pompously exhorted to the amusement of Megan. Cassidy, standing by the fireplace, solemnly nodded his head.

"Listen to you," Megan mockingly pointed to Sean. "Do you actually believe that what you and the other idiots like Cassidy, idiots that they really think what they are doing is for the good of Ireland?"

Cassidy rushed across the room and, before McGuire could stop him, cracked Megan across the mouth. Megan slumped back against the couch, blood flowing freely now. Again, refusing to wipe the blood away, Megan sat back up and smiled at Cassidy.

Cassidy, infuriated, brought his hand back to hit her again. McGuire, stepping between them, shoved Cassidy back. Reluctantly, Cassidy backed off.

"Megan," McGuire said adamantly, "your mouth is going to get you in trouble. The next time, I won't stop Cassidy."

"Just five minutes, Sean. That's all I need with the bitch."

"Calm down," McGuire repeated. Then turning back to Megan, McGuire continued as though nothing has happened. "All we want, Megan, is an equal distribution of wealth and to put an end to the horrible poverty that has gripped people for centuries. We want every Irish man and woman to have a home of their own on land they can call their own. And we want amnesty for all political prisoners. Is that too much to ask? You yourself believed in that once, Megan. What happened?"

"I saw you and the others for what you were, Sean. You talk about helping the Irish people and what you really want to do is continue this insane battle you have with the North and the British." Megan paused, seeing that what she had said had not registered with McGuire. "All the Irish really want is peace," Megan replied wearily.

"This is the way to peace," McGuire responded. "Like I said, it's very simple. I don't know why everybody is fighting it. It's going to happen."

"Not with guns."

"With ballots or bullets, Megan. Sure it will. It's the only way to peace."

"Does that include the killing of innocent men and women?" Megan asked. "Like Kit Fallon, for example?"

"That was an unfortunate accident, Megan," McGuire answered uncomfortably. "We are not about killing our own. It's the fortunes of war."

"Peace is the only way to peace."

"Will you listen to the Buddhist now, Sean," Cassidy sneered.

"She's no Buddhist," McGuire said. "She's for the Yank. And I have a sneaking suspicion the Yank's agenda includes collaborating with the British. I still haven't figured that one out yet." There was confusion as well as concern in McGuire's voice. "Just where does the Yank's sympathies lie, Megan?"

"You're a fool, Sean," Megan said disgustedly. "You still don't get it, do you, Sean. This has nothing to do with the Irish, the British, it's not a question of who's right or wrong, our side against theirs. This isn't about politics, the IRA, Ulster, or the British. This isn't even about American noninvolvement. This is about John's sister Kit and nothing else. If you can't see that, then I feel sorry for you."

"Well now, it's about me," McGuire lashed out, throwing his glass into the fireplace. The anger that showed on his face was evident to Megan and Cassidy. Megan knew she had struck a nerve. Cassidy, unnerved by McGuire's tantrum, nervously went over to the window looking out into the darkened night.

"Jesus, Sean," Cassidy said, tentatively eyeing McGuire. "Sure it's raining to beat the devil. I can't even see the boys out there."

"Shut up, Cassidy," McGuire lashed out again, turning back to Megan who was sitting silently watching him. "And, Megan, when did you become so naïve? Everything in this country is about politics. Fallon's sister was killed accidentally because there is a war going on between the British and the Irish. Remember?"

"Sean, you don't really believe that, do you?" Megan asked.

"Yes, I do."

"Sean, it's not a war when innocent people are killed and they are not even a part of it." Megan continued before McGuire could answer. "You and your goons are doing this to continue to keep Ireland and her people fighting a war that only a few people like yourself want to keep going. Again, Sean, what about the innocent?"

"No one is innocent in Ireland. You don't understand what this fight is all about, Megan," McGuire answered.

"I understand all too well," Megan replied.

Megan and McGuire had both forgotten about Cassidy. He was still standing by the window, his hand resting on the iron tucked into his waist. "All I want is another go-round with your bloody Yank boyfriend," Cassidy said, trying to sound at ease, but wasn't. "It isn't just about the IRA fighting the British for me. I'm going to take pleasure in killing your man, Megan. Then I'll take care of you."

Cassidy angrily moved from the window, stopped in front of the fireplace, and froze. Megan and Sean, puzzled by Cassidy's actions, watched as the color drained from his face. He had an expression of someone who had seen death walk over his grave.

"What the hell is wrong with you, Cassidy?" McGuire asked. "You look like you've seen a ghost."

Cassidy, his mouth hanging open, didn't move. McGuire noticed that he was staring at the back entrance to Megan's house. McGuire turned. Like Cassidy, McGuire stood like a statue, looking in the same direction. Standing in the doorway, the Uzi slung over his shoulder, was John Fallon. In his hand, he was holding two guns, each with silencers, pointing at both of them.

Megan's heart skipped several beats. She bolted from where she was sitting on the couch and ran to Fallon's side.

"Oh, John! I'm so glad to see you, darling," Megan said, pressing herself against Fallon's arm. "I was so afraid you were dead."

Fallon noticed the bruises on her face, the dried blood that had clotted on the side of her mouth. "Are you all right, Megan?"

"I'm fine, John."

"Who's responsible for this?" Fallon asked, his ice-cold voice splitting the room.

Megan didn't want to answer. She just shook her head.

"It was me that rearranged your whore's face," Cassidy blurted out, the false bravado evident in his voice. McGuire was startled by Cassidy's outburst. It was evident from the catch in his voice that what he said sounded hollow.

Fallon knew that Cassidy was a coward and a bully. His attempt at sounding tough and hard only made him look weaker. He looked at Cassidy and nodded. "It figures that it would be you. Megan is just about the size of woman someone like you would hit." Fallon smiled viciously, and cold chills ran down Cassidy's back.

Megan laughed a hard laugh. "That's just the way I feel about it, John."

Cassidy narrowed his eyes, and Fallon knew that he was contemplating on making a move. In his slow-witted mind, Fallon couldn't help but smile to himself thinking that was going to be a chore.

Fallon also noticed that McGuire and Cassidy were packing handguns. If they were going to try anything, Fallon was sure that was where they would make their move to. He knew both of them were trying to figure out what the play was and when they could make it. Fallon decided he would help them along.

"Listen, Fallon, I just wanted to talk," McGuire started. He didn't know about the three men outside who were history; he was looking to buy some time. "Don't mind Cassidy. Sometimes his size gets in the way."

Cassidy did not reply. Neither did Fallon.

Fallon nodded his head. Taking Megan by the arm, Fallon moved her to one side of him, keeping her from standing between him and Cassidy and McGuire. Fallon didn't miss the look in Cassidy's eyes.

"Okay, McGuire," Fallon said, relaxing his grip, letting the Uzi hang loosely in his hand. This did not go unnoticed. "Talk."

Fallon could feel Megan's hand clutching his arm tightly. "By the way," Fallon interjected before McGuire could say anything, cocking his head to the door. "If you're stalling for time, waiting for your men outside to make a move, forget it. They have moved on to a better place."

"You bloody bastard," Cassidy hissed. "You've killed them, haven't you?"

"Yes."

Cassidy, out of control now, not thinking about the consequences, rushed toward the table where the automatic weapons were. Fallon calmly let him get to the table. Then bringing the Uzi up in one swift motion, Fallon squeezed the trigger, sending Cassidy backward into the fireplace. Cassidy was dead before crashing into the fireplace.

McGuire stared, frozen where he stood, as Fallon swung the gun on him. There was terror in his face. McGuire, holding his hands out in front of him, began to sob.

"Please, Fallon." His voice was barely audible. "Don't kill me."

Fallon stepped closer to the table. Looking over at Cassidy, Fallon's bullets have all but ripped him in half. He turned to Megan. There was a look of disbelief on her face as she stared at Fallon, as though seeing him for the first time. She remained silent.

Struggling to get himself together, angry and ashamed that Megan had witnessed his display of cowardice, McGuire made an attempt at bravado. "So you're on a killing spree, Fallon. I assume the men outside are dead too?"

"Very," Fallon answered.

"And I'm next?" McGuire nervously asked.

"It looks that way," Fallon answered.

"John," Megan pleaded. "John, hasn't there been enough killing? What you are doing now is not going to bring Kit back."

Fallon turned to look at Megan. He realized how much he loved her. There was sorrow in his voce when he spoke. "I'm sorry, Megan. Someone has to pay."

"Why is that you are laying the blame for what happened to your sister on the IRA," McGuire offered, having somewhat regained his composure. "What about the Brits? Don't you feel they had anything to do with it?"

"I could tell you anything at this point, McGuire," Fallon told him. "And at this point, you're ready to believe anything."

McGuire sneered at Fallon. He felt that as long as he kept Fallon talking he could either talk his way out of this or come up with some plan to kill him. "Don't think me too scared, Yank. I've been in tougher situations before."

Fallon nodded his head. "I'm sure you have. That was evident in the way you were sniveling just a moment ago."

"You bloody arrogant bastard," McGuire said, his face red with rage. "Don't—"

"You men in the IRA are tough," Fallon cut McGuire off quickly. "It takes a lot of stomach to do what you do."

"It does indeed."

"Killing innocent people is always hard," Fallon said sardonically.

"You keep referring to us, Yank," McGuire retorted, angry now and feeling that he was much on steadier ground. "The Brits aren't innocent lambs, you know."

"I find it rather hypocritical the way you keep mentioning the British," Fallon said with some disgust. "I don't excuse them for their part in what transpired, but what puzzles me is you keep railing on about Ireland and yet it doesn't seem to bother you that you are killing your own people."

"There are always casualties in a war." McGuire was beginning to gain confidence. "The way it is, Yank, you are either with us or against us. That puts you with them. They aren't the innocent victims you seem to be portraying."

Megan, who had kept silent during the exchange between McGuire and Fallon, pointed her finger accusingly at McGuire. "You are nothing but killers, Sean. Kit wasn't the only spectator that was killed that day. You and your mercenaries care nothing about Ireland other than keeping this senseless war going."

"There was a time you were with us, Megan." McGuire looked accusingly at Megan. "Have you gone over to the other side too?"

"Yes, that's true. It was when I was foolish enough to believe that what you were fighting for was freedom for Ireland," Megan said sadly. "I see you and the others now, Sean, for what you really are."

Sean stared at Megan in silence. The hatred in her eyes was so evident. Megan held his stare in a defiant manner. Before McGuire could say anything, Fallon jumped in.

"So you sit in the pub with your cronies and talk about the cause. About love of country and honor to the Irish people. You get drunk and toast your victories and talk about all the good you are doing for the Irish people."

"We do at that," McGuire answered proudly.

"Eire Nua. A thirty-two-county Irish republic. The Irish language of the people," Fallon said.

"I see you are familiar with our language," McGuire said, surprised.

Shrugging his shoulders, Fallon saw no need to reply. He waited for McGuire to continue.

"That's because it is. It was."

"What you're saying, along with the British occupying Ireland, if the Irish language dies, the people die?"

"I would agree with that sentiment too, to some extent. As a matter of fact, to a great extent," McGuire said and laughed. He had settled into a relaxed, almost laissez-faire attitude about his predicament. It was almost as if he was just chatting with Fallon and had nothing to fear.

He wasn't even trying to think ahead. He was going to ride this out moment by moment. He was underestimating Fallon, having forgotten that John Fallon was going to kill him. Fallon could see this in his eyes, feel it in the room.

The rain was still hammering down on the roof and appeared to be getting worse. Cassidy's body still lay in the fireplace like some obscene object, discarded and forgotten. Fallon was enjoying McGuire's false sense of security.

"We Irish are reined to the fact that what we are doing is harsh and dangerous," McGuire said. "We know that many of us will die in this fight. But if that's the price we must pay, then so be it."

"There's nothing glamorous about dying," Fallon told him. "Dying is just that, dying. Dead is just dead whether it's for some lost cause or ending up on the street with a bullet through the head. And to be killed is to have everything you own and love taken away from you by someone who doesn't deserve the right." Fallon paused, letting what he had just said sink in. "That's usually how it happens too."

"War is hell," McGuire admitted.

Fallon felt the movement before he heard the sound. McGuire and Megan were unaware of the presence that had appeared in the doorway. Fallon knew even before turning around who it was.

Shifting his eyes away from McGuire, who by now was plotting in his mind how to get out of this bind he was in and was not cognizant of the fact that someone had entered the house, Fallon looked at the two men standing in the doorway, both with iron in their hands pointed directly at him.

"Hello, Al," Fallon said.

Al Reynolds and Jack Harris, coming in at different angles, entered the living room. Harris, stationing himself to the left side of Fallon, had taken himself out of Fallon's field of vision. Al Reynolds, standing directly in front of Fallon, kept the gun leveled at him.

McGuire and Megan, both standing with puzzled looks on their faces, watched as the drama unfolded. They were both unaware of who they were, but both sensed a feeling of foreboding. Megan rushed to Fallon's side, her eyes never leaving Reynolds's face.

"John," Megan asked nervously, "who are these men?"

Fallon, knowing this was not going to end up pleasantly, tried moving Megan out of the way of danger. But Megan was unmovable. Fallon, knowing he had to have room to maneuver, told Megan, "Don't worry, Megan. These are just a couple of people I work with. You have nothing to fear."

"Hello, Johnny," Reynolds said, cautiously breaking the silence. "It's been a long time. How have you been?"

"I figured it was just a matter of time before you showed up," Fallon said. "I was hoping I would have a little more time."

"From what I gather, Johnny, you have created quite a bit of havoc already."

"What do these men want, John?" Megan, over her initial shock, now displayed anger and disdain.

"They want me, Megan. They want me back." Turning to Reynolds, giving him his full attention, Fallon asked, "That's right, isn't it, Al? Or does Childers have something else in mind? Never mind. You don't have to tell me."

"Al." Harris spoke for the first time. There was impatience in his voice. "What are we waiting for?"

"Your girlfriend is getting impatient, Al," Fallon said, smiling at Harris.

"Why, you—" Harris answered, bringing his gun up, pointing it at Fallon.

"Jack." Reynolds wheeled on Harris, the look on his face stopping him in his tracks. "I'll say when."

By now the room was filled with tension. The only person seemingly not affected was Fallon. Still standing with the Uzi dangling from his shoulder and the deadly automatic in his waistband, he appeared to be removed from everything that was going on around him.

"You're not going to try anything stupid, are you, Johnny?" Reynolds asked.

"Maybe if we concentrate on his girlfriend, Mr. Fallon will be more susceptible to listening," Harris said harshly.

"You touch her and I'll kill you," Fallon said softly.

Harris was taken aback. He tried holding Fallon's stare, but was too unnerved. There was a look of fear on his face.

McGuire, all but forgotten since Reynolds and Harris showed up, piped up. "Sure and it seems you lads have lots to discuss. I'm thinking maybe I should leave." McGuire was trying to keep the tone light, hoping this was his way out.

"I don't think so," Harris told McGuire, the threat in his voice unmistakable. "What I think would be a good idea would be for you to just sit there and drink your tea for the time being and shut the fuck up. We'll get around to you."

"So, John, what do we do about the guns?" Reynolds asked, giving his attention back to Fallon. "I assume this man is one of your targets." Reynolds nodded to McGuire.

"Yes, he is," Fallon said.

"And if we let you raise that gun on your target, you'll kindly drop it to the floor. Without putting us in harm's way?" Reynolds said with amusement.

Fallon didn't bother to answer.

"And the woman?" Harris asked.

"There won't be any trouble, Al. Let her go. She isn't a part of any of this. I just want the man in the chair," Fallon told Reynolds and realized it was the truth. Anything after that, he was prepared for. Even dying. He just wanted to finish what he started. He wanted to take from McGuire what was taken from him—Kit.

Fallon, knowing how the company operated, wasn't looking for any breaks or favors. Being true to himself, Fallon knew he had crossed the line. Anything that came down the path, Fallon knew was coming to him. His only hope to take out Sean McGuire was Al Reynolds. If anyone was going to let him have this, it was Reynolds.

"You know how it works, Johnny," Reynolds said sadly. "After you lose the guns, we'll discuss the woman."

Fallon said nothing. Reynolds and Fallon kept staring at each other. Fallon knew Reynolds was lying. They were going to kill Megan, and if he didn't come up with something fast, there was nothing he would be able to do. Looking at the way Harris and Reynolds had stationed themselves, Fallon could see that it was textbook.

Meanwhile, McGuire's eyes did not rest. They went from man to man, gun to gun. He knew that if Fallon didn't kill him, these two strangers would.

"We're wasting time, Al," Harris said. "We should have taken this guy as soon as we came in. He's just a gun."

Fallon looked once at Harris, a look of disdain on his face. He turned back to Reynolds, a wry smile on his face. "Childers must love this one," Fallon said with cold amusement. "You must be scraping the bottom of the barrel hiring clowns like this."

"You bastard," Harris hissed. The gun in his hand had all but jumped, ready to pump one into Fallon.

Reynolds smiled for just a fraction of a second. Harris narrowed his eyes, his hand trembling on the trigger. He wanted to take the shot, Fallon could tell. But Al Reynolds was still calling the shots. Protocol. Hierarchy. They were useful, and Fallon knew Harris was not going to do anything without Reynolds's okay.

Megan, who had remained strangely silent as she watched the unusual goings-on around her, had started to get up. She noticed Fallon's eyes telling her to stay put.

"Before smiley gets trigger-happy, Al," Fallon said, not bothering to look at Harris, giving his full attention to Reynolds, "you better think about it."

The puzzled look that crossed Reynolds's face told Fallon that he had grabbed his attention. "What do you mean, Johnny?"

"You don't think I haven't covered myself in case something like this happened?" Fallon said.

"He's bluffing," Harris said.

Ignoring Harris, Fallon continued talking to Reynolds. "Johnny, you're not trying to run one on us, are you?" Reynolds asked skeptically.

"A few years ago, about the time I began seriously thinking about packing it in," Fallon continued, "was when I began documenting the operations. It also contains the names of all operatives, right up to and including Childers."

"You don't believe him, do you, Al?" Harris asked.

"Shut up, Jack," a frowning Reynolds said. "Let me think."

"Who are you people?" McGuire asked Reynolds.

Ignoring McGuire, Reynolds pressed Fallon. "I'm not saying I buy it, John, but just what have you got in the way of documentation?"

"Everything that I have ever been involved in," Fallon answered calmly. Fallon was also not unaware that Harris and Reynolds had not disarmed him yet. "You are also in there, Al."

Reynolds, a thoughtful expression on his face, looked hard at Fallon. There was hesitation and uncertainty in his look. He knew from years in the business they were in that someone like Fallon was sharp enough to cover himself. "I'm assuming that if you end up dead, everything becomes public knowledge?"

"You can count on it," Fallon answered, smiling.

"Al, let me take a crack at this punk," Harris said. "You give me five minutes with him and I'll break him."

Shaking his head in disgust, Fallon looked at Reynolds as he gestured to Harris. "Al, clue this loser in on how it works."

"What it means, Jack," Reynolds explains, "is that more than one person has access to whatever Fallon had stashed away. Is that about right, John?"

Fallon nodded his head in agreement.

"I'm sorry, John. But that's not going to fly. We have to take our chances that you really are bluffing. You know that."

"Goddamn it, man," McGuire anxiously blurted out again. "Just who are you people? This fuckin' Yank wants to kill me. If you can help me at all, you should. He's killed off almost all my friends and now he wants me dead. If you Yanks are the authorities, please help me. All I want to do is leave. I had nothing to do with what he says I did."

"Who is this guy, John?" Reynolds asked.

"He's the leader of the local IRA group," Fallon said. "My guess is he's the head of the ASU. His cell was the one that led the bungled attack on a British target in the middle of the morning in a crowded part of town. Neither the British nor the Irish had secured the hit, and consequently three people, civilians, were left dead in the street by stray gunfire. One of them was my sister."

Reynolds nodded his head in sympathy.

"What about the one on the floor?" Reynolds asked, pointing to the fireplace where Cassidy was lying half in and half out. Fallon looked over at the contorted body, blood oozing from where he had shot him.

"That's one of McGuire's men. He was all talk and bluster. Cassidy tried bracing me on the beach one time," Fallon continued. "It didn't turn out too well for him and since that time has had a grudge out for me."

Megan was looking at McGuire, unable to keep the disgust from her face. The anger was just smoldering beneath the surface. She didn't say a word.

"The other two we found outside," Harris asked, his piece still aimed at Fallon. "Were they part of this?"

"Yes."

Looking back at Megan, Fallon saw concern in her face, maybe worry. Fallon could understand. Megan was in the room with four gunmen and a dead body on the floor. That was what made him remember the day at the beach.

"And that, Al, brings us to where we are now," Fallon said and shrugged. "Look, Al, all I'm asking is you let me take him out and I'll come with you peacefully. Just let the girl go. She isn't a part of this."

"No, John," Megan cried, rushing to him. "I'm not leaving you. If they kill you, they are going to have to kill me."

Reynolds looked at McGuire.

"What do you have to say to all this?" Reynolds asked.

"The only thing that's true in what he said," McGuire pleaded, "is what I'm fighting for and that's for the cause of Ireland. On that day, we went to the prison to free the men who had been jailed improperly. But the British had laid a trap. Unknown to us, there had been an informer in the group."

While McGuire was talking, Fallon was scoping out the situation. He knew there would always be an opening, and when the time came, he had to be ready.

McGuire was still talking. "Eight of my men died and three others were shot down in the street by the British. Then this madman"—gesturing to Fallon—"came after me and started killing the rest of my men. He's crazy."

"Not without provocation?" Reynolds asked.

"My men only tried to protect themselves," McGuire said haughtily.

"With restless guns, Al," Fallon said, his voice still barely above a whisper. "Then these so-called heroes came here and took Megan hostage. The dead one on the floor made the first move. Now it's McGuire's turn. The trouble being, Al, you and your girlfriend showed up just a little sooner than expected."

Fallon saw the cold look from Harris. He was counting on him being the Achilles's heel. If he could keep pushing him, Fallon was sure he would lose his cool. That was when Fallon planned on making his move.

"Keep pushing, Fallon," Harris said through clenched teeth.

Fallon could see the wheels spinning in Al Reynolds's head. It was just a matter of time before he decided whether Fallon was bluffing or not. Whatever he was going to do would have to be soon and quickly.

Getting Megan out was uppermost in his mind. If he could convince Reynolds to let her go, Fallon would feel better about what was going to come down. The one thing he was sure of was that no matter what else transpired, he was going to kill McGuire.

"Al, if you let the girl go," Fallon started, "I'll come with you."

Reynolds, confusion showing on his face, had already made up his mind.

"I'm sorry, Johnny," Reynolds said sadly. "You know the rules as well as I do. We can't leave any loose ends."

"Christ, Al," Harris said impatiently. In that split second that Harris turned to face Reynolds, Fallon saw his opening. "Let's get this over with and get out of here."

McGuire, terrified now, started pleading. "Please, I have nothing to do with them. Let me go and I promise I won't say anything."

Reynolds and Harris both turned to McGuire.

"What do you think, Jack?" Reynolds asked.

"I say we take them all out. One thing we can't afford, Al, is to leave anyone behind." Turning to Fallon, a vicious gleam in his eye, Harris continued. "All I'm asking, Al, when the time comes, I get to off this smart-ass. This is one I am going to take particular pleasure in."

"You can't do it!" McGuire screamed. His face was contorted now, the fear evident, and he resorted to pleading. "You can't just kill me. Please, I have nothing to do with either of them. Kill them both. No one will ever hear it from me."

Reynolds smiled. "It looks as though you don't have a fan in McGuire, Johnny."

The wind and rain had become more severe, slashing hard against Megan's house. Suddenly, the door to the living room swung open. Everyone but Fallon turned to look. Fallon saw his chance.

So did McGuire. Bolting toward the kitchen, McGuire tried to make his escape. The Uzi jumped to life in Fallon's hand. Swinging it up, level with his hip, and shoving Megan to the floor at the same time, Fallon squeezed off a burst. McGuire took the full brunt of the bullets, sending him sprawling into the fireplace.

At the same time, Reynolds and Harris turned back to Fallon, pulling the triggers on their guns at the same time.

Fallon saw this coming and did what he did best.

After shooting McGuire, Fallon dropped to the floor, and a slug from Harris's gun hit him in the right arm. The Uzi slipped from his hand as he rolled behind the sofa, taking cover. He saw Megan crawling toward him. There was a gash above her left eye. Fallon was not sure if she had been hit or if it was from the fall to the floor.

Pulling Megan toward him, Fallon saw that the wound was superficial.

"Are you all right, Megan?"

"Yes," she answered, leaning with her back against the sofa.

Fallon, knowing they were caught in a crossfire, tried to asses their position. Reynolds and Harris, being professionals, knew they were in the catbird seat. They just had to play the waiting game.

Fallon did not know if he killed McGuire. One thing was certain—he had to find a way of getting Megan out. Right now, his options were nil. Pulling Megan closer, Fallon whispered in her ear, "Megan, I want you to stay low and not move from where we are."

"What are you going to do?" Megan asked.

"I don't know yet. The first thing is try to get you out safely."

"I'm not going without you," Megan answered.

"Megan, listen," Fallon said gently. He knew they were in a precarious situation. All Reynolds and Harris had to do was wait. They were professionals and knew that Fallon and Megan were right where they wanted them. Fallon had to get Megan out and free himself up to draw them out.

"Listen, Megan," Fallon whispered in Megan's ear. "We have one chance of getting out of here alive. But you have to do what I say." Megan started to protest. Fallon placed his hand over her mouth.

"Megan, it's the only chance we have. When I say go, you stay low and head for the kitchen," Fallon instructed her, knowing time was running out. "I'll draw their fire, and when you make it to the kitchen, keep going out the back door. The rain will help you. Don't worry, Megan, I'll be right behind you."

Peering over the couch, looking to get a fix on Reynolds and Harris, Fallon spotted Harris. He was hunkered down by the entrance. Good move on his part. It cut off the other exit out of the house. He couldn't see him, but Fallon figured that Reynolds was on the other side of the room. Turning back to Megan, Fallon gave her arm a squeeze and nodded.

Fallon, having taken the other gun from his ankle holster, cocked both handguns. Turning once more to Megan, he said, "Are you ready?"

Megan hesitated, then nodded her head yes.

Fallon braced himself against the couch. "Now," he said to Megan. Fallon, pushing the couch over on its side, came up with both guns blazing. He was firing in the direction of Harris and where he thought Reynolds was.

Megan, crouched down, dashed for the kitchen.

Fallon, rolling over to the coffee table, felt a burning sensation on his cheek. He was hit, but the bullet had only grazed him. Gunfire was coming from both sides of the house now. A second bullet, fired by Reynolds, caught Fallon in the leg. Reaching up, Fallon pulled one of the weapons off the table before pushing it over on its side. It was a sawed off double-gauge shotgun. Cracking the gun, he saw that there were two rounds in the chamber.

His leg was burning now, and he knew the table will not be protection for long.

Glancing to his left, he spotted McGuire. Lying near Cassidy, his eyes open in terror, Fallon saw that he was only wounded. McGuire looked over to Fallon, a look of disbelief on his face. Fallon raised the automatic, hesitated, giving McGuire time to think about what was coming. Then he pumped two slugs between his eyes. McGuire's body jerked once, then slumped forward, dead.

Laying the shotgun on the floor, Fallon slipped two fresh magazines into the two handguns. He froze. Megan was lying in the doorway of the kitchen. He saw blood by her arm. Megan was moving. Fallon could see that she was still alive. He knew he was going to have to get to her before she was killed.

"Johnny," Reynolds's voice pulled Fallon back. He gripped the shotgun and waited. He didn't answer Reynolds.

"Johnny," Reynolds shouted again. This time there was some uncertainty in his voice. "Johnny, come on out. We just want to talk."

Fallon remained silent.

The living room was deadly silent. The smell of cordite filled the air. Fallon, his leg on fire now, had pulled off his belt. He knew the makeshift tourniquet would only last so long. Slowly backing up, moving toward Megan, Fallon kept the table between Harris and Reynolds. Harris called over to Reynolds.

"Al." The nervousness was evident in his voice. "He's not coming out. Let's just take him out and get the hell out of here."

It was now or never for Fallon. It was just a matter of time before Reynolds and Harris closed in. He hoped Megan had made it out the back door into the night. They wanted him, and he was sure they wouldn't chance going after her. Then he heard Harris. His heart went cold when he shouted to Reynolds.

"Al," Harris said frantically. "I've got the girl spotted. She's trying to make it out the back door."

"Take her out," Reynolds replied.

They just made up Fallon's mind. Coming up just as Harris fired off two rounds, Fallon cut loose with both barrels in Harris's direction. He saw his face explode before another slug from Reynolds's gun caught him in the shoulder. The shotgun dropped from his hand, sending Fallon sprawling toward the kitchen.

With his one good hand, Fallon rolled to his right, bringing the iron up quickly and firing in Reynolds's direction.

The blood was flowing freely now as Fallon tried to crawl to the kitchen. Reynolds's voice cut through the room.

"Johnny. I know you're hit. All I have to do is wait you out."

Fallon, stalling for time, answered Reynolds. He knew he had to stop the flow of blood or he was going to pass out. "How is your girlfriend doing?"

"Good shooting, Johnny. You blew his head off." Fallon could hear Reynolds moving from his position behind the chair.

Fallon stopped cold. Just inside the door to the kitchen he saw Megan. She was lying on her back, blood flowing from her chest and forehead. Two of Harris's bullets must have hit her.

Fallon, his stomach tied up in knots, moved toward her. He knew she was dead, but he had to get near her. He knew Reynolds's vision was limited; several of the bullets that were spread around the room had taken out most of the lights. It was just a matter of time before his eyes adjust to the darkness.

It doesn't matter. Before Reynolds took him out, Fallon was going to kill him. The rage that was smoldering in Fallon rose to the surface. Reaching over, Fallon touched Megan's hand. The dizziness was beginning to overtake him. Fallon, leaning against the wall, pain shooting through his body, willed himself up to a standing position.

Catching Reynolds off-guard as Fallon spotted him reloading, he opened fire, emptying the gun. Reynolds went down. He took the last clip from his pocket, rammed it into the gun. Fallon turned back to Megan. Slumping beside her, Fallon took her in his arms. The tears fell freely.

He sensed the movement behind him. Turning slowly, still holding Megan, Fallon looked up to see Reynolds standing over him. He was holding his shoulder, his iron held steady on Fallon. He moved closer.

"You don't die easily, Johnny," Reynolds said softly.

Fallon looked down at Megan. When he looked back at Reynolds, he shuddered. Even close to death, with just the automatic for a weapon, Reynolds could see the fire in his eyes. He knew like a tiger that Fallon was still the most dangerous man he knows. He kept the gun leveled at Fallon.

"I'm sorry about the girl, Johnny."

"Why?" Fallon asked weakly.

Reynolds frowned. Looking at Megan and Fallon, blood stained and one dead and the other going to die, Reynolds searched for an answer. "It wasn't supposed to happen this way. All we were going to do was come in and take you out. The rest of it, Johnny, you brought it down on yourself."

"What about Harris and McGuire?" Fallon asked.

"You killed them both," Reynolds said.

That gave Fallon some satisfaction, but seeing Megan lying there, the life drained out of her, his will to live has passed.

"About the records you say you kept, Johnny," Reynolds asked. "Did you really document all that stuff, or was it just a bluff?"

"Does it matter now, Al?"

"I guess not," Reynolds said, the sadness evident in his voice. "But you know the rules, Johnny."

"Right. No one ever leaves the organization."

The rain has intensified. The wind blowing in from the sea blew the front door open. Momentarily, Reynolds, spooked by the sound, turned for a fraction of a second. Fallon, bringing the gun up weakly, got off a round. He was off the mark.

Reynolds, his shoulder grazed by Fallon's bullet, turned back, kicking the gun from Fallon's hand. Fallon slumped back against Megan. A smile crossed his face. "Almost got you, Al. It would have been nice to have offed all of you."

"I'll give you credit, Johnny," Reynolds said, shaken by the close call. "If you did nothing else, you created enough havoc here in Ireland to start a war."

"One question, Al."

"Yes."

"Do you really believe that I would have ratted anyone out in the organization?" Fallon asked, his voice but a whisper.

"No, Johnny," Reynolds answered earnestly. "But you know how Childers and the others operate. They don't want to take any chances. As long as you were running around free, they saw you as loose cannon. Remember, they don't know you as well as I do. Loose ends and all that stuff."

Fallon nodded, resigned to his fate. He turned to look at Megan. Painfully, Fallon took her in his arms again, holding her close to him. The only sound that could be heard was the rain and howling wind.

"Take it easy, Al," Fallon said to Reynolds.

"Nothing personal, Johnny. It's just a job." Reynolds raised the gun and put two slugs into Fallon's forehead.

Fallon, falling, clutching Megan to his breast, died instantly.

A look of sorrow crossed Reynolds's face. He looked down at Fallon and Megan. A fast glance around the room, at the carnage. Harris, McGuire, and Cassidy, all dead, scattered like so much debris around the once cozy room. Reynolds thought of the other three dead men outside and shook his head in wonderment.

"There will never be another one like you, Johnny," Reynolds said out loud to no one. "You were a mover and shaker."

"Freeze."

The voice cracked the silence like a bolt of lightning. Reynolds, still holding the gun loosely in his hand, stiffened where he stands. The voice was familiar, and for a moment, he was unable to put a face to it. Then it hit him. The gun started to come up in his hand.

"Don't try it, Al. You'll never make it."

"Dan," Reynolds managed to get out.

"Now drop the piece," Dan Morehead's soft voice said. "Be easy, Al, or I'll take you off at the knee."

Reynolds let his gun drop to the floor. He waited nervously.

"Now turn around slowly," Morehead said.

Reynolds, his mind racing, turned to face Morehead. Dan Morehead was standing at the entrance to the house. Water was dripping from his raincoat. In his hand, the .45 automatic he was holding aimed straight at his stomach made Reynolds flinch. The cold blue eyes never waver.

"Hello, Dan," Reynolds said. "It's good to see you."

"Why?"

Flustered, Reynolds searched for a way to answer him. "Childers said he might be bringing you in for backup."

"Is that what you think?"

"Yes, Dan." Reynolds racked his brain, hoping Morehead was there for that reason. Deep down, he knew that it wasn't so.

"You're a liar," Morehead said quietly. "Childers told you I was out of the picture. You and Harris came over here to terminate John."

"That's not true, Dan," Reynolds said hastily. "We were told to talk to him and get him back in the fold."

"We both know better than that, Al. Childers didn't want to have Fallon off the reservation. When he bolted, you were given the order to kill him."

Reynolds was sweating now. Looking at Morehead, the gun beginning to look like cannon, he was scared. "What now, Dan?"

Stepping into the room, Morehead gestured for Reynolds to move in front of him. He left the door open, the room now almost dark.

"Look, Dan," Reynolds started. "Let me—"

The first slug tore into his stomach, and clutching his gut as he slammed back into the chair, Reynolds looked at Dan Morehead in disbelief. The second bullet caught him in the eye. Reynolds was dead before he hit the floor.

Morehead walked casually over to where Reynolds was lying. Looking down, Morehead shook his head. "Nothing personal, Al. You go to a better place."

Morehead moved over to where Fallon and Megan were. Looking down at them, Morehead was overcome with grief.

"I suppose it had to end this way, kid. You were always a thorn in their side. I hope you and the girl find the peace you always wanted."

Turning, Morehead started for the door. Turning back once to look at Fallon, he stepped out into the blistering rain, disappearing into the darkness.

EPILOGUE

A SUDDEN SNOWSTORM TWO DAYS earlier had blanketed New York City in a sea of white. Snowplows were making their way around the city, slowly and tediously. They were in for the long haul. The storm had dropped twenty-six inches of snow, and in a city like New York, that meant everything and everybody had been brought to a standstill.

Schools were closed, businesses did not even attempt to open their doors, and the few emergency vehicles that patrolled the city were moving at a snail's space. It was eerie seeing the stillness that hovered over the giant metropolis that breathed twenty-four hours a day. The one business that thrived was the gin mills.

In the building that housed the offices of World Wide, most of the offices were closed. Childers and his secretary, who had holed up in one of the hotels near the office, had made their way in. The one thing you could take to the bank was when it came to business of life-taking; there were no snow days.

Childers, pacing his office frantically after having ended a call from a high-ranking member of Congress, was hoping he had tap-danced enough around the Ireland debacle. Just about every paper in the country had carried the story, what the press was calling "a bloody massacre."

According to the senator, the one saving grace had been it had not yet been traced back to World Wide.

Since World Wide was deep cover and very few people were even aware of its existence, Childers was given instructions to make sure they were distanced from any involvement. It was his responsibility to see that all the right notes were struck and make sure the oversight committee was off the hook for any wrongdoing that might have occurred. It always rankled Childers that when a crisis presented itself, these self-righteous bureaucrats suddenly became deaf, dumb, and blind.

He had his explanation of why nothing inappropriate had occurred and why they were completely in their rights to be confused. He hated to acquiesce to the righteous bastards. But one thing Childers had learned from his years as head of World Wide was how to play the game. There would also be plenty of agents' reports to back decisions taken by World Wide that might seem inappropriate.

Childers felt better about his situation and secure enough in the knowledge that the media reports had labeled the killings in Ireland as part of the war between the IRA and Greta Britain. The bodies of Reynolds and Harris, with some manipulation on Childers's part, had them down as "soldiers of fortune," brought in by the IRA. Fortunately, Harris and Reynolds could not be traced back to World Wide.

All in all, Childers was feeling very pleased with himself. Grabbing his hat and coat, Childers decided to go for a drink and congratulate himself. In the outer office, his secretary, Ms. Franklin, had a puzzled look on her face when she spotted him. Rarely did Mr. Childers leave the office in the middle of the day.

"Ms. Franklin," Childers said pleasantly, "why don't you close up the office and take the rest of the day off. I doubt we are going to have much activity with this weather."

"Thank you, Mr. Childers," Ms. Franklin said. "I just have these few invoices to get off and I'll be able to close up the office."

"Just make sure you change the message on the answering machine. Let people know we will be back in the office tomorrow."

"Yes, sir."

Childers turned and headed for the elevator. It was strange seeing the halls so deserted. Waiting for the elevator, Childers's mood picked up. On the way down in the elevator, he felt sure he had covered all the bases. He was sure he had left nothing to chance.

The Ireland fiasco had not been handled the way he had originally planned it, but now that it was over and having talked it over with Senator Wallis, it looked as though it must have been a blessing in disguise. Wallis, the only man aware of World Wide and what they did, was the only one other than Childers whose head would be on the block if the oversight committee uncovered anything about World Wide.

Childers, smiling to himself, knew Wallis was not about to jeopardize his position. Childers thought it was pure genius turning the story around to make it look like the IRA had hired a couple of mercenaries in their fight against the British. Since Reynolds and Harris did not exist, there was no way of tying Childers in to anything. He would go on running World Wide, existing as an import-export company, the one he had founded after his resignation from the army.

Leaning against the back of the elevator, the ever-present pipe clamped firmly in his mouth, Childers began planning for the future. Finding people like Reynolds and Harris, guns for hire, would be easy enough; and with Raven out of the picture, the organization would continue to flourish. Childers saw even bigger better things in the future.

As the door swung open in the parking garage, Childers found it rather amusing that after sifting through the bodies at the farmhouse, when they came across Fallon, he was found to have been a citizen of Ireland. The cops had come to the conclusion that he was just another IRA gun. Childers's face turned grim as he walked to his car thinking how pleased he was that Fallon had met such a fitting end. He had always been a thorn in his side. Of all the people Childers handled, Fallon was the one that acted autonomously, the one he was unable to control. Well, he didn't have to worry anymore. He was dead.

Walking through the almost deserted parking garage, Childers debated whether to take his car or walk. He decided on the car. The snowplows would have most of the main thoroughfares cleared, and he knew there would be very few cars on the road. Reaching his designated parking spot, a voice from the darkness stopped him in his tracks.

"Childers."

Turning to where it was coming from, Childers saw Dan Morehead walking toward him. In his hand was a Walther automatic, with a silencer on it. He approached Childers slowly and deliberately.

"Dan," a flustered Childers exclaimed, shocked to see Morehead. "What are you doing here?"

"I just came to see you."

"Look, Dan, if it's about Raven, forget it," Morehead answered him nervously. "I appreciate your coming down, but the situation has been taken care of."

"What do you mean taken care of?" Morehead asked innocently.

"Raven has been neutralized," Childers said, sure now that Dan Morehead did not hear about Ireland. They had isolated the problem and were sure that no names were released to the press. "My men have talked to Raven and should be bringing him back soon."

"What men?"

"Harris and Reynolds," Childers answered. "Like I told you, Dan, all I want to do is get Raven back in the fold."

"You're a liar."

"What are you saying?" Childers couldn't take his eyes off the gun that has not wavered from pointing at him.

"Get in the car." Morehead gestured to Childers.

Childers, hesitant at first then realizing his options were limited, shrugged, opened the door, and got in. Morehead climbed in the passenger side, the gun still on Childers.

"Look, Dan. Do we really need the gun?"

Morehead remained silent. He rest the gun in his lap. Reynolds, knowing he has a piece in the glove compartment, had to distract Morehead long enough to get to it. Something was not right, and his mind was racing ahead.

"What's this all about, Dan?" Childers asked, sounding indignant.

"What's it about, Childers," Morehead said coldly, "is that Reynolds and Harris are dead. They won't be bringing anyone back."

"How do you know that?"

"Because I killed them."

Morehead sat quietly, letting what he has said sink in. He watched the color drain from Childers's face. Morehead could see Childers thinking how he can disarm him. He found that amusing.

"You killed them." Childers was stalling for time now. He knew Morehead was aware of what went down in Ireland. His only way out of this was getting to the gun in the glove compartment. "What about—"

"Raven is dead too. Reynolds killed him in cold blood." Morehead was speaking deliberately now. "You finally got your revenge, didn't you, Childers?"

"What do you mean?"

"What I mean is that you have always hated Raven. All the years he worked for World Wide, Raven was given the hardest jobs and carried them out." Pausing to let what he had said sink in, Morehead continued. "The problem was, you couldn't control Raven and that was the one thing you couldn't handle. It was your pride, Childers."

"What are you talking about?"

"You wanted everyone who worked for you to stand in awe and fear you," Morehead said. "When you saw Raven wouldn't, your ego got the better of you. You are a phony, Childers. A phony and a coward. You were nothing but a desk jockey, and when someone like Raven went out on a job, you knew deep down what you were."

Childers was a ball of fury now. His hatred came streaming out. "Yes, I wanted Raven dead. Who was he to think he was bigger than the organization. We were a team, and he never fit in. I'm glad he's dead."

"That's all I wanted to hear," Morehead said.

Childers, sensing this was his only chance, threw himself against Morehead, driving him into the door. A heavy man, Childers tried pinning Morehead against the door as he fumbled with the glove compartment.

Morehead, managing to get his gun hand loose, shot Childers in the side, sending him back, his hand gripping his side in disbelief.

"You shot me," Childers said incredulously.

"Say hello to Reynolds and Harris when you get to hell, Childers," Morehead said, bringing the iron up and pumping one into the side of Childers's head. Childers slumped backward toward the door, his head falling forward obscenely as it landed on the steering wheel.

Morehead, looking at Childers's body, pocketed the automatic and climbed out of the car. Stepping out into the still deserted parking garage, Morehead looked back once and then walked slowly out of the garage.

The snow had started falling again. Morehead, pulling the collar of his coat up, whispered softly to himself, "It's over now, John. I hope you can rest in peace."

Morehead, head down, started up Broadway, disappearing into the follow-up snowstorm.